PAIR of FOOLS

LILLIAN LARK

Pair of Fools

Editor: Ellie, My Brother's Editor
Proofreader: Rosa Sharon, My Brother's Editor

Content Warning

***

Dear reader,
Pair of Fools includes
mentions of suicide and past sibling death
and depictions of the trafficking of sentient beings,
violence, and gore.
Be kind to yourselves,
L. Lark

***

This is for Cat, the first to request Sophia's and Mace's book, but luckily, not the last

And always, to my amazing husband

Prologue

SOPHIA

"What are *you* doing here?"

There is a demon on my doorstep, and it isn't my newly acquired brother-in-law. Instead, it's the demon who's been in direct competition with me. The one stealing my clients.

He's the reason I've been taking jobs that I'd normally reject. Jobs that landed me in the hellish situation I'm in now. The mark on my wrist burns as if in reminder.

Mace Reynolds doesn't respond to my vitriol. He leans against the doorjamb, and I stiffen my spine, unwilling to give any ground.

"Why wouldn't I visit the family of a friend?" he teases.

Leave it to my sister that the one time she leaves the house she gets mated. An anomaly for harpies already. Let alone the fact that she mated to not one, but two men. In a way that makes me wonder if I've angered the gods, one of those men just happens to be best friends with my adversary.

"Because I don't like you, and we are definitely not friends," I say.

"Ouch. I think we could be friends if you got to know me." Mace's dark eyes have a playful glint in them. "And we have a matter we need to discuss."

"If this is about Alice—"

Mace interrupts me with a bark of laughter. "No, this is not about your attempt at sabotage."

Having Alice feed Mace incorrect information had seemed like a good idea at the time. Now, with bigger issues plaguing me than this demon, I can admit that it was a bad idea.

But Mace doesn't seem angry.

"It isn't an attempt if it's successful," I say, miffed.

Mace nods as if conceding his point. I deliberate. If he's here about something other than my shot at his business… My ever-present curiosity claws at me. What could he possibly want? And how can I turn that to my benefit?

"Are you going to let me come inside?" Mace asks.

"Do you have to be invited?" Curiosity has the question out of my mouth before I can help it.

Mace quirks a dark eyebrow that has a scar running through it. I take note of the detail. For all that I've named this demon as my adversary, I've barely been in the same room with him.

Mace's dark hair flops on his forehead in a way that would be considered dashing but his features lack the refinement for it. His face can only be described as strong; the errors of it contributing to the overall look rather than detracting from it. His nose is crooked in the way that comes from being broken before. His jaw is just a touch too prominent, and his dark eyes are slightly asymmetrical. How can someone with the healing abilities of a demon have so many imperfections?

"It's good manners to not go into other people's homes unless invited... but it won't keep a demon out, if that's what you're asking," Mace says.

I glare at Mace and open the door wider. "I guess that was too much to hope for."

"You've been watching too much *Buffy the Vampire Slayer*," he says in passing.

I gasp as I close the front door; the demon now strolling around my apartment. "I take issue with that statement. There's nothing wrong with *Buffy the Vampire Slayer*."

"I implied no such thing!" Mace dramatically presses a hand over his heart. "But it's fiction and won't help you in the face of an actual vampire."

"Have you met one?" I haven't. I had only began meeting rarer creatures than witches or the odd shifter when I started my business. The older generation of harpies hadn't been pleased. Isolationism is practically a part of the harpy code.

Maybe that will change with all the help Asa is giving to the different harpy branches. Amara has even gotten to know other types of creatures through working at Greg's bakery. If my oldest sister can unbend enough to eschew our elder's isolationist requirements, then maybe there is hope for our kind.

My knowledge of other kinds of creatures had to be built from scratch.

Mace shudders. "Yes, they are less common than they once were. A bunch of snobs really."

I bite my lip to keep from peppering my rival with questions. The demon moves with ease around my space. The studio apartment is small but it's my sanctuary. Other harpies rarely come into my territory, and I like it that way.

The walls are a jumble of photo frames of places I've been and places I want to go.

Mace stops at my shelves full of knickknacks from my adventures. Some items are gifts from previous clients and others are souvenirs.

"Why are you here, Mace?"

"We have a debt to discuss, harpy."

I blanch. "What?"

How could he possibly know about that? I'd just barely returned home from that awful meeting. Mace is well connected, those who deal in information like we do have to be, but for him to work that quickly is near impossible.

Mace lifts a brow. "Did you already forget about the favor you asked for?"

My exhale is shaky. He's not talking about the other debt I owe. He's talking about that trick he pulled. Taking the thoughtless words I'd said while drowning in guilt as a demon deal. My relief is short lived.

"How much do you know about demons?" Mace asks.

Next to nothing, but this man is still a rival, a threat. He could lie to me, and I'd have no way of knowing.

I tilt my chin up with bravado. "Enough."

Mace's mouth twitches.

"Quite. Well, then you'll know that some demons need to have soul bonds to reside in this plane. Asa and I have been bonded for much of our lives but now…" He trails off before clearing his throat. "Now Asa is bonded with Zeph and Greg. Which means that I'm in need of someone to soul bond with; to act as an anchor in this plane."

"You can't stay bonded with Asa?"

Harpies may not take mates, my mother and sister being an exception, but many paranormal beings bond that way. There are different types of relationships in our world, couples, throuples, and more. I've never heard of a soul bond limit.

Mace grimaces. "Yes and no. Demons are sensitive to bonds and to be bonded to not only Asa, but to your sister and Greg all at once is… uncomfortable."

I can't even imagine. It puts a different meaning to feeling like a third wheel, or fourth wheel in this case. Mace picks up an acorn from my shelf. A community of dryads had given that to me when I'd retrieved enough blackmail to stop a developer from uprooting their forest.

"Why are you telling me this?" Suspicion stirs. As much as I'd love a lesson on the intricacies of demons, no one speaks about the particulars of what they are unprompted. Information is valuable and secrets about weaknesses are premium.

Mace puts the acorn down carefully, almost reverently, before turning to face me. His face a cheerful mask but his eyes alight with interest, with challenge.

"I'm here to call in that favor you owe me."

Chapter 1

MACE
Many Months Later

Frustration brews in me; it tightens the muscles in my back and has my teeth gritting. The emotion simmers as I toe a bottle cap across the dirt-covered floor.

The marks in the dust tell a story. It won't do any good to carefully analyze them as I would have in the past when my hunting would trek through wilderness. There is no trail that I can pick up and follow by sight. No wheel ruts of wagons full of captives. There are only a number of different size foot and shoe prints on the floor of this damp basement that reeks of fear and suppression collars.

I hiss out a curse at a particularly small set of prints, the toes tiny and obviously bare, losing the hold on my anger for a moment before I reel it in. Letting myself become furious will not help accomplish the things needed.

I spin in a circle and catalog the rusty cages hanging open like cheap jail cells. The scents on the air are not stale.

I bring my phone up to my ear and the call is picked up immediately.

"What did you find?" Gage asks. No preamble needed.

"I'm in the basement of the tenth location on your list. They were here. Very recently. Two days ago, at most."

Gage hisses on the phone. "Gods dammit, this group is moving fast for how many people they must have."

There are eighteen folders of missing people on our shared drive. There are more than that if the tracks are to judge. As if the traffickers are waiting to have a mass auction instead of finding buyers one-by-one.

A faint but familiar draw hangs in the air.

"They're using portals," I say and Gage curses again before going silent. The typing on a keyboard reaches me over the phone.

"That's useful information. I'll check with the certified portal retailers to start but I don't know about the black-market ones."

I nod and hope starts to build. It's small, but it's a lead all the same.

"I have a contact who can get me a list of black-market retailers for portal spells."

A sigh of relief comes from Gage. "Good. I'll send out a message to the team, so we know what we are looking for now."

Gage's business serves many needs in the paranormal community and is the party contracted for these missing persons. Having a public organization that the families can hire is useful. Asa, Gideon, and I should have done something similar a long time ago instead of relying on word of mouth.

Our trio was more informal, which worked at the time, but modern times call for modern measures. My friends are out of the business now, for the most part.

Gage continues, "I had to pull Kane and Leo for an abduction that just came in."

"Do they need any help?" I ask.

For those types of cases, the chances of retrieval decrease as the clock ticks.

"It doesn't look like it's a part of this trafficking ring. They already report having a solid lead. I'd rather use your skills in checking these locations. We might get lucky and stumble on one in use." There's a pause. "If you don't mind, that is."

I smile ruefully. "I'm happy to help."

Gage is used to directing his team. My presence and ability to teleport are incredibly helpful, but collaborating has taken some getting used to for this group since I'm an independent party. I'm happy to work with them but have no interest in being a part of their team in the long run.

Not for the first time, I wonder if I should accept Gage's offer to join them… no, it wouldn't be the same as working with Asa and Gideon. I'm not quite ready to move into a completely different organization. I'm too stubborn and independent to mesh and act as a team player.

We say our goodbyes and I go over the scene again, doing my best to suppress my rage. I have a list of other locations to check tonight.

I drop some sensing charms in the cages, on the off chance this location is used again. Innocuous objects, a bobby pin here, a button there, geared to pick up a certain level of distress and send an alert to my phone. Technology has added much to doing this job.

I've placed the last one when I feel *her*. Warmth spreads in my chest. The vibrant Sophia Shirazi is nearby. Her presence through the bond we have is like a swarm of bees, humming and dangerous and incredibly irritated with me.

I'd thought that the harpy may eventually settle in our arrangement. That had been wishful thinking. I'd underestimated the stubbornness that is Sophia.

Such a mysterious woman with secrets behind her stunning green eyes. Secrets that my demon side wants to possess.

The pull of curiosity is too much to resist. A small break before going back to my long list of locations won't harm anything. I learned a long time ago that burning yourself out with the never-ending tasks that come with chasing these sorts of criminals doesn't serve anyone in the long run.

A tiny detour to check on my bond-mate. It should only take a moment.

Chapter 2

SOPHIA

"Fucking demon," I whisper, but no one hears.

The nightclub is a clash of color, shadow, and above all, music.

The primal pulse coaxes the dancers onward. Uninhibited bodies twist like smoke on a breeze. Some dancers move as if they're in a human establishment, not showing any bells and whistles. Others fully embrace the freedom that comes with being in a club that caters to the inhuman.

A slender being with blue skin twines around a bulky man-shaped creature with tusks. A woman with snakes in place of hair twirls, the crowd giving her whatever space the hissing creatures on her head require. Others standby, watching the dancers with hungry eyes.

The ache of curiosity has me wanting to mingle.

Going to places like this was why I started my business rather than staying isolated with other harpies.

Just last year, this would have been one of my favorite places to be in a long list of other favorites. I was carefree and finally making my own way in the world.

A lot can change in a year.

My phone weighs heavy in my jacket pocket. The text message from earlier deleted, but still present in my thoughts.

Ms. Shirazi, my employer requires a meeting to discuss your debt. Please contact to schedule.

I mentally throw dealing with the polite message on the shit-I-have-to-deal-with pile and resist rubbing the inked spell on my wrist. Even after all this time the magic of that spell doesn't mix well with mine. No, no more thoughts of that tonight.

Avoidance is the name of the game.

I wipe my sweaty hands against the dress I'd changed into just for this outing, and tug on my jacket as if I'm here on a mission.

Maybe I am.

My leather jacket is beautifully designed and charmed for utility. It had been a birthday present from my best friend. Alice had used all of her witchy skills to make the pockets able to hold any number of charmed objects.

Most importantly, the lining of the jacket suppresses the sensation of magic against my skin. It isn't as capable as what we're aiming for. I'm still affected by the magics I pass from day-to-day, but they're a mere itch rather than the sting that some of the more potent spells can cause.

It's not the surrounding magic that's causing an ache in me. The stroke of the scented air against my skin, my curiosity, and the lively dancers are almost enough to quiet it, but nothing eases that particular sensation.

A sensation caused by my enemy.

I shake my head, trying to dispel thoughts of broad shoulders and that irritating smile.

I'm on a mission to forget.

Forget how naive I'd been. *Reckless.*

Forget that I'd assumed when clients mentioned a demon who undercut my time and price estimates, that he was moving in on my territory. Nearly a year later of being more integrated in the paranormal community, and the truth is embarrassing.

I had been the one floundering in *his* space.

Tonight, I'm looking to feel something other than that damn pull. To think of anything other than the dreams that feast on my mind.

Dancing isn't going to make me forget anything.

I have a different release in mind.

An orgasm will do nicely. Not sex, I've tried that since being bonded. The result was unsatisfying and seemed to make the issues bugging me worse. But an orgasm when frustration over my current state reaches a zenith? That hits the spot.

I could have stayed home and handled the issue myself, but… something about being alone in my apartment amplifies my current condition. As if the silence has teeth.

At least when I'm around people, the required vigilance makes it so I don't notice every single new weakness I develop.

I cast my gaze around the club, letting my eyes stroke over the men. Some of them make eye contact with me and look away quickly, cowards. I may have a reputation for being a love-them-and-leave-them type.

I'm a selfish lover.

Those who don't know me by my reputation but recognize me for what I am are wary for a different reason. My kind aren't known for our cuddly personalities.

As one of the few harpies that interact with people outside of the harpy community, I have the responsibility of upholding the reputation we bear.

My eyes reach the face of a man at the bar. He has sandy hair and some bulk, the way he moves makes me think shifter. I've gotten much better at identifying what people are since my first days of stumbling into these communities.

I haven't seen this man before and the way he looks at me sets my teeth on edge, all smug arrogance. Good.

I head toward him.

"Oh, hello there," the man says when I reach him.

Even the tone of his voice is irritating. Even better.

I lean an elbow on the bar and the stranger moves near me. Cutting through any preamble. Reluctantly, I admire the efficiency of it.

"Hello," I say with narrowed eyes.

"Let me buy you a drink?" he asks.

I make a show of considering the offer. "I'm not interested in small talk."

The shifter's smile grows.

A look and a tease later and he's pressing me into the wall of the empty hallway near the emergency exit. Very efficient.

I gasp in relief at the grind of our bodies.

His form is nice enough. The man knows just how to roll his hips and swelling erection against me. His shoulders aren't quite as wide as—

I snarl and pull the shifter by his collar into what could resemble a kiss.

I'd do anything to silence my mind right now.

The shifter freezes in surprise at the clash of my mouth on his before relaxing and trying to battle my tongue and teeth with his own. It's... nice. Different.

The shifter's tongue slides against mine, the flavor not immediately off-putting. My whirring mind starts to quiet.

Thank *fuck*.

The shifter is talented with his tongue. Maybe I'll let him lick me to completion. I dig my nails into his shoulders and the man grunts. He takes the cue to lift my leg up around his hips, grinding harder into the cradle of my thighs.

He moans into my mouth at the friction. I push him back, breaking our kiss.

"Fuck me with your fingers," I say.

I want the release I'm looking for. Depending on how nice it is, maybe I'll give him a hand with his cock afterward. Probably not... I'm not here to get him off. If he were smarter about this, he would have pushed for sex rather than run his hand up my inner thigh with a smug chuckle.

I guess he's never had a woman leave before returning the favor. Everyone should experience new things. This shifter's time with me will be an education.

The shifter stops and spits on his hand in a way that may have been sexy for some but leaves me nauseated.

I hold back my squeamish feelings as his knuckles press against my thong, the underwear made for easy access, and he rubs in circles before slipping under the fabric. The stroke of fingers on me finally stirs something. Is it arousal? Probably not, but feeling anything rather than the draw in my chest is such a relief that I moan.

"Yeah, that's it. You knew I'd be able to give you what you needed," he says.

I barely keep from rolling my eyes. The ego on this one. I'm starting to look forward to leaving him with blue balls.

But the man won't stop talking.

"A little birdie told me that your sister got mated." The man huffs a laugh. "Get it? Little birdie?"

I glare at him. The shifter has the nerve to chuckle, like my annoyance is cute.

"Is that the best your fingers can do?" I taunt.

A look crosses the shifter's face, and he presses his fingers inside me, using his thumb to rub circles around my clit.

Should I worry that he knows about Zeph? No, there aren't many harpies in this city and the whole story had run through the community like wildfire.

But I don't want to talk about Zeph right now. Her abduction and rescue had been more than nine months ago, yet the guilt of putting my sister on the radar of a trafficker is still as fresh as ever. That guilt is what made me vulnerable to a certain demon.

A demon I'm bonded to.

"For all the things we hear about harpies," the shifter starts. "That you're maneaters and gut people on sight, imagine my surprise to learn that your sister settled down with two men. I guess it just takes the right kind of man to tame a bird."

"*Fuck* you." My words lack heat because the shifter twists his fingers just right and the stretch of them is getting me to where I want even as alarm bells are ringing in my mind.

"We could be together forever. My life span matching yours. It would just take a little nip from me."

The brush of teeth on my throat goes from being mildly pleasant to causing a blast of icy panic.

So reckless. Again.

Fury comes second to the panic and my actions are quick. The shifter hits the opposite wall.

"Hey—"

My hand squeezes his windpipe and he fights me, but his strength doesn't compare to mine. I'm a harpy, a creature of myth with my own magic in my veins. My abilities exceed a shifter who is subject to an inner animal.

The shifter freezes and lets out a canine whine when the talons of my other hand penetrate the fabric of his pants, digging through the skin of his balls. His fear is a sticky scent and I want to slash upward and gut him as he'd joked about.

My hands are no longer human appearing but have shifted in my rage. The skin of my forearms to fingers are covered in rough, protective black scales, each finger ending in a deathly sharp talon.

Harpies don't wear weapons. We are one. Aunt Fairuza's words always come back to me when I'm tempted by a beautiful blade. But her meaning is undeniable. There is nothing quite as terrifying as watching someone be torn apart by talons and rage alone.

And if people fear harpies, then altercations such as this don't happen.

This is why we don't take mates. This is why we can't afford to be seen as *soft*.

Because then pompous, second-rate shifters think they can get a longer lifespan by biting us. Because when the illusion of strength is broken, people see harpies for what they are. A small race that's fierce, but ultimately vulnerable.

My heart races with adrenaline and rage. I sink my talons deeper into the man's balls. I fight the urge to gag at the squishy give of his flesh and the spread of wet on my hand. *Don't think about the fluids, Sophia. Think scary harpy thoughts and don't think about the blood and everything else.*

The shifter responds instinctually to the display of dominance, no matter the amount of pain he's in.

"N-no need to resort to violence." His voice is wobbly but not nearly as scared as what my instincts desire.

A part of me is screaming that it's my duty to show this man why people speak in whispers about harpies. But killing this shifter will cause more problems than it's worth. Harpies have no representation on the Council that rules over paranormal beings. The Council is only made up of witches and shifters; those beings that are the majority of the population.

A cheerful voice breaks into the struggle I'm having with my instincts.

"Oh, hello, bond-mate."

No fucking way.

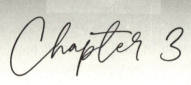

Chapter 3

SOPHIA

My head snaps toward the voice.

Mace Reynolds, thorn in my side, leans against the wall next to us. His dark hair and imperfect face are undeniable.

Words won't come to my mouth.

Mace's eyes trace my predicament. His lopsided smile morphs into a wince when he reaches where my talons have stabbed into the shifter.

I find my voice, my rage bleeding through. "What are you doing here?"

Mace shrugs in a way that stretches the fabric of his suit coat over his wide shoulders. I've never seen him out of a suit. It doesn't look formal on him even in the sea of T-shirts and jeans. It fits, as if the way he dresses is the only nod he gives to the fact that he's a couple hundred years old.

"I sensed you in the area and thought you may be in need of assistance," Mace says.

The audacity of this demon. My cheeks burn and anger has me lashing out.

"I don't need your help," I snap.

Mace rocks back on his heels, his jovial nature slipping when he looks at the shifter again. A cold, deadly expression passes over his face before it's gone. I'm half convinced I imagined the look when he grins at me again.

"I see that you have things… in hand."

The shifter sputters, believing now is the time to make his case. To Mace.

"I-I didn't know she belonged to you. I'm sorry, man."

Disbelief taints my rage. This stranger is more afraid of Mace than me, the one stabbing his balls? Would it really be that inconvenient to kill this shifter?

My muscles tense, waiting for Mace's response, expecting humiliation. As per our agreement, this demon owns a part of my soul. Why shouldn't he claim he owns me? Why shouldn't he chip away at the reputation of harpies everywhere for my flawed favor exchange?

Mace scoffs. Loudly. He gives me a *can-you-believe-this-guy* look, as if we're on the same side.

"I'm not the one you should be apologizing to. The lady shish kebabbing your family jewels holds that honor. Have you never met a harpy? They make what I can do to you look like child's play."

I blink, my muscles easing with each word he says.

Mace shakes his head. "And anyway, you're very much mistaken."

I frown. Where is he going with this?

Mace continues, "If anything, I belong to her."

The sentiment would sound romantic if my frustration with the man didn't give me heartburn, sleepless nights, and an unwanted soul bond.

That's what this shifter wanted to force on me, a soul bond. I pull my attention from the drama happening between me and the demon who's haunted me since I made my ill-fated request and focus on the issue facing me. How do I deal with this shifter in a way that stays beneath the Council's notice?

"I-I'm sorry." The apology from the shifter is hesitant, unsure. I sink my talons deeper into his testicles, there's a popping sensation that does have me gagging but the shifter is too busy screaming to notice.

The sound would have attracted attention if Mace hadn't covered the man's mouth. The muffled scream is horrifying, but the demon only tsks.

"Now, now, don't be dramatic. You'll probably heal by morning. If you make it that long," Mace says with a good-natured grin.

When the shifter only whimpers, Mace pulls his hand back. A string of saliva and mucus sticks to it. More fluids cover my hand and disgust finally overwhelms me.

I release the shifter and stumble backward. He crumples, clutching his bleeding crotch.

"You bitch," he spits out before hiccuping a sob.

Great. Another enemy made, another miscalculation, just one more fucking mistake to heap on my head. *Reckless.*

Mace fists the shifter's hair and yanks the man's face to look him in the eyes with a ferocity that I've never seen from him.

"What did you call this harpy who has every right to end your life?" Mace asks.

The shifter freezes.

"I heard every word that you spoke. I witnessed what you intended. Do you really think you can force another to soul bond?"

My eyes widen at the vehemence behind Mace's words. The fury peeking out behind his lackadaisical mask.

Embarrassment crawls over my skin. *How long has Mace been watching?*

"A soul bond requires at least a moment of *intention* on both parties. To even attempt to force such a thing is such a violation that it's taking everything in me not to strike you down on principle."

The shifter releases another canine whine at the sharp words.

Mace snarls. "Don't think you've escaped anything. Your alpha will be told exactly what happened tonight, Nick Rogers."

My brows shoot up as the shifter babbles an incoherent apology. The fury in my chest eases in the face of this version of Mace. Having the alpha of this shifter address the issue is a solution that didn't occur to me.

It's rare that I have all the knowledge and weight to outsource something like this. Going to the alpha will ensure this stays off the Council's radar and my lack of action won't be seen as weak. I admire the tidy fix.

Mace casts an asking glance to me. *Is this enough?*

My ruffled feathers smooth. I may not like that I'm bonded to this man, but he can be useful.

I nod for him to continue.

"Now, get out of her sight before she decides to fully neuter you." Mace's tone is cruel, and an impossible stroke of heat hits my belly at the brutality of it.

The shifter scrambles away and Mace disappears in the blink of an eye. Teleporting is such a rare skill that I forget it's one he possesses. The adrenaline is slow to recede. I jump when Mace reappears holding a *bar towel?*

Mace tilts his head and smiles in a silent apology for startling me before handing over the towel.

"My lady," he says, the ferocity in his voice is gone and he's back to being the irritating demon I've been dealing with for the past nine months. Before that, before we even met, I had to deal with this man causing issues in my business.

The towel is soaked, stinking of disinfectant. I snatch the gift and start to scrub the gore off my hands. The black scales start to shift back to skin as my heart rate begins to slow.

The disinfectant blocks the smell of the blood and fluids that I refuse to think about. The gratitude that swells in me is undeniable.

"I hope my presence didn't interrupt the job you're working," Mace says, the words careless but there is a gleam in his eye.

My cheeks burn. A job. That would be a good excuse for being in this situation. Not that the debts I'm dealing with and the bond between us have destroyed the life I've known and spurred me to seek out a distraction.

I sniff and attempt to deflect. "So, what are you really doing here?"

My neck itches and I look down the hall, there's a smear of blood from where the shifter used the wall to support himself and I yank my eyes away. Mace tilts his chin up and, somehow, he knows. He knows I'm not here on a job, knows he interrupted a situation of a more personal nature.

I tense, waiting for jokes, castigation, something.

Instead, Mace shrugs.

"I was actually in the area and sensed you." He leans in and the impossible happens. It almost distracts me from his words. "And I was curious."

In the breath of Mace's proximity, the awful drawing sensation in my chest *eases*. I take a deep breath and there's no restriction, no discomfort. I blink. How had I never noticed this before?

This is… not good. The dreams are one thing, but to be weakened when separated…

"Sophia?"

Mace's brows are furrowed and I force my mind to move onward. Later. I'll figure this out later when this demon isn't right next to me, invading my senses with his scent and providing *comfort* with his presence.

Sensed you in the area. Frustration spikes in me, and I grit my teeth.

"This bond between us is not what you said it'd be. You said I was just an anchor. That I'd probably *barely notice*."

Mace smiles and the slow satisfied movement of his lips strikes a chord of lust in me. It pisses me off.

"Do you *notice* me, fierce harpy?" The words are hot honey, burning and sticky.

The frustration almost boils over, and I blink to keep rage-induced tears from my eyes. Notice him? My entire life has been thrown out of whack, and it's as if Mace doesn't know a thing.

Because he doesn't, and I'm not going to tell him.

I won't share whatever weakness he's caused in me.

The only answer is to get out of this.

"Didn't you say you needed my assistance with something?"

Mace doesn't respond for a breath, looking at me as if he can see every thought I'm hiding from him. He leans in.

"So many secrets," Mace whispers, as if savoring the air between us.

Something throbs in me. Is it fear that he'll see through me? Or anticipation?

I squash that sensation quickly.

"At the birth?" I grit my teeth.

Mace blinks as if I've distracted him.

My nieces had been born almost a full month ago. A month ago, Mace had dropped the detail that he *needed* something. It was the first glimmer of hope that I could get leverage on this demon since this whole soul bond ordeal had begun.

Since then, we've barely been in the same room and the times we were had been for family functions. Functions that this demon had been adopted into as Asa's best friend.

Mace's lips purse into rare frustration. "I did say that. I do need your help, but this particular quarry is proving harder to pin down than I planned. Have no fear, bond-mate, your time will come."

I've never been patient, but the concept of being in this bond for an interminable amount of time destroys what patience I do have.

"Who's to say that I'll be available to help when you finally get around to needing it?" I hear the irritation in my own words, but I won't hide it.

I am not a convenience. It's better to give the impression that I won't wait around for him to figure out his shit.

Mace's brows shoot up. "Being connected through our souls doesn't give me priority?"

To figure that the man had that assumption and to have it confirmed are very different things. The insult burns between my shoulder blades and my talons itch to swipe out again.

I grit my teeth. "No, it doesn't. I am running a business. If you need my assistance with something, I suggest you book my paid services ahead of time."

Mace tilts his head and I see the other assumption rolling around in his mind. He thought I was going to do whatever he needed me to do for free.

This fucking demon.

"Mr. Reynolds." I spit the honorific. "We are soul bonded. That is the extent of our interaction. I don't work without compensation, and I don't live to serve you at the drop of a hat."

There's a glint in the demon's eyes, as something I've said thrills him.

"I have no expectation of you serving me, bond-mate."

The words are suggestive, and I forcibly look down the hall again to keep from blushing.

"I do admit, I took for granted that you'd want to help," he says.

Curiosity pulls my gaze back to Mace in time to see something dark pass through his expression.

Mace continues, "I've been made aware of a group that traffics individuals of rarer species. This involves the mysterious buyer Henderson arranged for your sister when he took her. I'd assumed that bringing this group down would be satisfying for you."

Yes. Satisfying doesn't begin to describe what it would be like to be involved in this. To do some good with the guilt haunting me.

But... I have other concerns.

More concerns than this soul bond.

I clench my jaw. "I'm not in a position to take on charity work."

Mace's eyes widen in surprise. "Is that so?"

I freeze. I've shown too much of my hand.

"How curious." Mace's eyes dilate and he leans in. "What have you been hiding, Sophia Shirazi?"

I'll never tell.

I glare at the demon, refusing to cower under his scrutiny. We stay like that for a moment, Mace analyzing my face like he can see more than I'm showing.

The lick of lust from before is back. It's a distraction that I literally can't afford.

"Don't wait too long, Reynolds." I spin, leaving this encounter before I show this demon any more than I mean to. I shout back. "And figure out what you're going to pay me!"

Chapter 4

MACE

I watch Sophia leave.

Her scent of sunshine disappears with the last swish of dark hair.

Curiosity and temptation vibrate in my veins. What has my harpy gotten herself into?

The dark circles under Sophia's eyes have somehow gotten worse since I'd last seen her, and that had been right after she'd fainted at the triplet's birth. Her soul energies are all over the place with worry and distress. The golden threads of her soul that braid with mine have frayed.

It doesn't weaken the bond we have, but the state of stress is unlike the woman I first approached. Her mischievous nature had been what had called to me. Her fiery strength added to the attraction. Fate must have intervened to serve up such a delightful anchor right when I needed one.

There's an ache in my chest. I wish I could keep her.

I shake my head at the impossible thought. I have nothing to offer her. Our bond will hold for now, until she finds a way out of it. It might be this year, or in a hundred, but I have no doubt that Sophia will find a way to be free of me.

When that happens, I'll need to find a different anchor, maybe one of the rare objects that can operate as such. Until that time, I can play this game with my harpy. Even if the world around us isn't a game at all.

With my detour complete, it's time to go back to checking locations.

Now with the memory of Sophia's hips moving on the other man's fingers, a moan breaking from her lips. The sight had been intoxicating.

Not just because Sophia Shirazi is exquisite, she is, all olive skin and plush lips that could drive an individual mad. But because it's so rare for me to see her at ease, with her guard down.

And then that shifter had suggested such a violation as bonding to her against her will, and I'd seen red. Our bond was not done with force. If Sophia had gone back on the favor she owed, I wouldn't have bonded her. Our bond depended on the fact that Sophia is a proud creature.

Before I could act, Sophia had skewered the shifter.

That was when my lust flared.

Since our first meeting, I've wanted Sophia Shiraz, but creatures such as I don't usually get what they want. If my harpy and I make it into bed together, I'll enjoy it while it lasts.

But now something is going on with her. She's keeping secrets…

I can't do much about that tonight though. I slide my phone from my pocket and pull up the list of locations, picking the next one. I upload the address into a maps app and compare my mental map of the target area to the satellite image before centering myself.

I breathe out and disappear into the shadowy in-between like a wisp of smoke.

Chapter 5

SOPHIA

"Are you walking back on the favor you owe?" Mace raises a brow.

I crease my brow. "No, I just—what will it be like?"

Mace rolls his lips, entertained. As he should be, I'm stalling. It won't matter what it will be like because I owe him this favor for finding Zeph. I made the request and now it's time to pay up on this demon deal.

I won't run away from this… until I can figure out a way out of it. There is always a way out. Just like there will be a way out of the other debt weighing on my mind.

"Well, we will be bound together on a soul level, but most people don't notice anything different. Once we make the bond, we'll both be a little drained, but it's nothing a little sleep shouldn't solve."

"Most people don't notice?" I repeat.

"Most." Mace pauses. "There is the chance that we'll feel each other's emotions, but probably only for distraught moments."

That doesn't seem that bad.

"Okay." I nod. "How do we do this?"

Mace's eyes light up and he crooks his finger toward me. I wait for a moment before approaching, already regretting this. I'm a fly caught in a spider's web.

"So brave," Mace says, and I don't think he's just teasing me. "May I touch you?"

"Where?" I ask.

Mace grins. "And cautious, I'll just be touching your shoulder, near your neck."

I nod again, this time narrowing my eyes.

Mace places his palm exactly where he stated. His thumb tickles the bare skin over my collarbone before his fingers stroke over the muscles from my back to my neck.

"Relax, fierce harpy," he whispers.

I swallow and the room feels hot. His touch stokes something I won't dare name.

My reaction to him is just nerves.

Something in my very being tugs and my knees go weak. The edges of my vision darken. A man embraces me, his arms firm and warm. The physical connection feels deeper and whispers of reassurance. The man speaks words that I don't catch, the world spins as I lose my grip of what is real and what is this new thing. I'm placed on something soft before my consciousness leaves me.

***

"Weakness when separated, sleepless nights, and discomfort, anything else?" Alice writes in a spiral-bound notebook.

"What?" I ask, startled. Did I doze off or merely get lost in the memory? It's hard to say sometimes now. After the bond, I woke on my own couch the next day with the

terrible sensation plaguing me. Like someone sucking a
Capri Sun.

I shrug. "Weird dreams, but that's been for months."

"Dreams? You haven't said anything about dreams.
What kind of dreams?"

I hesitate.

"Oh." Alice blushes and coughs. For having a very large
romance book collection, the witch could be quite shy
about sex.

I blow out a breath. There have been some sex dreams.
Nothing incredibly explicit, but enough to leave me aching
when I wake.

Sex dreams aren't really the issue.

The disturbing dreams are those filled with a wanting
for warmth. *Comfort.* A wanting that rips at my lungs
and yanks on my heart. Like trying to catch wisps of
satisfaction. Of happiness, only to wake with the sense
that there is something missing. Someone.

Those dreams are subversive. Dangerous.

"Why won't you tell Mace about how the bond is
affecting you again?" Alice asks.

I glare at her, but she doesn't look at me. Instead, Alice
has moved from the spiral-bound notebook to an aged
piece of parchment featuring a meticulously drawn circle
design. She frowns at her hand as she starts to draw a line
before stopping to grab a raised ruler.

I blow out a breath. We've talked around this before,
but Alice tends to forget to be as on guard as me when it
comes to people's intentions.

"Why would I tell my biggest rival that I'm weak
without his presence?"

Alice finally looks up at me. The flatness of her mouth communicating that this was not something she had forgotten, just something that she thinks is senseless.

"One, he may be able to fix it," she says with a raised finger.

Oh, she has a numbered list for this.

"And demand a payment for it—"

"Two," Alice cuts me off. "I'd say that Mace is not your biggest concern."

That silences me, a sick feeling rising in my gut. Alice is the only person I've told about that *other* situation. Alice cocks an eyebrow.

"I've worked with Mace for years. He'd treat you fairly and he's practically been adopted into your family's inner circle." Her words are a little bitter with that.

It's completely incongruous, but somehow Mace has won over my mother. Alice has been my friend for years and only gets the polite treatment in the presence of my family.

"You know that has more to do with you being connected to me versus Mace being connected to Zeph." Favoritism, harpy, is thy middle name. "My aunt still hates him," I offer, as if that makes it better.

Alice snorts. "Fairuza hates anyone who isn't a harpy." She shakes her head. "He found Zeph when she was taken. Give him credit where it's due. Mace is an ally."

"He extracted a demon deal from me for that!"

Alice rolls her eyes. "You gave those words freely—"

"I know! But he didn't have to take them!"

We glare at each other. This is an old argument. After Mace soul bonded with me, I fled straight to Alice. She made me recount my exact words repeatedly, trying to tease out a loophole for the debt I had stumbled into. In the end, it's as simple as I made a request and he accepted it.

Sometimes I wonder why I didn't push my luck and put off accepting the bond. The real consequences of betraying a demon deal are unknown. Could Mace have forced me into this bond? Could he demand my skin to walk off my body as with some myths I've heard?

Honestly, I don't know.

Whether or not Mace could enforce our contract is a moot point. I've repaid my favor to him with our bond. He never specified I had to stay bonded for our agreement.

"And anyway, I thought you were working on fixing this bond. You said it's possible." I wave a hand over Alice's worktable, trying not to let my voice take on a demanding tone. Trying not to push away my friend in frustration.

The surface is littered with various tools Alice uses for the craft and some of the more precision projects she's working on.

Alice's face softens. "I'm trying, Soph. Soul energies aren't my forte. I can't see them or even feel them like a demon would be able to."

"I know, but you've already figured out so much about harpies."

Alice has a lot of goals around experimenting with the boundaries of magic and I'm the perfect guinea pig.

Harpies are incredibly sensitive to magic. It's how Alice and I started working together. It had started when we were teens. After Amara had broken her wing and was on the mend, boredom had gotten the better of me and I had started frequenting the shops that I knew catered to magic folk on the sly. My parents wouldn't have stopped me from going there, my father is a witch and keeps his own workroom in our family home. But my sisters' and my harpy training had been handled by my aunts, as is custom, and it would have caused more conflict than it was worth for them to know about my adventures.

Alice had been in one of those shops full of books and crystals. Her family's shop, actually. Before her father had lost it. I'd picked up an item from the shelf, wanting to inspect it further, and the next thing I knew I was flat on my back, looking up into the pale face of a witch near my age, frowning at me.

Alice and I just clicked. Our curiosity of the world went hand in hand with our goals. Alice wanted to learn things to use in her projects while I was more interested in gorging myself on new sights, meeting new people. A friendship was born.

Amara never went out adventuring with me, even after she healed, and Zeph was more of a homebody than both of us put together. I love my sisters, but we have hardly anything in common.

Alice's main goal for years has been to somehow make a spell that completely blocks magic, something to nullify it. A spell like that would mean that harpies wouldn't have to be as vulnerable as they are.

"It's not enough." Alice scowls.

"It's made a world of difference."

In the last few years, Alice has accomplished some very useful spells, under a pseudonym, of course. Even after all these years, her father's reputation casts a long shadow.

I've covertly spread these spells through the harpy community and some other types of paranormal communities that don't react well to magic.

My amazing jacket was designed just for me, but there are a number of invaluable spells circulating. A way to put a person under that won't result in a hangover that lasts days. A healing spell that won't make a harpy, me in particular, vomit afterward.

I distribute these in ways that can't be traced back to me because, like Alice's father, my reputation is more of a hindrance than a help.

Wild Sophia. Irresponsible Sophia.

I huff.

"I actually have something to test!" Alice says, brightening.

Excitement hums at the same time as nerves clutch my stomach.

"How strong do you think it will be?" I ask. Each test symbolizes a possibility of success, but side effects are a bitch.

Alice's excited face winces and the nerves squeeze a little tighter. I bite my lip before committing to the unknown with a shrug.

"Well, I guess I only have a family dinner tonight. I could just not attend," I say.

We stare at each other for a moment before I shake my head. We both know I won't risk my mother's ire by skipping family dinner.

"I could go with you," Alice offers weakly.

I scrunch my nose. "My aunts will be there."

Alice blanches.

Yeah, that's how I feel about it too. Our familial relationship is a tangle of contradicting emotions that bite.

"Okay, let's get this over with." I push forward, brave face in place.

Alice gives me a smile, trying to reassure me. We both know the risks. She goes to her cabinets before returning with a simple polished stone with gold tiny painted marks on it. She gets the charm about a foot from me before I'm falling over backward to get away.

The interfering static clashes over my skin and drags painful, invisible claws through me.

"No!" I shriek without meaning to, my hands coming up to keep her away.

Alice freezes and retreats, her brows crease in concern.

I gasp as the awful experience starts to fade.

Alice puts the charm away with the snap of a small drawer. "That was not the intended effect."

I make a weak sound, the result of the drain hitting me with the way the world tilts. "That's the third time we've had a failure in the last few months. What is going on? These are meant to block magic."

Alice starts to pace, chewing on her thumbnail. She doesn't respond immediately. I flop on the old couch, dizzy and needing a moment. My eyelids flutter shut, and the darkness is such a relief I have to bite my lip to keep in a whimper.

In the darkness, there is a small tug in my mind. *What the*—the bond. Mace is on the other side of the soul bond… checking on me. I've never been able to feel him before. My mental snarl must reach him because there is a responding sensation as if I've made him smile and the tug disappears. The demon retreats.

Alice sighs with aggression. I open my eyes to see her flipping through a lab notebook she keeps. There is frustration on her face with an undercurrent of wariness. Unease bleeds through my already tired body when she looks up at me.

"Sophia…"

I wait. And wait. The unease rises with each moment we stare at each other.

"What?" I ask when she still doesn't respond.

"I think it's getting worse."

"What is? The design?"

"No, my design has been consistent. I think you're becoming more sensitive to magic."

My skin goes cold.

"No—" I cut myself off, stopping the thoughts in my head from spilling out of my mouth.

No, no, no. With how susceptible to magic I am... I already have to deal with the buzz of every ward I pass; the disorienting effect of a stranger's glamour when they get too close. To be even more sensitive would be devastating.

"You said that the soul bond is starting to affect you more these past few months."

I rub my hand over my chest. "Yes. It hasn't ever been comfortable, but it's definitely gotten worse."

Silence stretches between us. The way I could feel the bond just now making more sense as the fact of the situation settles.

"Sophia..." She doesn't continue.

I blink at a pale Alice. She knows how debilitating this would be for me.

When I finally open my mouth, there's only one thing I can think to say.

"Fuck."

Chapter 6

MACE

Sophia's snarling response through our bond is a sharp whiplash and has me smiling. I retreat from my curious prodding and open my eyes. The kitchen is bright with a homey feel to the place. It hums with positive energy in the way that many houses passed through witch generations do.

"What are you smiling at?" Gideon asks, exasperation clear in his voice.

"Hm?" I hum, as if not understanding the question.

That's what you get when you pop in on your friends with no warning. Exasperation.

In actuality, the exasperation is because I'd interrupted Gideon and his lovely mate when I popped in with no warning. Something that I will now think twice about. I'd considered the kitchen a common area not meant for intimate games.

Joke's on me and now it will be hard to see the table in the same light.

Gideon, a once immortal sea monster, rolls his eyes at my deflection and continues typing at his laptop. Rose enters the kitchen, now composed but still blushing.

"Apologies for dropping in without notice," I say to her.

"She doesn't mind being watched," Gideon teases before giving me a look that puts rethinking dropping in without notice higher on my priority list. If his mate didn't have an exhibitionist streak this may have ended in a very different way.

Rose glares at him. "It's not the same thing and you know it." She shakes her head. "How about we start over? Hello, Mace, it's nice to see you. What brings you to our home?"

I bite my tongue to keep from automatically saying it was nice to *see* her too. Rose's blush deepens as if reading my mind.

Gideon's mouth twitches.

Rose sighs loudly. "I'll make sandwiches."

"I'll do that." Gideon jumps up, the chair scraping against the floor with the force of it.

"No." Rose makes a staying gesture with her hands. "I'm not helpless and Mace needs something from you."

Now Gideon glares at me as if I'm the reason he can't wait on his pregnant mate. Which is true.

Rose walks to him and presses his shoulders until my powerful friend is sitting again. He wraps an arm around her, hugging her body to him and slides a hand over the swell of her belly.

I cast my eyes away, giving them a moment of privacy. My chest brimming with a mix of emotions.

Asa and Gideon both deserve to enjoy their happiness. I'm happy for them and also… it's not jealousy, not really. There's an ache that I won't ever have what they do.

Not the young, I could do without those for the next few hundred years if ever. But, I'd had a passing thought not very long ago that I'd eventually find a mate for myself.

And then Zeph was taken from Asa.

He had gotten her back. Asa is a powerhouse. He could burn the world down around him to protect the ones he loves.

I wouldn't be able to do that.

I am the weak one.

The demon who has to resort to soul bonds as to not fade away. There would be nothing more terrible than to have the gift of a mate and fail to protect them.

I've already lost someone who I was supposed to protect. I won't do that again.

I clear my throat. "You should get that ward against teleporting put in place. I'm not the only person who has the ability."

The couple breaks away from each other. The moment they're having disrupted like a pebble dropped in water, the cascading ripples bringing them back to my presence.

Rose's face pinches in discomfort. "It's been on our to-do list, especially with this one" —she gestures to her belly— "on the way, but we've been having some… awkwardness with our ward master."

"I'll handle it." Gideon nods to me. "I also emailed you that list."

"What list?" Rose asks.

"A list of all the places one can get a portal spell without going to a registered retailer." Satisfaction oozes from my tone but transitions to excitement. The hunt continues.

Chapter 7

SOPHIA

"The story you want to go with is that you were day drinking with Alice?" Amara says as she taps against the steering wheel. My sister broadcasts her disbelief with a certain economy of words. It's a skill.

At the same time, I pick up Amara's frustration from being lied to, the stress on her face from helping run Greg's bakery, and nerves from the imminent family dinner.

One of these times I'm going to need to instruct Amara in the art of not showing every thought on her face. Or maybe I can see every struggle because I know her so well.

A casualty of being triplets.

"I figured getting a ride with you was the responsible thing to do. I wouldn't want to fly into a building or anything."

Amara doesn't completely disguise her shudder at the thought. My sister doesn't hide her fear of heights nearly as well as she should.

The truth is that I'm too tired to drive or fly to the family dinner. I haven't trusted myself to operate a vehicle since a close call a month ago. Drowsy driving isn't safe driving and all that.

Alice's place is on Amara's route from the bakery, so I called her. I could have used a ride-sharing app, but I'm not in the position to be spending money.

I delete another sternly worded text message from the untraceable number.

"How has it been going at the bakery?" I ask, trying to distract myself from impending doom.

Amara's face softens and a smile starts to curve her lips.

"It's been good. Really good. The catering orders are starting to take off and Greg has started coming in more often. Sometimes just to show off the clutch." Amara good naturedly rolls her eyes.

I snort. "Of course he does. You'd think he was the one to carry them for nine months instead of Zeph."

"It's kind of adorable to see Asa and Greg fall all over each other for those babies."

I tilt my head and Amara's smile freezes at my look.

"Not that having fathers underfoot is natural for harpies," she says.

Now I'm rolling my eyes. "You sound like Fairuza."

We groan in unison.

"Being around her already isn't comfortable, but since Zeph…" Amara blows out a breath.

I shake my head. "That's an understatement. At least she's stopped bothering Zeph."

"She doesn't want to risk being cut off from the girls," Amara points out.

"And she's stopped bothering us about adding to the harpy population."

Harpy fertility is a strange thing. Conception is at will, but once one sister conceives it becomes less of a sure thing. As if having young around suppresses our biology. It's probably a holdover from times that flocks were instrumental in protecting the next generation.

"She's been stopping by the bakery lately," Amara admits. "Watching me interact with the staff."

"Oof, like how?"

The tapping of Amara's fingers on the steering wheel takes up a nervous rhythm. I make a face at the idea of having Fairuza watching over my shoulder.

"Like instructing me in ways to be a better leader."

"…And?" Morbid curiosity has me prodding.

"It mostly revolves around the subject that I'm too soft on them." My sister snorts. "That I need to assert my dominance."

I blink. "It's a bakery. Not battle."

Amara's lips flatten. "To hear Fairuza talk about it, it's one and the same."

Something occurs to me. "Is that fae still bugging you? I can't imagine his backtalk going over well with Fairuza there."

Amara's brows crease. "He's fine. Strange, but I think it was just a culture difference." She brightens. "Thankfully, he has a way of disappearing when she shows up."

I huff a laugh before getting serious. "So, Fairuza is starting to groom you for the matriarch role then? Making sure you'll uphold the harpy values once she's gone."

"It's ridiculously early. She has like another hundred years in the role. At least." Amara adjusts in her seat.

"Yes, but you're the eldest and she probably wants to make sure you aren't going over to the dark side like Zeph did."

"I'm just glad Zeph is happy." Amara sounds wistful.

"There." I point. "Don't ever let Fairuza know you think that. Ever. That's a recipe for having her show up all hours to try and mold you into the perfect harpy."

I rest back against the seat. "You already stress yourself out doing that anyway."

Amara waves her hand. "I just… I want her to be proud of me."

I nod. That's how Fairuza gets what she wants. By withholding her emotions from us. Making us strive for her approval. Our other aunt, Jasmine, is a little more relaxed about that kind of thing, but Fairuza is head of our branch.

"You've had so many accomplishments to be proud of," I say.

Amara sighs in exasperation.

I shrug. "Just because they aren't what Fairuza wants for you doesn't diminish them."

Amara's brows crease and unhappiness paints her features.

I realized a long time ago that I couldn't be happy and have my aunt's approval, her conditional affection. It had hit me sometime between her beratement of my "weakness" as a teenager about my curiosity and the cold disapproval when I claimed a witch as my best friend.

Harpies don't intermingle with other kinds of paranormal beings.

It's drilled into our psyche that it's for our safety, for the safety of harpies everywhere. The less the world knows of our weaknesses the safer we'll be.

It's the one rule I've never been able to keep.

Wanderlust is what Fairuza calls it. I've always had it. The want to know more, see more, experience everything. There's a special kind of joy in meeting other paranormal beings. I won't be getting best harpy of the year awards, so why twist myself into something my aunt will approve of?

Fairuza always did say it would get me into trouble. I'd rather skewer the balls of twenty shifters before admitting that she had been right.

Amara grips the steering wheel harder. "I will show Fairuza that I can do the work I do, know the people I know, and still uphold all the harpy values. I've got time."

"That's the spirit," I say, but my cheer is shallow.

The determination in Amara's words lingers.

Chapter 8

SOPHIA

The familiar scents of Mom's cooking hit me when I open the front door. Saffron, rose, and cumin flavor the air and have my mouth watering. Some of the tightness I've been carrying in my shoulders loosens. Amara and I push each other like we're still kids as we move from the entryway. We're the last to get here according to the noise coming from the kitchen.

I may have moved out of the family home, but there's still something unique about it that signals safety. Here I don't have to worry about the debts I owe. I can put aside my issues for a short time and enjoy Amara bickering with our brother, Luca.

Along with the rest of the new family we have picked up.

The living room next to the entryway is empty except for Asa. Zeph's mate is swaying back and forth, talking into a phone while cradling one of my nieces in an arm. Amara is correct in that seeing Asa and Greg melt over the babies is a tiny bit adorable.

It's not something I want in my life, but I can appreciate it. Or appreciate watching a powerful demon show his marshmallow center anyway.

Asa catches sight of us in the hall and makes a gesture of lifting eyebrows and the baby in his arm at the same time. The kid squirms and Amara swoops in to take a hold of the swaddled heap.

Asa flashes a grateful smile, covering the receiver with a hand. "To Zephyrine, please. The little miss is demanding her dinner."

Amara makes a silly face at the baby as she moves with me to the real hub of action, the kitchen.

"Is that right? Are you hungry?" she asks in a weird voice.

"I don't think she understands what you're saying," I deadpan and Amara scowls at me.

"You don't know that. Harpies develop early."

I roll my eyes, but don't fight the issue. Everyone tends to be a little on edge when it comes to the clutch.

I've always been an outsider to my family. The things I'm interested in, what drives me, seem to be so radically different than everyone else that there were times growing up when I thought I was adopted. That outsideness amplifies around the babies.

I love my nieces on an instinctual *I will rip out the eyeballs of whoever hurts you* level, but I don't turn to mush around them. If anything, I wish they'd grow up faster so I can have a conversation with my new blood. Or maybe not. The faster this clutch grows, the sooner Amara and I will need to stumble through the motions of training the next harpy generation, as tradition demands.

The clutch can stay squirmy peanuts with squished faces for now.

Everyone looks up when we arrive.

Dad and Zeph are playing cards on the dining table while Luca feeds a bottle to another niece and coos. My mouth twists at the sight of my overconfident brother becoming completely undone. Mom and Greg are in the kitchen area moving smoothly in tandem, not hampered at all by the fact that Greg has my last niece attached to his chest with some contraption.

Amara heads that way. "Delivery! One hungry baby bird."

Zeph groans, wrapping her arms around her chest protectively. "I've got nothing left. She'll have to have the formula."

"I'll get it!" Greg says and rushes over to the open diaper bag on the table.

Mom's brows crease. "You are drinking those drinks the midwife gave you, aren't you?"

"Yes, Mâmân." Zeph glares.

"Well, it's just supposed to help—" Mom starts, and I see the absolute frustration on Zeph's face with a tinge of hopelessness.

"So, what are we having?" I interrupt loudly with a playful smile that I'm lacking the sleep to feel.

Mom frowns at my interruption and looks at my empty arms. "Sophia, where exactly is the salad?"

Fuck. I knew I forgot something.

Lately, I've been lucky to remember where my phone is with how the drain has been affecting me.

Heat rises in my cheeks, but I keep my face blank.

"What salad?" My innocent tone has Mom pursing her lips and I've succeeded in deterring her and Zeph's impending contention. At a price.

Irresponsible Sophia.

I've once again managed to disappoint my family. My emotions are closer to the surface than they should be. It's just a salad but I blink my eyes against the sting of tears. What is wrong with me?

Some of what I'm feeling must show on my face because the skin around Mom's eyes crinkles in concern.

Mom blows out a breath. "It's fine—"

"I can pop out to get the veggies," a voice says from behind me, and I spin. Mace gives me a *wink* before disappearing as if never there.

I spin back around. "What the *fuck* is he doing here?"

Zeph snorts at my outcry. She's the only one who has been privy to my contention with Mace over my business. No one in the family knows about the soul bond.

Mom's head tilts in confusion. "Mace is family. He's always welcome here."

I bite the inside of my cheek to keep from releasing heated words. The unfairness of it still burns. Mace is family. The friend of a mate that Zeph was never supposed to have is *family*, but the best friend I've had for half of my life is treated like a visitor.

"That's just great," I mutter.

The sound of the front door opening travels through the house, and my roiling emotions freeze. Multiple people around the kitchen stiffen, as if sensing the impending tidal wave of whatever our aunts bring.

It hadn't used to be like this. Or the tension hadn't been so obvious. There used to be times growing up that I'd be excited to see my mother's sisters. Times when Fairuza's feelings hadn't been so obvious.

Now, after Zeph's decision to buck harpy tradition and commit her life to her mates the hostile air around Fairuza infects everything. Was this what it had been like for Mom when she had abandoned the rules of being a harpy to keep Dad as a mate?

Had it been worse then?

Mom straightens. "Fairuza." She nods. "Jasmine."

I turn to face my aunts. Fairuza nods to my mother in a way that has me bristling while Jasmine smiles awkwardly.

"Hester." Fairuza greets Mom before turning to me. "Sophia, a word, please."

It isn't a question, but a statement. Always the dominating force; a request from Fairuza is an order.

Mace is quickly forgotten, and I bare my teeth in a smile.

"Of course," I say.

Jasmine gives my shoulder a reassuring squeeze when I pass her to follow Fairuza down the side hall to the family library. She's always been the more nurturing one of my aunts. I glance back at Mom and the worry on her face has me snapping my eyes forward. What could Fairuza possibly want to talk to *me* about?

I drag a finger along the wood paneling of the unlit hallway as I walk and rack my brain. What trouble could I have caused that would result in a lecture? No fun nights dancing with different kinds of paranormals in public, no stealing, and only a moderate amount of lying.

Most nights I drag myself home and wrap myself in a blanket, forcing my eyes open enough to do research for various cases I'm working before tossing and turning in bed for the rest of the night.

Damn demon and this damn soul bond.

Is this about that shifter I maimed?

News travels fast, but that kind of thing shouldn't have reached Fairuza's ears with the circles she runs in. Harpy circles with only the smallest contact with those she works with in relation to the Council. Fairuza is one of the three harpies that represent the interests of our kind to the Council.

"I don't know what you've heard, but it isn't my fault," I say as I step into the library.

This room had been Zeph's favorite growing up. It was a quiet place for her to hide in our noisy family. I spent time in here as needed, the shelves hold what history had been recorded about our family line. I'd been more interested in the tomes from Dad's witch side of the family. Those books told a more well-rounded history, or a less secluded one anyway.

His books helped give me the very basics about other beings in this world. Witches always acted as the neutral go-between. The majority of the paranormal population other than shifters, their organizations are much more integrated into the wider community. It's more acceptable for witches to marry or mate outside of their own group.

Dad's side of the family is more distant. As if he ceded his place in their family to be a part of the harpies. My witch grandparents visit once a year, still pinching our cheeks no matter that we're all adults, but they don't really feel like family the way my aunts do.

Fairuza turns to face me, her eyes narrowing on my face as if she can see every sleepless night, every single attribute about myself that she finds less than.

"Sophia—"

"Aunt Fairuza."

I meet her steel tone with my own. I may be exhausted and have a list of failings as long as my arm, but to cower in the face of my aunt would be the exact wrong thing to do. Instinct knows how to react to the matriarch of my branch even if I'd rather turn tail and run.

Fairuza's pursed mouth softens in satisfaction, and I blink.

Everything is a test with this harpy.

"We have things we should discuss," she says.

"Like what?" I ask.

My business performance is at an all-time low. With the drain of the soul bond being how it is, I haven't taken any jobs that have had a whiff of danger. It's a vastly different business model than I started with and not nearly as lucrative as I need it to be. Anger at a certain demon burns in my chest even as I face down my aunt.

"I haven't received any complaints of your behavior from the Council of late."

I keep my eyes from widening in surprise. So, not the shifter then.

"I'm not being the troublemaker you expect me to be? I should work on that," I say.

An exasperated expression passes over Fairuza's face. "I'm saying that your improvement has been noticed."

There's a bitter pang in my heart. I've only *improved* because I can't risk going into an iffy situation in my current state.

"And?" My smile is brittle.

Fairuza lifts her brows. "And I think the time has come that you start being trained to someday be matriarch."

My ears would ring less if she had smacked me.

"What?" My question comes out with a squeak.

"You need to prepare to serve the harpy cause," Fairuza says, her brows now creasing.

"B-but I'm the youngest. The youngest doesn't become matriarch."

Fairuza's lip curls with a trace of disgust. "Traditionally, no, but Zephyrine has chosen to forsake our way of life."

Disbelief has my head shaking back and forth.

"Zeph isn't the oldest—"

Fairuza cuts me off with an indistinguishable sound. "Amara isn't a good choice for matriarch."

I gape at my aunt who folds her arms, showing a small sign of discomfort.

Fairuza continues, "She is… timid. She doesn't go after what she wants. Zephyrine has provided a new generation of harpies and you've created your own business, no matter how sordid, but Amara hasn't shown the mettle required to be matriarch."

Rage on Amara's behalf swells in my chest. How dare Fairuza make these sorts of judgments about my sister. How dare she find Amara wanting when Amara is the one who combats her anxiety every day to show a brave face to the world.

"Amara is the only one still trying to win your approval. She actually follows the rules." My words are practically a hiss.

Fairuza stiffens. "And those who follow the rules aren't the ones that are born to lead."

Speechless. I am speechless that Fairuza would bring this kind of conflict into our family. How dare she try and pit us against each other just to fit the picture she has of what a harpy *should* be.

My anger finally melts the tangle of emotions stilling my tongue.

"Is your pride worth your family?" My voice is fierce. I keep myself from shouting by pure will alone.

Fairuza jumps, as if surprised that I'm not clamoring for the approval she's finally extending.

I continue, vehemence pounding each statement. "I'm not going to rearrange my life to your satisfaction, Zeph has her own priorities now, and Amara… maybe it's better you push her away because you don't deserve how hard she tries to please you."

I can't stay here. I refuse to sit around a table with my aunt and pretend she hasn't shown me her ugly hand. I throw the door open to storm out and face an audience of two. The worst people that could have overheard the exchange.

A pale Amara blinks before a mortified flush spreads up her face. She looks over my shoulder at Fairuza and my own chest cracks with the heartbroken expression in her eyes before she shakes it away.

A sound of regret comes from Fairuza, but it's too late.

"S-sorry." Amara's voice is low, as if her throat is too tight. "Dinner is ready. I'm just going to—"

Amara's sharp inhale breaks the blank mask and my sister rushes into the dark of the hallway. Pushing past the demon waiting in the shadows. Mace's brows are high, and he lets out a whistle.

"That was brutal."

I chase after Amara. Barely resisting the urge to jab at my ball and chain for his unhelpful commentary.

My concern for Amara has me searching every room. It's no use.

Amara spent a long time trapped indoors when she was younger, waiting for her wing to heal. Long enough to know every secret hiding place. If she wants to hide… I have to let her.

I make a tired mental note to try and talk with Amara later, to check in on her. Fairuza's words had been ruthless.

Amara may be the eldest, but this had been the first time in her adult life that Fairuza had outwardly disapproved of her, and I know that sting as intimately as the cracked plaster on the ceiling above my bed that I'd covered with a poster of the Florentine dome. The memory always there even after trying to bandage it with newer things, better things.

I'm trudging down the steps when I sense his presence.

"Why are you everywhere I turn?" I ask, spinning to see him a step behind me. The stairway is lit by moonlight and the shadows are deep, but his carefree flash of teeth is visible enough.

Chapter 9

MACE

"Maybe I just love your company," I say.

Sophia's emotions are vibrant even in the dark. They reverberate toward me with a mixture of frustration, anger, and a splash of violence. I have no doubt that had Sophia found her sister, there would have been caring there too, hidden under a thick layer of brusque behavior.

I wonder just how much alike Sophia and I are.

Her mischievous nature may have been what called to me but the longer we're bonded the more layers of her personality become known.

I regret putting off working with her.

Sophia blows out a breath that lifts her hair out of her face and communicates her dissatisfaction all at once. The breath itself is a little weak and I catalog the detail. Another piece of evidence of what Sophia's hiding.

"I'm surprised you're not downstairs eating dinner with the rest of the *family*," she snarls.

I rear back. "Your aunts left, if that's what you're wondering."

Sophia's shoulders drop a little at that.

"You were magnificent, by the way." I don't mean to say it, but it rings with truth.

Sophia snaps her face to mine. The darkness showing more emotions on her face than she usually displays. She probably doesn't know how well I can see her versus what she must see of me.

"So fierce and bright." I drop my voice lower and a breath shudders from Sophia at the growl of the words. I continue, "I'd want you in my corner every time."

The core of loyalty that strums through Sophia attracts me. She's shown so many faces to the world but hearing her protective vehemence for her sisters is the cherry on top of a delectable pastry. A magnet for my sweet tooth.

The gleam in Sophia's eyes sharpens. "Could have fooled me with how much hemming and hawing you've done about having me help you."

My face stretches wide with a smile. "True, true, true."

Sophia takes a step up so that we share the space. Her frustration boils over, and her tone is deadly. "Make a decision, Mace. Now."

Violence roils through her energies. The sensation is so delicious that I almost miss a crucial detail. She *brightens* at the proximity of our bodies. Her soul threads ease as if slackening after having been strung taut and some of the tension in her face calms.

Curious.

"Mace," Sophia calls my attention back to her statement with angry exasperation that lacks the utter exhaustion that's painted my harpy as of late.

Sophia had admitted she'd been having dreams about me. A detail I had found delightful… I hadn't been concerned about the effect of the bond on her. I should have.

I step forward to check my suspicion. Our fronts brush and Sophia's inhale is deep.

"You're strung a little tight, fierce harpy. Did that sad excuse of a man not provide the type of release you were looking for?"

Sure enough, the swell of Sophia's anger is more energetic this time. She goes to take a step away and I catch hold of her wrist. The sensation of touching her is always similar to brushing a live wire. Electric and stinging in a way that makes me want more.

Experiencing Sophia is a little like the clearing beauty of pain.

Sophia rips her wrist from my grip and moves into my space. My back presses against the stairwell and talons prick my throat, a mimic of the shifter last night.

"*You* don't grab me," she says.

"I don't grab you," I agree quickly. "My apologies."

I am sorry. I'd moved without thinking and it had been rude. The confirmation of my suspicions is also rude. Sophia obviously doesn't want me to know the secret I've divined.

The secret that the bond between us is pulling at her stronger than it should. That it's draining her when we are apart.

No wonder her anger with me is so strong.

Why hadn't she said anything? But that is hardly a question I have to ask. Why would Sophia Shirazi expose a weakness to me?

Sophia's talons disappear and she backs away again, as if sensing my contriteness in the air. Or rather, through the bond.

She wouldn't be able to pick up from me as much as I can from her, but if the pull of the bond on her has

increased over time.... The longer we're connected the
more sensitive she will be. This is a little bit of a mess.

To admit or omit my rudeness. The stolen secret... I
sigh. This isn't a game.

"Sophia—"

Something about my tone must clue her in because she
looks away.

I continue, "Believe me when I say that the bond wasn't
supposed to pull on you like this."

Sophia clenches her jaw before shaking her head.

"It doesn't matter if I believe you." She snaps her mouth
shut but opens it again. "Can you fix it?"

I gnaw on my lip in consideration. "No."

A vulnerable hopelessness passes over Sophia's face,
and it draws me in.

"Not right now," I say. "I'd have to break the bond to
even be able to try and remake it. It would weaken both of
us, past the point of what you're experiencing. I can't risk
that with the trafficking case I'm working."

Something about that statement has Sophia perking up.
"But after that's resolved?"

I pause before nodding. "I can rework it after it's
resolved, but we'll still be bonded."

Sophia's eyes narrow as if taking that as a challenge.

We both jump at the echo of dishes clattering in the
sink downstairs.

"Perhaps we should rejoin—" I start.

"No, I'm leaving. I... can't deal with hanging out with
my family right now." The admission sounds painful, but
honest. I'm shocked that I'm the one she's making it to.

Then she curses, casting a look up the stairs.

"I need a ride home. I don't have my car." She waves
her hand up the stairs to wherever Amara went. "Amara

brought me, and I planned on tagging along with Zeph but…"

"Well, isn't it great that you're bonded with a demon who is exceptionally skilled in the area of transportation." I waggle my brows, trying to cut through her frustration.

"Oh." Sophia tilts her head. "You don't think it will make me feel sick?"

I tilt my head in thought. Teleportation can make people sick, and harpies are sensitive to magic, but this isn't just any harpy.

"I don't think so. Our energies are closely tied and there are fewer things that we'd be as close as teleporting together," I say.

I don't mean the statement to be suggestive, but it is. Sophia licks her lip and I stifle my groan at the action.

Sophia straightens and holds out her hand. "Then let's get out of here before they come looking."

I slide my hand into hers. The bond between us pulses in time to the thrill echoing in my chest.

"Take a breath, Sophia." I wink. "And enjoy the ride."

Sophia's eyes widen. "What—"

I pull her into the shadows.

Chapter 10

SOPHIA

Darkness envelops me, swirling around like a tempest. A tornado of shadow whips my hair in every direction. It's like a free fall. I can't see a thing. The sensation of the wind catching me is an eerie one, and my body tingles with goose bumps.

A hot hand still holds mine and I start to be able to see some things. The inky darkness that flows over my skin lightens to transparent indigo smoke in places and I think I may see pinpricks in the distance. *Stars?*

It's as if I can see everything in the world and nothing at all. The pure exhilaration of it has tears pricking my eyes and my laugh is lost to the dark wind around me until I fall against a chest, strong arms catching me.

The world of shadows is gone now, and my mind starts to take in the sights of the real world. The texture of the sidewalk under our feet, the glow of the nearby streetlights, the blink of a neon sign for a ramen shop I live a few blocks from.

The demon holds me against him, an avid look on his face as he watches mine.

I'm breathless and dizzy with glee. "What was that?"

Mace tilts his head. "I didn't know if you'd experience it the way I do. Most people say it's instant."

"That was not instant. It felt like it went on forever."

Mace grins. "I'm glad. Congratulations, fierce harpy, you've now been to the in-between."

"The what?"

"There are the planes. This plane, the demon plane, and the fae plane. As it was described to me, how I teleport is by traveling in the space between them."

My heart starts to slow, and my body registers the grasp of Mace's arms around me, cradling me. I hadn't realized how cold the trip had been, like being dropped in an ice bath, but bit by bit my body thaws. The heat of him bleeding into my skin through all our layers.

There are fewer things that we'd be as close as teleporting together.

Mace's face is close to mine, giving me an up-close look at all the imperfections that mark him. It's as if I'm in a trance. A trance that breaks at his smirk.

I push away from the warmth, and he releases me easily. As if all I had to do was ask.

I look away, not wanting to be tempted into touching this man again. Some of the cold clings to me but I let it.

"You missed the mark if you were trying to take me home." I force a drollness into the words.

"I thought we could take a lovely walk," Mace muses, his eyes still on me.

"A walk?" I blink at him.

Mace slides his hands into his pockets, playing the impossible part of bashful suitor. My lips twitch without my permission.

"A walk to talk."

Suspicion starts to chase away the high of excitement. "What are we talking about?"

"About business of course." Mace is quick to answer. "We're to discuss what you're going to charge me for your service…"

I start to relax.

Mace continues, "Maybe mention how many issues the bond has been giving you."

I tense.

"There are logistics to cover now that we are both aware how our distance is causing a drain on you."

I frown. "That's unavoidable if you can't restructure the bond."

Mace hums, holding out an elbow to me. "Weakness would be avoidable. If you're willing."

His elbow and words are a dare, a challenge, a play. I'm aware of it but my soul rebels at the notion of losing ground even in this small way and I grasp his elbow with narrowed eyes.

I realize it quickly and my eyes widen.

Mace snorts but I don't care. Since the trip through the in-between, since being close to this demon, the weakness has been absent. My energy is normal, there isn't a pull draining me.

I feel like myself again.

All I have to do is be near Mace.

"*Fuck!*"

Mace has the gall to laugh. Which cuts off when I jab him in the side with the hand that had looped through his elbow. I walk away with purpose. I'd run away if I could.

Mace stays where he is, as if divining the purpose of my movements.

I get about five feet away when the draining sensation starts, it's light, but it will increase with distance. I turn toward him again and the look on his face is apologetic.

"Fuck." This time the word is thick with emotions I'm trying not to show.

Mace's expression softens. "We'll figure this out, Sophia, I promise."

"And in the meantime, I need to follow you everywhere you go? Like a pet parakeet? Because I don't have another solution to this, do you?"

Mace winces.

"More of a pet falcon than anything," he says. "I'm joking!"

Talons stretch from my fingers at my anger.

"It's not funny!" I throw my arms wide. "This is my life! Do you even have any idea how much it's taken to be as independent as I am? To be able to see the world as me and not a harpy in a cage!"

Mace's smile drops. "A cage?"

I'm trying to will my talons away. The street is empty but it's bad practice to walk around with claws out where any human may wonder why there are scales on my hands. Frustration has words spitting from my mouth.

"There are expectations that come with being a harpy; rules that the community follows. To have my life is to invite danger in. I had to fight for it." I think of Fairuza tonight. "I'm still fighting for it."

I won't go back to having to answer to someone. My life is my own. I need to figure out a way to get out of this.

"Gods above, I could never trap you, Sophia. There is no cage that could possibly hold you."

Mace's words hold an awe that has the rage draining from me.

He continues with sincerity, "You are uncageable."

The sentiment is a beautiful one and said with complete seriousness. My anger starts to dissipate and my lips twitch.

"I don't think uncageable is a word," I say.

Mace looks down with an abashed smile. "I never said I was good with words."

We stay like that; the space between us practically humming.

I have to be near Mace until he can bust the trafficking ring he's working on. The truth of the matter doesn't make it better, but it is concrete. Now what?

I close my eyes as hopelessness starts to bleed in. My proximity to this demon is something I *need*. I've lost all the bargaining leverage I had for payment.

"What do you want, Sophia? What would make this better?" Mace asks.

His face is drawn, guilty.

Guilt is useful.

I need to make my ask big. I need to get as much from this as he will possibly allow. I think of the financial debt riding me. I can figure out a solution for that. I technically have some time. Not much, but some time.

I *need* a way out of this bond.

"In payment for my service to you, I want a favor." The words are strong, betraying none of my fear.

Mace has the upper hand.

"What kind of favor?" Mace asks with suspicion.

I clear my throat. Am I praying?

"An open-ended favor."

Mace's face goes blank, and I count the seconds it takes for him to respond. This would be a big concession on his part. He knows what I want more than anything.

"With one stipulation," he finally answers. "I hold veto power on the request."

It's a fair stipulation for a deed that I haven't fulfilled yet. I didn't honestly think that he'd give me that much. Maybe Alice is right; Mace could be an ally.

I close the distance between us and solemnly hold up my hand to shake on the agreement. The formality isn't necessary to make the deal. Apparently mere words can be binding to a demon, as seen from my currently bonded state. But I want this as official as possible.

Mace's smile is coy as his hand grasps mine. "Is that a threat, harpy?"

I don't know what he means until I glance at our hands. My talons are still on display. They aren't full length with the deadly curl, but currently look like an over sharp manicure. The dark scales of my skin scrape against Mace's calluses, contrasting to his pale hand.

The gnarled ugliness of them against his human features has insecurity taking over my actions.

My cheeks burn and I start to pull my hand away, but Mace catches my fingers and surprises me by raising them to his mouth. The kiss he gives the back of my hand is courtly and wicked all at the same time.

The touch is dulled through the hardened layer of scales, but the sentiment is not. Mace's direct stare leaves no room for misinterpretation. He means to make my body heat. To seduce.

"Deadly and beautiful," he says. "My favorite."

I squash the fluttering feelings he inspires in my chest and try to focus while pulling my hand away.

Mace can veto my request.

Now I'll just need to figure out how to make it so he doesn't.

Chapter 11

MACE

"I should pack a bag." Sophia's words break my focus, and she starts walking down the street.

The focus I had on the pretty blush that spread across Sophia's face. Which is also the focus of trying to piece apart her motives for her request. She wants to get out of the bond we have.

My chest aches at the concept of losing this bond. It may be inevitable, but this is time I've been given with Sophia, I won't waste it just because I can't keep her.

"Ah, yes. It seems as if the two of us will be like glue for the foreseeable future."

Sophia's mouth thins.

"We can allot blocks of time for your clients while we work on this case," I offer.

Sophia's brows raise. "Um, thanks, but I'm currently between clients."

Now my brows are the ones raising. "Is that so?"

Sophia's business was booming when I had enacted the soul bond. It had been what had put us in direct competition. I hadn't been aware that we were fighting for the same clients at the time. I would have backed off if I'd known. Not that Sophia would ever believe that.

Sophia scowls at me but continues walking.

It's not until we reach the end of the block that she answers me.

"In my current state, I haven't accepted any jobs over a certain level of risk."

"Smart," I say, but wince.

I wish she had told me about the bond sooner, but trust doesn't grow from nothing. With the way our interactions started, our trust is a seed in barren soil, or concrete rather. Perhaps with this forced proximity I'd convince Sophia that I have her best interests at heart even if I have my own parasitic needs to contend with.

Something scratches at the back of my mind. My demon nature whispering to my instincts.

Sophia starts to slow her pace. She feels it too.

We're being watched.

"Pissed anyone off lately, fierce harpy?" I ask. My tone is cheerful even as I slip a hand into my side pocket to grasp my favorite dagger.

Sophia doesn't respond to my question but stops walking to turn to me. "We should go. Now."

She offers her hand up, ready to dive back into the darkness with me.

I frown. "You don't need to pack?"

Worry starts to emanate from the harpy. "I can buy supplies elsewhere."

"Sophia—"

"Please!"

I jump at the urgency in her voice and do as she asks, gripping her hand and we plunge into the in-between. The darkness welcomes us like we're coming home.

This space has always felt like mine. I've only known a few people who share this ability and one of them had been my half brother. The association of that has me distrusting the few others who can teleport.

I don't mind sharing this experience with Sophia.

I travel the distance, an intention in mind and hand clasped in hers. The shadows cling around my harpy, playfully tugging her clothes and hair. I wonder not for the first time if the in-between is sentient but discard the thought in favor of getting us to our destination.

We arrive in an alley instead of on a street corner, in a different city. I have an innate glamour that usually diverts attention when I appear out of thin air, but I do try to be discreet.

Sophia spins, eyes wide. "Where are we?"

"New York."

I analyze her expression, waiting for fear to bloom at having been brought across the country in the time of two blinks, but the fear doesn't come. Instead, Sophia's smile is blinding, and she rushes toward the commotion of the street.

I stand, stunned in the face of her openhearted delight before trailing after her.

"Sophia!"

"I've never been to New York!" she calls back.

I almost trip in surprise. *Never been to New York? What sort of travesty is that?* Sophia stops when she reaches the street. Taking in the tall old buildings and narrow streets. A few people walk around Sophia, snickering at her wonder.

Because Sophia is avidly taking in the sights of a convenience store and some novelty shops full of I Heart New York T-shirts.

Her first time in New York and I bring her to an alley in Lower Manhattan. An older Asian woman makes a sound at Sophia, and the harpy stumbles back so she isn't blocking the sidewalk. I shrug. An experience is an experience.

Sophia's brow knits. "It looks different than in the movies."

I snort. "If we have time, I'll take you to some more recognizable places. Welcome to the divide of Little Italy and Chinatown."

"What are we doing here?"

"Well, neither of us had dinner for one."

Sophia's mouth drops open. "We came to New York just to eat?"

"Now I know that you've never been to New York if that's what surprises you."

Sophia blushes and I take pity on her. It's hard to remember that not everyone can travel in the blink of an eye.

"We are also here on business."

That catches her attention. I offer my elbow. She takes it with none of her previous hesitation and we begin walking as I explain.

"Since we've discussed your compensation, I figured we'd best get started. The group I'm tracking is moving very quickly. That, and the feel in the air in locations they've used, indicates that they are using portal spells."

"Do you think if you get to their supplier, you'll be able to get their current location?"

I hum in satisfaction. "Or at least the identities of the traffickers. Our world is a small one. If we can get some details about them, finding out identities should come easy and—"

"Identities lead to connections they have, which leads to possible locations," Sophia surmises.

"Exactly."

"Don't portal spell merchants have to be registered?" Sophia asks.

I smile. "Yes, retailers need to be registered with the Council, but those retailers have to file records for every spell they sell. There is a market for off-the-book portal spells."

"Black market?"

"Exactly. A friend of mine has given me a list of all the retailers known to trade in portal spells."

Sophia trips over nothing, too busy taking in the sights to focus on walking, but recovers quickly. "That's a valuable list."

"It pays to have informed friends, and Gideon is the best at knowing where valuables are being sold."

Sophia frowns.

I continue, "I'm working with an organization that is checking the legit avenues. They don't need person-to-person contact to check those. This list isn't one where we can just call the individuals up."

"How do we make sure that the people we meet with are telling us the truth? They deal in contraband; they don't have an incentive to flip on a customer."

My smile is wide and vicious. She said *we*. Perfect.

"Have no fear, I have some skill with telling truth from lie and I recognize some individuals on the list."

"Can I see the list?"

I steer us to the edge of the sidewalk and pull out my phone. Tapping away until Sophia brings out her own buzzing phone.

"How do you have my email—never mind." Sophia rolls her eyes at herself.

Of course I have as many details about Sophia as I can readily get. I did research before deciding on wanting a bond with her.

"This is the big leagues, fierce harpy. How are you feeling?" I ask.

Sophia's breath catches. "I feel good." She blinks rapidly and looks away. "Like before we bonded. I have energy, my mind is clear—"

Sophia stops talking and shakes her head before she gives any more details of her condition away.

"I can get the job done," she finishes.

So very cautious.

Caution is a good trait to have in our line of work, so I push my desire to dig into every detail Sophia is trying to hide from me aside. There will be plenty of time to delve into the depths of Sophia's secrets later.

"Good. Now, how do you feel about noodles?"

Chapter 12

SOPHIA

I moan, tilting my head back and chew the noodles. The heat of the chili flakes with the punch of flavor from the sauce hits my tastebuds. I swallow and am able to speak.

"Oh. My. Gods."

Mace leans back in the booth seat; the light over the table not quite reaching his face. He's committing the atrocity of ignoring the dish in front of him in favor of watching me. His mouth curves in a smile, but there's a glint in his eyes that sparks a heat in my body.

It's probably just the noodles. There's no way I'm susceptible to his charm.

Any heat sparked in my body by this demon can be blamed on the bond and the dreams that have plagued me. It has nothing to do with his actual person; who he is.

I pick up more noodles and shove them into my mouth to keep my mind busy. The flavor profile of the dish is like the best things I've had and nothing like I've experienced at the same time.

It's not Chinese food but some fusion creation without a name. Mace had laughed when I'd naively assumed that we'd get Chinese food while in Chinatown. He reassured me that what we'd get would be just as good while patting my hand in the crook of his elbow. He'd asked me to trust him.

I went with it, and now reap the benefits. The bar that had been hidden in a tiny alley, behind a heavy glamour, clammers around us with activity. The seats at the bar and most of the booths are full of a variety of other paranormals.

This is a neutral territory, much like the club I visit, and I soak in the company we're in.

An androgynous figure with twitching fox ears and the fluff of several tails leans against the bar, rolling their eyes at a shorter burly man with a gnarled face. A group of what I'd guess to be trolls take seats around the only table equipped with huge backless benches. The better to hold the men's bulk. One of them scowls and pulls his long hair back with some sort of clip to keep it from the noodle bowls.

And a majority of beings I don't recognize. They all looked different from each other. With differing tones of skin, from shades of red to green and some purple, some are lithe and others bulky, but they *feel* similar. They give me the same feeling I'd had when I'd met a goblin artist I'd worked to get out of a bad contract.

Mace had to push me into the booth we're in now with a muttered comment about staring being rude.

This demon whose name I had been cursing for months has given me an experience so far out of what I know, I could kiss him. I won't. Even if he keeps watching me with eyes that taunt me.

I swallow the noodles.

"Now, who is the one being rude?" I ask.

Mace's smile widens instead of shrinking in shame.

"Apologies, I just love seeing a woman enjoy her food. The sounds are… heavenly, even without the look of bliss on your face. Consider me struck dumb." The glint in Mace's eyes shines.

"Dumb seems apt." It's a terrible comeback; my cheeks burn in embarrassment.

Mace chuckles and picks up the chopsticks with graceful fingers before beginning to eat. I cast my eyes away from seeing if his face would show the amount of rapture mine did, but the heat kindled isn't dissipating. Instead, the interest persists with the excitement flowing through me.

So many people, so many different types of paranormal beings of completely different heritage than the ones I've met in the city I live in. A group of women enter, their musical laughter inspiring a taste of euphoria.

When they drop the glamoured appearances they walk through the streets with their skin takes on a paler hue and iridescent scales show on their cheeks. Sirens.

"Eat, Sophia." Mace's words are teasing. "We still have business to attend to."

I shake my head. "You take me to a place like this and tell me to eat."

Mace tilts his head. "I thought this would be quite average for you with all the adventures I assume you have. You became very competitive in a short amount of time on a circuit that took decades for me to build."

I duck my head and poke my food with the chopsticks.

"That was strategy. I took jobs from the most influential people who would give me them."

"That seems rather…" Mace trails off.

"Reckless?" *Irresponsible?* How badly would either of those words sting coming from this demon? I'm aware of the truth of them now, aware of how risky it was, but I hadn't known any other way.

Mace hesitates. "Nothing I can say is going to sound good. Either I can tell you I didn't expect that your movements would be so strategic with how much of a free spirit you are, or…"

"Or what?"

"Or I admit how shallow of an experience I think that would give you of the world." Mace winces.

I blink and watch the drops of oil flow in the noodle sauce. "You're just being honest. I plan on reevaluating my strategy when we are done with this job."

When I can be free of this bond.

The expression on Mace's face is searching. "Why did you start your business, Sophia? From what I've learned about harpies, it's clear that the work you do doesn't fit into that community."

My mouth twists and I shrug. "I've never really fit in that community. I know that my family cares for me but everything about being a good harpy feels restraining. Like, I'm on top of the world and can see it all but have boundaries drawn around me saying I can only go this far."

"A cage." Mace muse, referring to our street conversation.

I sigh. "I just, there's something about being out here that makes me happy. When I have to stay put for any period of time it's as if everything around me *dulls*."

Mace nods. "That wanderlust makes sense with how far flung your kind are. There must be others in your line that longed to explore before now."

My laugh is a little sad. "If that's true, they aren't around anymore."

"I've never considered what it must be like to come from a community that wants you to stay with them. I never had any structure. The world has always been wide and dangerous." Mace's face has an openness to it while he speaks, as if he's on the edge of getting lost in thought.

I want to ask questions, to get to know Mace and his history, but what would that invite in? *It could bring leverage.*

I open my mouth, but Mace shakes his head; the moment is lost.

"Are you done with your noodles?" he asks while reaching for my bowl.

I make a sound in denial and guard it from him. The demon laughs and whatever thoughts he'd been skirting seem to be far away.

"Well, finish! As I said, we have work to do, fierce harpy."

***

When we both finish eating, Mace pops a courtesy breath mint that had been brought over without a check. He pockets the second one when I refuse it. The demon has quite the sweet tooth.

Mace gathers both of our bowls and stands.

"Now, let's feed some of your wanderlust," Mace says.

I follow the demon as he makes his way toward the back of the establishment, nodding to the bartender, a giant man with tusks, before pushing open a door to the kitchen. Mace doesn't pause in his journey until he puts our bowls in the sink and turns to face a slender man with a darker shade of green skin in an apron giving him the evil eye.

I get the same vibe that I picked up from the other patrons. Could they all be types of goblins?

"Carson, you're looking well," Mace says.

Carson straightens and wipes his hands on his apron. "What brings Mace Reynolds into my domain?"

"What, you aren't happy to see me?" Mace asks.

"I owe you. Of course I'm not happy to see you."

Mace's laugh is bright, genuine. This goblin owes Mace money? Then again, what I owed Mace wasn't money.

"I would have thought that you'd be happy to pay back your debt," Mace says.

Carson's mouth twists in something that resembles a smile, a reluctant one. "I only fear what you'll ask of me. You performed a great service for me. Paying the equivalent will hurt. Maybe I was hoping that I'd just keep you in noodles for the rest of your life."

"The noodles are fantastic, as always."

Curiosity has my head swinging back and forth with the conversation.

"And what did your lady friend think of them? I didn't believe you were on a date until I saw it for my own eyes." Carson lifts a brow.

Mace straightens. "This is Sophia Shirazi, and she can answer your question much better than I."

I wait for Mace to say that we aren't on a date, and wait. Mace lifts his brows.

"The noodles were the best I've ever had," I say and watch Mace nod.

Carson puffs his chest up and forgets to dig any further about Mace's and my relationship. Mace's closemouthed answer makes sense. It would be better to let the world assume we were on a date than to let anyone know about the nature of our bond.

There's a lot of strength that can be had from being in a soul bond but there is also weakness. If someone were after Mace, they'd only have to kill me. It'd weaken him, if not kill him outright.

"So, about that favor," Mace starts, and Carson stiffens. "I want an audience with your grandfather, and I want a guarantee that he'll answer my questions."

Carson hisses. "You don't pull punches."

Mace shrugs. "It's what I need. If I didn't, I'd be happy to gorge myself on noodles for the rest of my life."

The goblin clenches his jaw and Mace doesn't push.

"And we'll be square?" Carson asks.

"I won't even come back here again if that is what you'd wish; though, I'd miss your cooking."

Finally, Carson curses and removes the apron he wears. "Your girl coming too?"

Mace stiffens at that. "Sophia is my partner on this case, have a care with how you address her."

I blink, I guess we aren't pretending to be dating after all.

Carson tilts his head at me, the action is sheepish but respectful. "No offense meant, lady."

"None taken," I say. If I took offense to every passing address, I'd be skewering a lot of balls.

Carson sighs in relief and gestures for us to follow him out a door that leads to a narrow staircase. We climb and I make a note that Carson's steps are the only ones in our party to groan. Mace has skills in making his own climb as silent as mine and probably does it as much in instinct as I do.

We stop at the second floor and Carson pauses on the landing, moving his shoulders as if gathering courage before turning to us. "Stay here."

The goblin knocks before entering the apartment.

Mace leans easily against the stained wall and glances at me.

"We've got to stop meeting like this." He gestures to the stairway.

The smile breaks across my face before I can stop it. "You're the worst."

"Absolutely, but now you're more relaxed and that's what this encounter needs."

Mace is correct. There's a looseness in my body from his teasing that will allow for my movements to be quick if we do need to respond to an attack.

The questions whirling around my mind start to bubble over.

"What did you do for Carson to make him owe you?" I ask.

Mace's smile is slow and makes a tsking sound. "That is between him and me. I don't go around sharing secrets for nothing in return. Then they wouldn't be secrets."

Secrets. This isn't the first he's mentioned them with a seductive caress to the word.

From what I could glean in my research, demons usually have a type of vice. I have no idea how debilitating the vice is, but I start to wonder if Mace's has something to do with secrets.

It would make sense with the type of work we both do.

"What kind of being are they?" I ask, a little hesitant. It would be considered rude to discuss, but Mace and I are working together and safety is more important than politeness.

I tell myself that instead of admitting I'm just curious.

Mace tilts his head. "What do you think they are?"

"Well…" I start, hating to look ill-informed, but the need for knowledge drives me. "A lot of the patrons and Carson give me the same impression as a goblin I've met before, but they all look different."

Mace nods. "They probably all identify as goblins of some sort. There are different beings that hail from all over the world, but are similar enough that when they find others like them, they stick together, and new generations come from that."

"Power in numbers," I say.

"Exactly. It's better not to be seen as rare."

I jump when the door swings open, Carson's face is an even darker color of green and I think he's blushing. He steps to the side.

"Babble will see you now."

Mace's smile is wide, patently affable as if he hasn't forced Carson to do this, and we enter the apartment. The weight of spice in the air is heavy, it doesn't have the heat to it like the kitchen below, but a thickness.

As if the flavor of the various spellings has seeped into the walls. Photos hang on darkened wallpaper, black-and-white images of a couple in front of an ocean liner with garb that looks from the early 1900s.

We enter what must be a family room. In the corner, on a big recliner, sits an ancient goblin in a plush chair. His skin isn't as dark of green as his grandson's and his hair sticks out from his head as tufts of white.

The age and appearance of the goblin doesn't detract from his presence. The way his head tilts when his milky eyes turn my way gives the impression that he sees much more than I'd expect.

"Babble," Mace says with a formal bow. "It's an honor to make your acquaintance, spell master."

A yellowed fang flashes when the goblin's lips crook in a smile.

"Secret eater, I did not expect to ever meet you face to face."

Secret eater? There's amusement on Mace's face.

Babble continues, "What a surprise it was to learn of my grandson's debt to you." The man's gnarled hands wave. "Alas, the young do seem to fall into debt easily these days."

Carson stands against the wall, his features pinch in discomfort. Indignation at the comment swells in my chest and I open my mouth.

"Sometimes taking on a debt is the price of moving forward."

"And you would know something about taking on debt, harpy, with the weight of that bond and that mark, it's a wonder you can still fly," Babble says.

The hair on the back of my neck rises as the annoyance is doused with alarm. It's rare, but sometimes it's possible for others to identify what I am on meeting rather than by reputation. But the rest of it... he can see all of that? Mace raises a curious brow at me, but gazes back at Babble.

"We're not here to make conversation about my associate," Mace says. "I have a few questions."

Babble's brows crease before he shrugs with a huff. "I suppose that is an uncomfortable topic for the harpy. Ask your questions, secret eater, I will answer with honesty. I'm sure you'd be able to sense a lie."

"I want to know about the portal spells you've sold," Mace says.

Babble hisses; an angry flush coloring his cheeks, but Mace doesn't react.

Finally, the goblin smooths his expression to one that hides more of his emotions, but his voice is gravel. "That is a sensitive topic."

Mace's shrug is careless. "The favor I'm owed isn't light."

Babble scowls and his grandson shrinks under his glare before the goblin turns his face to us

"That it is not. Ask your questions."

"Start by telling me about the portal spells you've sold in the past year."

Babble's brow creases in thought. "Three."

Mace's head tilts. "That isn't very many. Who were the buyers?"

"I'm old. I don't do that sort of serious magic often these days." Babble chews his lips, not wanting to answer the question but he continues, "One went to a group of fae that wanted to settle far from any fae doors. They wanted to have a way to get to one if they needed to."

Mace blinks and waits.

"One to an ancient of some type. I couldn't divine what he was, but his motives were pure. It was a gift to his chosen mate while he traveled. An escape route in times of trouble."

Mace's brows lift in surprise. "And the last one?"

Babble looks at me then, his white eyes strike at my soul. "A harpy matriarch. The one with the white hair. A gift to a young harpy in her branch who had started her clutch."

My breath rushes out at the pang of mourning. It's not a mystery why a harpy might need a portal key. Vegadóttir lost one of her daughters to domestic violence. Harpies are proud beings that don't ask for assistance from others of our kind, but clutches are born as triplets and that's a lot to handle alone.

It's a bad combination for the modern harpy. There have been instances where the harpy secretly keeps the father involved. At those times it becomes a situation of the harpy not wanting to go to their own branch for support and admit that they kept the male around for financial or emotional support.

The harpy matriarchs have been working on making a built-in support structure for all young harpies. Zeph's mate Asa has even been offering his expertise. That Vegadóttir wouldn't want to chance what happened to her daughter to happen to any other harpy, even with the changes happening, isn't a surprise.

"I see," Mace says. "Why were these orders off the Council record?"

Babble scoffs. "Don't play dumb, demon. I have no doubt you've experienced enough as a rare being. We don't trust the Council. They don't represent our interests. My clients didn't want the information available to be bought. We protect our own. They wanted their privacy, their safety," he spits.

Mace ducks his head in easy acknowledgment.

Babble isn't the source of portal spells the traffic ring is using.

"Thank you, Babble. I consider this favor paid. If it settles your mind, trust the information you provided won't be for sale."

The old goblin deflates in relief. "I won't pretend to trust a demon, but your past actions help me believe in your good intentions. Your partner is unproven."

Babble eyes me.

I shake my head. "I would never put others in danger like that."

Babble sniffs. "Until a debt is called up asking that of you. Remember, young one, owing is a dangerous thing."

Nausea constricts my throat. Would I be asked to betray someone? Mace wouldn't have asked that of me, but Mace isn't the only person I owe.

Mace raises an eyebrow. "We will be taking our leave if you are done imparting your wisdom."

Babble cackles. "Who would say no to free wisdom?"

Chapter 13

SOPHIA

"He's not the one providing portal spells," I say.

The words are almost drowned out by the screech of the building door closing behind us. We've exited in a smaller alley than the entrance of the noodle shop. Night has fallen and the light over the door casts long shadows against the brick walls around us.

"He's not," Mace responds.

I stop walking and narrow my eyes at the easy answer. "Aren't you upset that you cashed in a favor for a dead end?"

"I've learned not to be. I tend to hoard secrets, but if I treat favors as a resource that can run out, it halts everything with indecision. We can cross off one name on our list with confidence. This is progress and there is always a cost to progress."

I watch Mace until he casts a glance to me; his lips curving in a sly smile.

"Anyway, I have no shortage of secrets." Mace's eyes darken. "Much like you. I wonder how Babble could tell the nature of yours when I can only get a taste."

Secret eater.

What a strange title.

"Are secrets something you need?" I ask. If they are something he needs, his vice, then that detail could be the leverage I'm looking for. That may be how I get out of our bond.

Mace's mouth curls at my question. Answering it would be giving me something. A gift.

A secret.

A shiver travels up my spine when he steps closer. The crunch of his step echoes as the shadows darken around us.

It's not the shadows that have my heartbeat starting to pulse in my ears. The way Mace's head tilts, considers me before he bestows this gift sends warning signals to my brain.

"Secrets," he says softly. "Are a currency, a thrill, and a passion for me. Nothing gets my heart racing quite like knowing something others don't."

Mace's mouth twitches. "Almost nothing, anyway."

The smooth innuendo in his voice has my patience snapping.

"But are they a need?"

If I let Mace dictate this conversation, we'll be circling all night, threads in hand until we braid a bracelet with all the hoops he'll make me jump. I won't be led that way.

I step forward and Mace stills in a combination of surprise and hungry expectation.

I'm surprised too. I'm supposed to be immune to this demon's constant teasing, but in the shadows it's easier to admit to myself that the way he pushes me has a responding pull that primes my body. There's a feel to our interactions, one that I ignore, one that I'm sure will go away as soon as this bond does.

The feel of the inevitable.

I'm close enough to smell the mint on his breath. My mouth waters to taste it. Mace's eyes darken when my tongue wets my lips.

"They are a need in the same way that sex is." Mace's words are threaded with wickedness and that damned pull draws tight.

I inhale at the intense way his voice reverberates through me.

Mace smiles at my inhale and leans forward, our faces almost touching. My own stubbornness keeps me still, keeps me from retreating.

"Each one is a special pleasure. A particular flavor beckoning me forward. Seducing me," he says.

Heat builds in my body, unmerciful and direct.

Mace breathes in, mouth open, and the draw of air over my cheek is an erotic caress.

"And you, dear Sophia, have such sweet secrets."

I stumble back then. The reminder of what I hide ugly and out of place here, but Mace doesn't give me the space to hide my embarrassment. The alley wall presses against my back as his body cages mine. Curls of smoky shadows from the in-between whisper around him. As if the few steps between us would have taken too long to bridge in any other way but to dive between planes.

My lower lip trembles; the heat from his body and the heat of mine gravitate toward each other.

Mace's lips graze my cheek with his next words. "Like sugar and cinnamon. I could just devour you whole."

That small touch cascades through me like ripples in water. Each wave growing larger and larger. The truth reverberating through me so loud it's undeniable.

I want him.

My body tenses to do something. Strike out or give in and grab him, I don't know, when a vibration breaks the moment.

The bricks behind me grit as Mace's hands tense against the rough surface before his head falls on a sigh. He pulls away from me slowly, regret in every stiff line of his body before it dissolves back into his usually carefree stance.

Mace slides the vibrating phone from his pocket and answers.

"Yes?"

A man's voice on the other end of the line is clear. "Is now a good time? I was wanting an update on whether you could get the list you mentioned."

Mace's mouth twitches, his eyes on my face. "Yes, I forgot to tell you that I was able to get the list and have checked with one supplier. I'll send it to you and flag the ones I don't have any connection to for your team."

The man on the other end agrees, there's a trace of annoyance in his tone.

"That's the organization you're working with?" I ask once Mace has ended the call.

Mace nods. "Gage's team is contracting me. I'm sure that we'll meet up with the rest of them when we start making headway. They are the company the families have hired to find their missing members." He smiles with self-depreciation. "It's been a long time since I've needed to report to anyone, and we are both having some growing pains."

I lift my brows. "It sounds like you're the one being the pain."

Mace stops tapping out an email on his phone to laugh. "You may be right."

Talking like this I could almost forget the tension that had strung us both tight only a moment ago. I had been about to kiss this demon. I try and shake off a swell of emotion.

For the life of me, I can't tell if it's relief or disappointment.

Chapter 14

MACE

Fierce Sophia. Delighted Sophia. Hungry Sophia.

Every facet of this harpy draws me in more. It had been difficult to pull away in the face of Sophia's lust; to dissipate the tension between us that still claws at me. It's better not to start anything that the need infecting my blood calls for in a dark alleyway.

It's better to give my harpy the time and space to consider what is going on between us, because I'd rather not see the expression on her face that I'd just seen if and when we truly give in to the pull.

Regretful Sophia.

I want her and she wants me in some way. It's obvious and not something that can be avoided by distance now. The particulars of whether or not we both give in to our mutual attraction is up to Sophia.

The next time lust drives us to the brink my harpy should have had enough time to decide whether sex between us will be something she'll regret.

Now, I get to experience *amazed Sophia.*

She turns in a slow circle, taking in the penthouse around us. There isn't much to see. It's decorated in all neutrals and clean lines.

"This is your place?"

I duck my head to hide my smile. "One of them."

I had noticed Sophia's weariness after sending Gage the details of the list. Our proximity helps with the exhaustion the bond caused her, but the dark circles under Sophia's eyes, the toll of months of drain, won't be solved only by proximity.

Sophia's hesitance when I held my hand out to teleport us to a place to stay tonight, reinforced that I need to give her time. Time and sleep for her to decide if she wants to fight our attraction.

"One of them? How many places do you have?" she asks.

"I keep real estate in a number of locations I frequent."

Sophia's brows raise. Probably at the expense of keeping multiple properties, but being longer lived, and friends with Asa, gives me a good financial foundation. Having multiple hideouts when dealing in secrets is an indisputable advantage.

"There are some supplies in the room on the right side of the hall."

"Supplies?"

"Extra clothes, toothbrushes, etc."

A deadly stillness falls over Sophia. "Do you have company over often?"

I bite my lip to keep from laughing. "Not in the way you're thinking. Have no fears, Sophia. Should you join me in my bed, you'll be the only one."

I stop before I make any promises that would alarm her. Monogamy is an easy promise to make. I'd give her much more of a commitment, a relationship, if she asked. But she won't ask for that.

Exclusivity is a territorial thing when it comes to sex. A relationship involves feelings. Emotions that I'd readily embrace for the time I'd have Sophia, but this harpy won't allow that.

Harpies don't date.

Sophia scoffs and looks away, but not before I catch the relief that eases her shoulders.

She'll decide the extent of our physical relationship one way or another, which brings a different topic to mind. One I'll need to address. My mind is on what errands I'll need to make when Sophia turns toward me.

"What kind of company?" she asks.

The question lacks the violence from earlier.

"In my work, there are always people needing a safe place to stay. All of my homes have some basic amenities along with the most important one. Secrecy."

Sophia's eyes narrow. "This isn't the first time you've gone after a trafficking ring, is it?"

I smile at Sophia's suspicion.

"No. Asa, our friend Gideon, and I used to do this often. We caused many problems for those organizations in the past. Some time ago Asa and Gideon decided to slow down before we drew more trouble than we could handle."

"Not you though." There is no doubt in Sophia's words.

I blink and struggle for a moment with the sensation of being *seen*.

It's a rare thing. I'm not like the people I surround myself with. My talents are useful, but ultimately, I'm a helper. I fade into the background so easily that it's a surprise for Sophia to notice me.

A warmth blooms in my chest.

"No." It comes out soft and I clear my throat. "No, I haven't. It's a slower process, and I ally with others instead of Asa and Gideon, but I haven't stopped."

There's a pause in the conversation and the back of my neck itches at the searching way Sophia watches me.

"They don't know that you haven't stopped."

I shuffle my feet. Sophia is good at getting information. I've admired her skill in the past with professional interest, but this line of questioning reveals things. Things I haven't thought about in a long time.

"They haven't inquired about it." I don't want to guilt my friends into risky actions when they've already decided to change gears. They aren't the ones running from bad memories or driven by revenge.

A thoughtful look passes over Sophia's face and her purpose for digging is suddenly obvious.

Nauseatingly so.

The warmth dies.

She's trying to find leverage. It's clever, actually. I'll owe her a favor at the end of this. All she has to do to get out of being bonded is find a way to make me grant it instead of vetoing it.

Simple. Then she'll be gone. There will be no more vibration of frustration or singing delight touching me through our connection. I'll be alone.

"It would do you no good to threaten to tell Asa. If he knows, he'll either help in my endeavors, putting him and his family at risk, or be conflicted about it all. This isn't the leverage you're looking for."

Sophia scowls and blushes at the same time.

"Get some rest. I have some errands I need to run first. I'll stay close and be quick so that the bond doesn't cause you any issues." There's a hollowness to my words.

Sophia's actions aren't a surprise, but the emptiness in my chest is.

For a moment, I thought she wanted to get to know me, but she is merely looking for a key to be free of me.

Chapter 15

SOPHIA

Sleep comes quickly but doesn't stay.

My dreams weave webs of guilt, indecision.

I wake to a dark, unfamiliar room. It takes me a moment to remember where I am. The sanctuary of Mace's city apartment. A place that acts as a sanctuary for others. There is more than meets the eye when it comes to my demon. *The* demon.

My curiosity prods me, but I temper it.

There's a winding guilt in my chest at the way I botched things before we separated for the night. The guilt is stupid. Mace should have expected me to have ulterior motives. He's keeping me trapped in a soul bond. There is no reason for guilt to twist my stomach at the memory of his face falling when he connected the dots about my questions.

I sigh in frustration and hit my head into the pillow with force. Hoping to shake off the useless feeling, the tickle of regret, and the curiosity that has me wanting to get to know Mace better for more than to find leverage.

There's a twist of pain that leaves me breathless and echoes of grief that isn't mine. *What?*

I sit up in bed, pressing my hand to my chest. Not all of these feelings swamping me are mine. Somehow, I'm picking up more from the bond. Which means that someone else is awake in this apartment.

I slide out of bed without another thought. As if there is a magnet drawing me in.

The dark apartment is empty, generic past the point of minimalism. There is no sensation that this is Mace's home and no trace of the mysterious demon. I let the odd tugging sensation lead me.

The balcony door is open.

The sounds and lights of the city at night draw me closer, making me forget my quest for a moment. An invitation. There's an itch under my skin to see the sights. This city is bigger, louder than the one I live in, and it sparks my need to explore.

I reach the doorway and can only stare, amazed. The balcony wall is glass, and nothing stops my view of skyscrapers and the haze of light highlighting the night clouds. Distant sirens and honking reach my ears even at the late hour. Or early hour.

It's all strange and beautiful. Full of life. I take a deep breath. The air is frigid as if we are high enough to be in a cloud.

A sound breaks me from my reverie. This is where my demon is. *The* demon, I correct yet again.

Mace reclines in a patio chair, balancing a coffee mug on the armrest. The mug is a secondary detail to the fact that the man is shirtless. I'm stunned for a moment, not expecting to see the expanse of his skin in the low light.

Mace is nicely made. The light caresses his muscles, highlighting the swell of his chest, the thickness of his arms. The curves of his body are traced by lines of black tattoos. Runes of some sort run over his chest, under his collarbones before trailing down his arms.

"Can't sleep?" Mace asks, but he doesn't look at me, keeping his eyes on the view as if lost in thought.

I wrap my arms around myself and shiver.

Mace's tone sounds *wrong*. The lilting teasing that marks his words is missing.

I don't like it.

"No, some asshole bonded to me keeps waking me up," I say.

That gets his attention. Mace blinks and looks me up and down. I'd taken the plain sleep set from the well-stocked closet of supplies. His eyes travel up my body, slowly moving over my bare legs until catching on my nipples pressing through the fabric before continuing to my face where my brow is raised.

I'm not self-conscious about my body. I descend from a long line of woman warriors. I'm beautiful and strong. If Mace doesn't want to see my nipples, he can look away.

"That sounds inconvenient." The words sluggishly dance but sound more like what I expect from Mace.

I snort. "You have no idea."

Mace's mouth twitches. He lifts the mug to gesture to a seat next to him.

"There's a blanket if you want to join me."

I shouldn't. I'm already forced to spend too much time with this demon because of the bond. I need to be wary.

Mace is dangerously enticing.

He's seen so much, knows detailed intricacies about things that drive my wanderlust wild. It would be easy to get too close to him. To become something that might resemble friends. Friendship combined with the burn of attraction between us is a bad mix.

I yank my mind away from the memory of the alley and the tension that held my body in a vice.

Lust is lust; compatibility is something completely different, something more. I'm bad at being a harpy, but I've never crossed the line of wanting to keep a man.

"I won't bite," Mace teases with a curve of his lips. "Not unless you want me to."

The hollowness of Mace's words is gone. In its place is a challenge I can't ignore. I'm never going to be a harpy who takes the safe way out, the easy way.

The risk adds to the appeal.

The concrete is rough under my bare feet as I near the demon.

The smile drops from Mace's face as he watches me approach, hunger lights in his eyes. I bend over and pick up the blanket, choosing not to angle my body away. Choosing to give him a view down the tank top.

Mace's face is tight with want but he relaxes it into a dark smile as I wrap the blanket around my shoulders and take a seat.

"Isn't it a little early for coffee?" I ask, and just like that, his smile falls and the desire on his face fades away.

Mace tilts the cup, as if trying to read tea leaves. "It's not coffee."

There's a pause before he offers the cup to me. "It's still warm if you want it."

I narrow my eyes at Mace before accepting the mug. It's mostly full of a dark liquid that I can't identify in the low light until the scent hits me.

"I can't decide if it's stranger that you're drinking hot chocolate in the middle of the night or that you made a whole mug and haven't drunk it." Suspicion laces my words. His sweet tooth is well known in my family.

The statement pulls a reluctant smile from Mace.

"I make it more for the memories than to drink it. It shouldn't go to waste," he says.

Memories that pull my own chest taut with guilt and grief.

"Curiouser and curiouser." I take a sip of the drink and the flavor bursts over my tongue. "What kind of memories? They don't seem pleasant with how the bond is pulling on me tonight."

Discomfort pinches Mace's face before he looks away.

"Apologies. I didn't realize you'd be affected," he says. His brow creases as if he's thinking.

"Is it a secret?" I prod.

Mace's face relaxes at my teasing. "Not a secret. It reminds me of someone who always dreamed of being able to drink such a luxury whenever she wished."

She. *Don't ask, don't ask, don't ask.*

"Who?" *Dammit.*

"My sister." Mace's words are soft.

My eyes widen in surprise. "I didn't think demons had siblings."

Mace smiles sadly at me.

"We were a rare occurrence on this plane. Twins."

Were. A sister in the past tense. The mere concept of it is catastrophic to me. I don't know what I'd do if anything were to happen to either Amara or Zeph.

"I'm so sorry." My voice is thick with emotion that I'm usually better at masking.

Mace puts his hand on his bare chest. "I know. I can feel your emotions sometimes. When they are strong and sharp." He takes a breath, his expression poignant. "Your pain on my behalf is—"

He breaks off before resuming. "Comforting."

"I don't know why."

Mace's smile is self-deprecating. "Because I don't feel alone. Because you can also understand the guilt of putting your sister in danger."

I rear back as if slapped. He's not wrong, but that part of my psyche is sensitive and the pain that follows is sharp. I can only be comforted by the fact that Zeph is fine, unlike Mace's sister.

The ache of that pain has me speaking.

"Do you want to talk about it?" I ask.

Mace shrugs, some of the hollowness returning.

"It was a long time ago and I shouldn't confide in someone who would use the information against me." The words aren't meant to hurt. There are no sharp edges, but I still gasp at it.

"Sophia—" Mace starts but stops. There isn't anything more to say.

I look out at the city. "I'm not going to apologize for trying to find leverage. I have to do what is best for me, and that's getting rid of this bond."

"I know. I … forget sometimes. Forget that we aren't on the same side. Forget that even though you paid up voluntarily, this isn't what you wanted."

I squeeze the mug.

Mace spreads his hands out. "I like you, Sophia. I admire your spirit and loyalty. I forget that you don't want to be friends or anything more." His smile is apologetic. "It would be easy to fall for you."

My cheeks burn at his easy admission. The guilt in my gut from before hints my own feelings and the moment between us stretches. The inevitable.

"I—I like you too," I whisper the confession in the night air and the bond thrums. It's a small thing, like the breeze of an unlocked door, disturbing the space between us with newness. It's as if I've sealed my fate, but it's honest.

I'm fascinated by Mace. It's a bad idea to be involved with him. To care about him, but on some levels, I can't help it.

Mace tilts his head, amused by my confession.

"It's not like I can pretend that I'm not affected by you. We have to spend a lot of time together," I snap.

"Your anticipation is flattering," Mace teases but his eyes are dark, considering.

"Just don't do anything stupid, like fall for me. That's not something on the table," I mutter.

With those words, I've opened a gate. The possibility of friendship, the possibility of acting on our attraction.

"I still don't trust you," I say, as if to hold up a single remaining boundary to *this*.

"What do we do in the absence of trust?" he asks.

I think on that; my curiosity begging me to come up with something. To get answers somehow.

"An exchange."

"An exchange? Of what?" Mace's glitter, his usual playfulness returning in full force.

"Anything," I say, letting myself think out loud. "Actions, histories… secrets."

Mace's smile is wide. "You're playing with fire, fierce harpy."

"You're tempted."

"I'm absolutely seduced. You'll start, truth or dare?"

I gape at him. "I was not talking about truth or dare."

"But the game fits."

I sit back. It does. My lips twitch even as a darker voice in my head whispers warnings.

I don't want to be telling Mace any of my secrets…

"Dare," I say.

The delight on Mace's face has me rethinking my decision, but I don't back down.

"I dare you to come closer," Mace says as he leans back in the chair, his eyes alight with challenge.

I'm confused, there isn't anywhere to sit next to him, until the spread of his thighs has his meaning clicking. It seems as if the demon is done with late-night confessions.

"Diving right in," I say with a lift of my brow.

"Are you going to quit?" Mace asks. The question settles some uneasiness.

He's letting me know that quitting is an option. He's giving me an out.

It just means losing.

I refuse to lose.

I let the blanket fall from my shoulders and stand slowly. Setting the mug of chocolate on the ground, I close our distance. Mace's dark eyes follow me.

I don't know for sure if he meant to have me kneel before him or sit on his lap, but my harpy nature refuses to do the expected. This demon wants to play. We'll play.

I place my hands on his bare shoulders as if to perch on his lap but slide my legs on either side of him in a straddle instead. The motion is smooth and uninterrupted by Mace sitting up and grasping my waist in surprise at the press of my softer parts to his hardening one.

Mace clears his throat. "Temptress."

"You asked for it," I say.

Mace's laugh is light and warms my skin. His thumbs massage into the bare skin of my waist where the sleep shirt has ridden up. His eyes meet mine, crinkled with his smile.

"I did."

Something catches my eye and I lean in. I take note that Mace's breathing goes shallow at our nearness, but analyze the gold medallion he's wearing.

"What's this?" My hand goes to touch it and Mace stops me. His hand wrapping around mine, warm and gentle.

"Careful, it's spelled; it shouldn't affect you but go slow just in case," he says and releases my hand.

I glare. "How much do you know about my sensitivity to magic?"

Mace shrugs. "I had to do a lot of research on harpies for Asa's proposal to your matriarchs. I know about harpies in general, but not about your particular sensitivity."

I swallow and slowly touch the medallion. It hums against my fingers instead of stinging.

"I'm not reacting to it. What is it?"

Mace nods. "Good. Is this the truth you want?"

I blink. I almost forgot about our game with the expanse of bare skin before me. *Bad harpy.*

I bite my lip, hesitating. Do I really care about his necklace? The way Mace's eyelids lower decides for me.

"Yes," I say.

Mace's slow smile is seductive. "I got it while I was out." His fingers press into my back muscles from their place wrapped around my waist. It's a tease. It would take no effort for them to slide down and grip my ass, but Mace doesn't go any farther.

I wait, allowing my body to press harder against him, a breath away from a grind. Mace's cheeks flush but his cool demeanor doesn't change.

"It's a charm against causing pregnancy," he says.

I stop, frowning. "I didn't think that was an issue for you."

"Let's just say I'd rather be prepared."

Prepared for the possibility that the tension between us will boil over, that we'll have sex.

I snort. "Harpies control their own fertility."

Mace's brows raise. "Would your sister agree with that?"

My brows crease. "That's different, her and her mates were... bonded."

The blood drains from my face.

Mace's mouth twitches like he's fighting the urge to smile. "You see my concern. I would have gotten you your own charm, but with harpy sensitivity to magic..."

Disbelief has my head shaking.

"Sophia? I didn't ruin your plan of stealing my seed like your predecessors, did I?" Mace teases, but concern lines his eyes.

"No! I just—I could have accidentally—" I stumble off his lap and Mace stands, gripping my arms to keep me from falling backward.

"Breathe Sophia. I wouldn't let that happen."

I gasp in a breath. The oxygen and Mace's firm hands keep the world from tilting as my demon continues to reassure me.

"This is the kind of charm I acquired for Greg and Asa. Zeph thinks that one set of triplets is enough for now."

I bark a laugh. "I'm sorry—you upset a fact that I considered truth and now—" I make a gesture in the air and Mace nods.

"I understand. I don't know for sure if it would have been a possibility, but I didn't want to take that chance."

"Me either." My heart slows. Gratitude is a slow rolling stone bringing an avalanche that fights back my panic. "Thank you. Even if it was presumptuous."

I tease and finally feel back in control of the situation.

"I prefer cautious," Mace says.

The sexy, teasing air of our game is gone. I already miss it.

I look out on the horizon and realize the sky has begun to lighten with a new day. I let the information sink in. Mace made the decision about us giving in to our attraction last night and planned accordingly. He went so far to get a charm that he guessed wouldn't make me feel sick.

Regardless of the instinct that something between us is inevitable, what do I want?

Chapter 16

MACE

The scent of sugar and vanilla in the air has my mouth watering. When I bite into the pastry, the burst of sweet lemon with the crunch of glazing, I moan in appreciation.

"You're being indecent."

I open my eyes and the look on Sophia's face is somewhere in between alarm and amusement with a light blush coloring her cheeks.

"It's an indecently good pastry," I say.

"You're praising a pastry," Sophia says and sips her coffee with an eyebrow lift.

"I give praise where it's due. It's hardly indecent to say something is delicious in public. I'm not calling the pastry a good girl."

Sophia chokes on her coffee and coughs, grabbing a napkin in the middle of the patio table to cover her mouth during the fit. I smile and nod as concerned people pass and mutter to each other in French. When she's recovered, she glares at me.

"You did that on purpose," she hisses.

"I don't know what you're talking about." Would Sophia like to be called a good girl? She lives her life in opposition to the ideals her people hold, always the rebel, never the rule follower. How often does Sophia hear how amazing she is? Not enough.

It's a curious thought that I save for later.

Sophia shakes her head. "Absolutely shameless."

I smile. "Especially with you."

Sophia blushes and turns away, taking in the scenery. When we arrived at my favorite patisserie, Sophia had gone through all the ecstatic reactions that I've learned to expect from her when she experiences a new place.

I'll never tell her that it's adorable. I like my spleen where it is.

Instead, I'll take her somewhere new every day that she lets me. Though I don't know how many other times I'll get the same reaction as Sophia experiencing Paris for the first time.

"Do you think the next on your list is more likely to be our supplier?" Sophia asks, breaking into my thoughts of other places I can teleport her.

I mull over the question before answering. "Yes and no."

Sophia tilts her head and waits.

"I think this person would be willing to provide the portal spells without asking questions, but his prices would be heinous."

Apprehension that I'd been attempting to avoid by coming to my favorite patisserie for breakfast starts to rise.

Sophia nods. "So unless this group has deep pockets, this isn't our supplier. And we are checking this—" She looks down at her phone. "Alton next because…"

"It will be quick, and he's a gossip."

"Then why are you tense?" Sophia asks. "That's why we're here isn't it? Loading up on sweets. You don't like this guy."

The harpy is astute.

"You don't like our trip to Paris?"

"I *love* our trip to Paris, but you have to bring me back to see more sights than just a bakery."

I freeze my face so that I don't give away my surprise. Sophia Shirazi just expressed that she wants to make future plans, with me.

"It's a patiss—"

"Mace, stop avoiding the question."

I press my lips together. "It's uncomfortable to be around Alton."

"Why?"

"Once upon a time I asked you what you knew about demons, and I believe you said 'enough.' Would you like to know more?"

"Yes." Sophia's cheeks are pink again in embarrassment, but her eyes are avid.

"I wouldn't be surprised if you had a hard time finding information because there are many types of demons that humans have named and types that don't have a name at all. We all use the term demon because we come from the same plane. Either we are born there, or we descend from those who are." I look down into my coffee.

"So, a succubus is a type of demon, but different from you?" Sophia asks.

"Exactly. Along with that variety, there is a distinction from those demons who are spawned in the demonic plane and those born on this plane."

"I've heard that demons could only stay in this plane by making deals." Sophia's face is open, hungry for knowledge. It's a hunger I want to indulge even if the details cause me discomfort.

"That bit of knowledge is true. In the beginning, those who dealt were mostly witches. A demon can only stay here if bonded to someone of this plane. In exchange, the demon can provide the raw power for spells."

"So, demons from the demon plane are stronger?"

I shrug.

"In a way. They are not of this plane and tend to struggle with staying here for long stretches of time. A lot can be done with more power, but that issue can't be solved without a bond-mate, or sometimes bonding to rare objects.

"As you know from the existence of your adorable nieces, demons are capable of breeding. Some of the demons who bonded to witches on this plane procreated with them. The most common demons on this plane are those who are first or second generation. Since Asa is second generation, that would make your nieces third generation if they weren't automatically harpies."

And now comes the important details. The truths of the world that scald.

"The distinction is a sharp one. Demon born are quite elitist about it. Alton is demon born."

Alton isn't a bad person, exactly, but being around him grates.

"So, demons from the demon plane are powerful and the further down the line it goes the less powerful the demon?" Sophia asks.

I give a hollow half laugh. "No. The first generation is weak in comparison to both demon born and second generation."

Sophia's eyes widen in confusion.

I make a flourish with my hands. "That would be my designation."

"But—how does that make sense?" she asks.

"It's thought that the plane you are born in determines the amount of power available to you. I am of this plane, but not. I have the weakness of the demon born without the power to overcome the issues. My existence is ephemeral on this plane, and the demon one. Not that I've ever been there."

Sophia sits back and the wrought-iron chair creaks. "And a second generation gets their power from this plane? That's… shitty for you."

She frowns suddenly. "What would happen to you if you weren't bonded?"

Ah, the hard-hitting questions. "Are you sure you want to know?"

Annoyance flashes over his face. "I wouldn't have asked if I didn't want to know—"

"I'd fade," I say, words soft. "With no anchor and no plane supporting me, my being would slowly disappear." I had been close to that fate once before. Asa had saved me.

Sophia looks sick at that.

"Have no worries, Sophia. You're keeping me safe and sound," I say, twisting my lips when her face takes on a greenish hue.

Chapter 17

SOPHIA

I'd fade.

I regret asking.

As we move through the in-between, I tighten my hand on Mace's. This demon who has allied with my family and busts up trafficking rings would disappear without an anchor. Not at home in any plane.

"Well, here we are," Mace says as we step into the sunshine of the human plane. There is a cobblestone walkway under our feet and cheerful scenic buildings around us. The one in front of us is a little worse for wear in the dinginess of the whitewash and faded paint. The open sign is a little hidden, but the window display is full of old leather-bound books. It's as if the shop is hiding in plain sight, wanting to appeal to only those who know about its wares already.

I don't think I'll ever get used to being able to just show up wherever I want. Mace had explained that eventually teleporting too much would drain him but that isn't an issue that we needed to worry about while we're bonded. He has access to tap into the power of this plane by being connected to me.

"Books?"

"This decade it's books," Mace says with a shrug and strides to the door.

The bell on the door echoes in the darker interior of the shop.

"Coming!" A musical voice comes from the back.

Mace's body stiffens before he forces his muscles loose with a grimace.

A tall, slender man with delicate features comes through the door to the back and stops. "Mason!"

Mason? I mouth the name at Mace but keep from teasing him about it. There's a sadness on Mace's face before he shakes it away.

"You know I don't go by that name anymore," Mace says.

"Yes, of course, how silly of me to forget. Not since that terrible business with dear Elise." The demon coos with a wave of his hand. "Forgive me, you know how long demon borns live. My memory is not what it once was."

The words ring false and it's clear why Mace doesn't like this guy.

Mace smiles but his body is bowstring tight.

"Elise?" I ask.

"Oh, why hello," Alton says as if just seeing me. "Mace hasn't said anything about his dear sister? She was the sweetest; I'm surprised he doesn't talk about her more. Well, there was all of that nastiness with Nero, so I guess—"

"Alton," Mace cuts in. "We're not here to dredge up old memories. This is Sophia, Sophia this is Alton."

Somehow when Mace had been explaining all the demon business, it didn't occur to me that their lives had been connected going back into Mace's history. All the time I'd spent researching Mace and I only would have needed to look up this guy who can't stop himself from spilling details left and right.

"It is my absolute pleasure." Alton holds out his hand, his eyes taking in my appearance greedily.

When I go to take the offered hand, Mace stops me and glares at Alton.

"None of that," Mace says.

"My my, Mace, you've done well for yourself. Such a strong anchor," Alton purrs and drops his hand with a shrug.

Why doesn't Mace want Alton touching me? The other demon somehow understands. Maybe it has something to do with our soul bond?

"Yes, she is. I'm assuming you have a new bond-mate." Mace forces the words out with nonchalance, and it takes me a moment to realize he's trying to go through the motions of small talk.

"Oh, yes! You know me, I like to switch it up every once in a while. Keep things from getting stale." Alton's smile is knowing. "So, what brings Nero's half brother to my door?"

I keep my eyes from bugging. Mace had told me about his sister but not about his brother. I must succeed at keeping my surprise to myself because Alton looks disappointed at my nonreaction.

The tension in Mace's shoulders reverberates from him, it's a bitter taste on my tongue. Alton doesn't notice it though.

"I'm calling in a favor," Mace says.

Alton's mouth pinches. "Now, Mace, we don't have to hold things like favors between us. If you need something from me, you only need to ask."

"That's because you owe me a few times over." Some ease enters Mace's words. This is what he's comfortable with. Not small talk with a demon with a penchant to run his mouth. A demon that seems to know everything about Mace's history.

Alton sighs. "Well, if you're sure you want to call in a favor, what can I do for you?"

Mace lifts his chin. "I'm looking for a portal spell supplier, one that's been selling within the last couple of years."

Alton's elegant face scrunches in distaste.

"Is this concerning that awful slavery business you keep getting involved in?"

"Does it matter?" Mace asks.

"I suppose not. I haven't sold any portal spells in a couple years. No one wants to pay the price for quality," Alton says with a shrug.

Mace nods without surprise. It had been a long shot, but I still can't help being disappointed.

"But—I could do you one better." Alton tilts his head. "As you've tactfully pointed out, I owe you a few times over. I could cast a look into your future if you would, say, strike another favor from my tab."

Mace frowns. "You can't cast for demons."

"No, that's still true, but you happen to be intimately intertwined with another person." Alton lifts a brow at me, and Mace stiffens.

"What?" I ask.

"That won't be necessary," Mace says.

"Why, Mace, how unlike you! I'm giving you the opportunity to get closer to whatever group you're chasing, and you refuse?"

"That opportunity may not be worth the price," Mace says.

"Oh, but it could," Alton taunts.

"What is it?" I grab Mace's elbow, demanding he answer.

Mace purses his lips before looking me in the eye. "Alton has the ability to search into the future. Sometimes he can pick up on useful things and sometimes it doesn't work at all."

"That sounds useful," I venture.

"It is!" Alton smiles.

"It can be." Mace clenches his jaw before continuing. "But he'd have to use his skill on you, and he'd possibly get more than you would be comfortable with. It'd be an invasion of privacy."

Oh.

I rock back on my heels.

"I'd be sworn to secrecy," Alton blusters as if offended.

Mace gives me a look with a raised brow, and I understand. Alton may not spread my secrets around, but he'd know about them, and people can release secrets in many ways that aren't directly telling other people.

Mace is right. It's a risk that I don't want to take.

But.

We're going after people who are selling others. Mace sent me the list of known missing people. A list of people being held against their will, away from the lives they built and their families.

Zeph could have ended up on that list.

Without some strokes of luck, it would have been Zeph.

If my discomfort could make it so we find them faster... I can't reject that option.

"I'm willing," I say.

Alton beams at me and Mace runs a hand up my spine before massaging the back of my neck. The casual touch comes as a surprise, but the comfort it offers is too good to pull away.

"There is always a cost to progress." I quote Mace's words from before.

Mace's face is soft as he takes in my own determination and nods. He understands why I need to do this. He releases me and turns back to Alton.

"If *anything* untoward happens, I will call in favors that will make you regret the day you came to this plane." Mace's cold tone holds absolute violence and Alton pales.

"I'd never—" Alton shakes himself to keep from inadvertently lying. "I am sworn to secrecy. I'll try to keep out of anything you're not looking for."

That would have to be good enough. Mace doesn't look satisfied, but he nods toward me. This is my show now.

I pull my harpy nature up like a shield. "If I find out that you've put me at a disadvantage in any way, there is nowhere you can hide from my rage."

Alton nods, looking like he regrets offering his services. "As it is spoken, it is truth."

I hold out my hand in offering and Alton clenches his own in nerves before taking mine. He closes his eyes and the stinging sensation of foreign magic spreads up my arm, like pins and needles amplified. I grit my teeth from the pain and my harpy side starts to react to the threat.

I breathe, trying to calm the race of my heart and the demand of my instincts to yank my hand from the demon's. My skin flashes nauseatingly hot and black dots appear in my vision.

A cool hand comes to the back of my neck, a firm, familiar grip holding me, supporting me. I almost whimper at the relief that spreads through my chest. Mace's face is stern but soft as his thumb digs into a tense muscle.

"It's almost over," he whispers.

I nod. True to Mace's prediction, Alton releases my hand and stumbles back, gasping. The demon waves off help we haven't offered and takes his glasses off.

"Interesting," Alton says. He removes a cloth from his shirt pocket and starts to clean the lenses. The action looks to be a meditative one rather than an urgent need to remove a smear. "Very interesting."

Mace breaks contact, dropping his hand now that I'm not fighting blacking out. For a single moment, I miss the touch, then I mentally shake myself. *Focus, Sophia.*

"Well?" Mace asks.

"I couldn't get much. The group you're hunting has demonic assistance. It's skewing what I can pick up."

Mace frowns. "Are you sure?"

Alton sneers. "Very." He looks to me. "Your debt is coming for you, harpy. That mark isn't done causing you trouble."

Anger blossoms in my chest. "I'm aware."

Alton just nods and places his glasses back into position.

Mace tugs my hand. "Good doing business with you, Alton. Contact me if you have any more information."

Mace's voice is tight, but I let him hurry me out the door. We are striding down the street until he pulls me into an alley. Always an alley with this demon.

Mace pulls me into his arms. "Are you okay?"

The contact of his body against mine stuns me for a second. One of Mace's large hands cradles my skull and the other sweeps some errant hair out of my face. Mace analyzes me, concern in his eyes.

"Y-yes," I sputter. "There was only a moment there that I thought I'd pass out."

The pulse of Mace's urgency eases and he sighs in relief before squeezing me to him with an arm around my waist. I should push this demon away, eschew the familiarity he touches me with, but his next words destroy that passing intention.

"So determined. So fucking brave," Mace says. Awe bleeding through every word.

My eyes widen. No one has ever called me brave. Reckless, yes, but not brave and not with utter sincerity.

Adrenaline from the magic contact rages in my blood like lighter fluid, his praise acting like a match. Now that the danger has passed, heat clamors for my attention.

Raw need and the press of Mace's body shreds my good sense. My fingers thread through Mace's hair and a growl of sound escapes his mouth.

I yank his face to mine.

There is no hesitation in Mace. Our mouths meet as if he had only been waiting for me to snap. For my fire to crack so he could devour me. The clash of us overruns my thoughts and the limits I'd placed on myself.

The kiss is a rough fight for dominance.

It's all desperate tasting and, *gods*, he tastes good. Vanilla and sweetness from breakfast and an underlying taste that is just him. I bite his lip and Mace snarls, so different than the grinning demon he shows the world.

I suck on the tender skin and Mace's groan is gratifying. My back hits the alley wall and the breath in my lungs rushes out. The impact spurs me to claw at his shoulders.

Now that I've dipped my toe in, there's no resistance to the inevitable.

I need everything and Mace is happy to oblige. I wrap my legs around his hips, and he drives my body against the wall, pinning me. The hard feel of his cock grinding against me has a sound escaping my mouth. I meet the roll of his hips with my own, my lower body clenching at the delicious friction.

"Fuck!" I break the kiss to gasp.

Mace starts kissing my neck. He uses the grip he's taken of my hair in one hand to bare the vulnerable spot and scrape his teeth against my skin.

I could yank out a chunk of his hair if I wanted to stop him. Claw him bloody with my talons for daring to handle me like this but I love it. I love the fierce way he licks, bites, and kisses the same area that an enemy would want to tear out to claim victory.

Every push and pull moment between us has been building to this and I want to triumph.

The distant laugh of a child has both of us freezing.

Gods above, we're about to fuck in an alley, in broad daylight.

Mace pulls back, his pupils blown. The air hisses out of his lungs as he attempts to rein in whatever impulses he's struggling with.

"This is, perhaps, not the most ideal location for this." His voice is gravelly, and I arch against him.

"Maybe we should go to a more ideal location," I say, hunger a harsh edge in my words. I squeeze my legs around him. Now that we've come this far, I don't want to slow. I need the thrill of us finally combusting. I can't imagine stopping.

I seem to be the only one.

Mace grimaces in regret. "We have things to do, Sophia."

Need has a whimper escaping from my lips. "But—"

"We can't stop now, Sophia."

"I don't want to stop now."

Mace gives a huff. "That wasn't the task I was talking about, and you know it." He looks up to the sky, taking a deep breath. "We have people relying on us and just had a break in the case."

"Fuck, Mace—" I stop before I start to beg. I grit my teeth and slide my legs down. The fire of arousal between us still flashing hot over my skin. Frustration isn't a good look for me.

"So, you're just going to walk around with *that*?" I gesture to his erection.

"It will pass… *maybe*," Mace mutters.

His struggle helps soothe my needs a little. I lean back against the brick wall. Willing the cold stones to seep away the worst of the want.

How Mace threatened Alton comes to mind. How many people owe this demon?

"Truth or dare?" I ask.

Mace frowns at me. "That's not the sort of game that will help in this situation."

"I'm making conversation," I say. *And digging.*

"Truth," Mace says cautiously.

"Why me? So many people owe you. Why did you choose to soul bond with me?"

The question surprises Mace. He tilts his head as if the answer is obvious.

"Sophia—" Mace breathes. "In a world of people who color in the lines, how could I resist bonding with you?"

I frown. "That's not an answer."

"You draw me in." A smile curves Mace's lips. "Your strength and cleverness are so bold. And that was before spending time with you."

My cheeks heat at his matter-of-fact tone. *Strength and cleverness.* How is it that this demon sees me so differently than anyone else? A detail sticks.

"You're attracted to me because I'm strong?" I ask.

Mace breathes out, a thoughtful look on his face.

"I don't think you truly understand the draw of power. I've lived all of my life being the weak one, not being able to protect the ones I care for. I've always needed to make alliances to be able to succeed in this world."

"You choose to surround yourself with people who don't need you to protect them," I say.

Mace smiles sadly. "I failed to keep someone who was the world to me safe. I won't let that happen again."

Chapter 18

MACE

A gust of wind whips away Sophia's laugh and I curb the urge to pull her back from leaning too far over the edge. The woman is a harpy, falling from the Eiffel Tower isn't going to hurt her even if we're higher than the tourists are free to go.

This short detour is to gain her forgiveness for not ravaging her in that alley. By the happy thrill reaching me through the bond, I think it's worked.

My body doesn't forgive me. I ache to feel her against me, savor her skin, and elicit those delightful sounds from her mouth. The taste I had of Sophia Shirazi is not enough.

The cold air clears my head and dissipates some of the heat. The darker part of myself that has been hungry for this harpy since setting eyes on her fights with the mask I display to the world. The temptation to take her, to consummate the seductive song we've been dancing to is pressing me hard, but I won't get Sophia in my bed only to do a rush job.

The lead-up between us deserves a deafening crescendo, even as the scent of her skin draws me in.

This harpy tests the control I hold over myself.

The anticipation is delicious.

Sophia turns back to me and catches me watching her. She holds my gaze, her mouth curves into a smug smile that I return.

"You should call the team you're working with," she says.

I snap my fingers, my cheeks heating. "You're right."

I dial Gage and put the phone on speaker.

"Gage, you're on speaker. My associate Sophia Shirazi who's been helping me in this case reminded me that I need to report in consistently."

"That's appreciated." Gage's words are dry and able to communicate his eye roll. "It's good to be working with you, Ms. Shirazi. I'm sure we'll meet in person as this case progresses."

"I'll be interested in meeting you and your team," Sophia says and gives me a significant look.

"Gage, I've checked a name off the shared document, but I also received some intel. The group we're after is receiving demonic assistance."

"Really? There aren't that many demons on this plane, are there?"

"Only a few hundred I know of, and maybe a couple dozen of those would be inclined to be involved in such activities. I'll draft a list after this call, but I don't personally know them all."

Gage hums over the phone. "Katherine or Leo may know some, I'll coordinate with them." We all pause for a moment. "This is a good lead."

I nod. "Sophia and I will continue checking suppliers and I'll send a few messages to see if I can't narrow down our demon fiend probabilities."

Gage snorts. "You do that. Thank you for the call, Mace."

Sophia lifts a brow at me when I hang up. "You really don't take direction, do you?"

"Of course I take direction."

"Is Gage your boss?"

"Gage... hired me."

Sophia rolls her eyes. "Here you are assigning yourself tasks and not calling in."

I shrug. "I'm an independent contractor."

"You must like to be in control."

I pause.

"Are we still talking about my work?" I ask with a tip of my head.

Sophia narrows her eyes. "You show the world this demon that goes with the flow, but I bet you have everything neatly managed. It only looks like chaos to someone who doesn't know your system. Do you always have to be in control?"

Now her tone is edged in seduction.

My smile is vicious. "I don't always have to be in control, but you'll find that out soon."

Sophia tilts her head back, her white teeth biting into her lip, and I clench my hand into a fist to keep from touching her. From pulling that lip from the grip of her teeth and sucking on it.

"Is that so?" Her voice has a breathy quality that I want caressing me daily.

"Oh yes, fierce harpy, but first, we hunt."

Chapter 19

SOPHIA

"I think I'm about to do something stupid," I say into the phone. I kick a rock across the tarmac. Mace is in the warehouse behind me, seeking out a recluse who could give us an answer for the fifth person on our list.

Each candidate has been routine since Alton, since the alley. Routine and exciting all at the same time. I'm becoming addicted to the ability to teleport and the withdrawal of it, going back to the world of airplanes and trains, is going to suck.

"How stupid?" Alice asks.

"I'm going to jump Mace." I've already decided. I think.

The chemistry between us is burning me alive. Eventually I'll get out of this bond, but until then...

"I'm pretty sure you can't break the soul bond with violence," Alice responds.

My mouth twitches. "That wasn't the type of jumping I was thinking of."

"Oh." Alice's exclamation is followed with a pause that she eventually breaks. "That was a quick development."

I snort. "Tell me how bad of an idea this is."

There's a pause on the other side. "You don't think you'll get attached to him?"

Just last week I would have laughed that question off. Now though…

"I don't know."

Alice inhales through her teeth.

"I'll just throw out that Mace isn't the worst man to get attached to, if you do get attached."

"It's not very harpy-like of me."

Alice guffaws. "Sophia, when have you cared about appealing to your aunts? Like, I know you're worried about how the world perceives harpies, but you can't control what other people think. We both know that reputations are a fickle thing."

Reputations are a fickle thing. I could put up the strongest front, be the fiercest harpy, and one event could unravel it all. If all it takes to ruin the reputation of harpies is a few instances of appearing weak, can reputation really keep us safe?

Why deny myself something I want for something so fragile with no guarantees?

She's right.

"So, bad idea?" I ask.

"Probably a terrible idea," Alice agrees.

"Good, good talk."

"But it sounds like a fantastic time," Alice adds.

Alice is always right.

***

The last teleport to the penthouse isn't graceful. We both stumble from the in-between gasping breathless laughs.

"I can't believe you said that to them!" I cry.

"You can't blame that on me," Mace says picking a spaghetti noodle from my hair and I shudder.

"You insulted the food, I'm blaming you. Even I know ogres are sensitive about their cooking!"

Mace smiles. "You said you were bored."

I gape at him. "I didn't say bored. I said I was tired."

Mace shrugs. "Well, I gift you with another unique experience then."

The slime of the sauce slides over my neck when I cast him a look of disbelief before I snort a laugh. "Please excuse me while I wash this experience from my hair, not to mention my jacket."

I point a finger at him as I walk to the guest shower. "Report to Gage where we are with your list."

Mace, the smart-ass, salutes me. "Yes, ma'am."

I'm still shaking my head when I get to wiping down my leather jacket. The garment could use a professional clean, or a spell from Alice, but my spot cleaning works for now.

I hang it to dry and strip. The red sauce on my skin is starting to itch.

I catch my reflection in the mirror and stop. My smile seems to be a permanent fixture to my face now. When was the last time I had this much fun? The bond had been a drain on me, but even before then, my life hadn't been carefree.

I thumb the black mark on my wrist. The ink under my skin hotter compared to the rest of my body. My harpy nature still attempting to reject the foreign magic even after all of these months.

Your debt is coming for you, harpy. Alton's words have a shiver of foreboding running up my spine. I only have to

put off that collector until this bond is dissolved, then I'll
be able to take bigger jobs to start paying off my debt.

It's not the best plan, but it's what I have.

I start the shower, waiting for the water to get up to
temperature. Droplets run down my arm and over the
insidious mark. Doubts and creeping affection whisper
alternatives to me. Alternatives like asking Mace for help.

I dismiss the thought sharply and dunk myself under
the cold water with a gasp. Bits of spaghetti and tomato
rinse from me. I shiver until the water becomes hot, but
the whispers are still there, persistent.

I can't trust Mace with the information, can I?

I close my eyes and start washing my hair. The
repetitive motion allows me to admit truths to myself. It's
not about trust. Every step in our interaction grows the
trust I begrudgingly have in Mace a little more.

I'm… embarrassed.

The demon on the other side of the apartment sparks
all sorts of emotions in me. The regard he has for me
soothes insecurities that lay just beneath my skin.

Brave. Strong. Clever.

I don't want to ruin whatever vision Mace has of
me with the truth. I don't want him to know about my
recklessness.

I want to enjoy this time with him, for the desire
between us to burn away every worry plaguing my mind.
My hands slide over my wet skin, sparking sensations.

I reach out mentally, curiously tugging on the bond
between us. Mace must sense something of my current
emotions, the need that's been toying with me since the
first moment our souls twined together. A wave of heat
hits me in response and I moan.

My eyelashes flutter shut as I squeeze my breasts.

The hot sensations recede with a teasing nudge. An underlying impatience for something.

A decision. He's waiting for me to make a choice of whether this happens.

There's a parting challenge in our bond before Mace leaves my senses completely.

I gasp at the absence, an answer clear in my mind.

Chapter 20

MACE

I blow out a breath in good-natured frustration. Sophia exploring the limits of our bond has stoked my arousal until it sings through my blood. My body primed to the point of pain, but I wait.

Maybe another day I'd pour desire and affection through our bond, driving Sophia to climax with nothing more than the magic that connects us. Tonight though, tonight Sophia decides whether she'll dive into those waters with me.

I'll accept nothing less than her enthusiastic participation.

The muscles of my body tense when the water of her shower shuts off. I run a hand through my hair, wet from my shower. I had been tempted to use my hand in the shower, to find some semblance of levelheadedness, but refrained. There's something marvelous about this ache between us. Something I want to tease and torment us with until the only taste on my tongue is her ecstasy.

Sophia walks into the room, the roll of her hips with each stride broadcasting her confidence. My eyes are drawn to the harpy. Her dark hair is damp, tousled from a towel, and hangs down her naked body. The wet ends tickling her brown nipples into tight points that have my mouth watering.

The orange of the sunset colors everything in the apartment with a warm otherworldly light. Leftover water droplets bead on Sophia's skin and shimmer. I pull my gaze up to her face and she tilts her chin up in defiance. A goddess deigning to be in the presence of mortals.

There is no doubt that the vision of my bond-mate in this moment is one that will live in my memory for the rest of my days.

Sophia has decided.

I'm before her in an instant, moving through the in-between to cross the room without a single thought.

Sophia gasps and wisps of shadows run over her skin lovingly before disappearing.

I stop myself from invading her space and straighten.

"You are stunning."

Sophia's breath shudders out, the only betrayal of her nerves other than a tickle through the bond and the race of her heartbeat. Her cheeks darken in color.

"Am I?" she asks. It's supposed to be a taunt but there's a note under her tone that speaks of insecurity. I want to crush whatever is burdening her. I want to be powerful enough to raze cities or defeat armies in her name, but I only have my words. And my touch.

"A goddess," I repeat my inner musings and run a single finger up her bare skin, catching a drop of water and bring it to my mouth, licking the trace taste of her off.

Sophia bites her lip and I continue.

"Unbelievably breathtaking. I'd worship you if you'd let me."

"How?" Sophia's curiosity peeking out from behind her seduction. The temptation for everything new so core to her being that it's endearing.

I bring our fronts close; my clothed body burns to press against her bare one. I hover my lips over hers, enjoying the way her breath stutters against my lips.

My voice deepens. "As anyone should worship a goddess, on my knees."

Sophia inhales my words.

I slide my hand to stroke up the inside of her wrist. Frowning at the hot skin there. Is she injured? I turn her wrist.

I halt, the magic connecting me to the wards protecting this place pulse a warning that has my head snapping to the door. Had someone brushed up against the building's wards by accident?

"What is it?" Sophia asks but my mind goes blank when I see her wrist.

The dark tattoo there is something I'd noticed in passing but hadn't seen up close. Tattoos are a common thing in our world, I've had the ones that decorate my skin for a century.

Sophia's tattoo isn't decorative.

"What is this?" I hiss, alarm rages through me.

Sophia freezes. "I-I—"

Fear bursts in my chest. The spell of the mark is an old one that I haven't seen in many years. Only the most powerful players would use this dark of magic. "Sophia, who do you owe?"

She yanks her arm away from me. "I'm dealing with it."

"Are they looking for you? You know they can track you with that mark, don't you?"

Her face goes white. "What?"

Shit.

The wards blare through my senses again

I grab a naked Sophia and she yelps as we travel through the in-between to the room she's been using.

"Get dressed! We have to go," I say.

Sophia scrambles away from me, rushing to the closet and I grab her leather jacket from where she left it drying. Luckily, there's the weight of her phone in the pocket.

The crash of the front door breaking open echoes through the apartment and I grab the decorative blanket on the bed and throw it around Sophia who drops the jeans she was attempting to step through.

"I need clothes, Mace!"

"Too late."

We pass into the in-between right as I hear the thunder of steps running into the apartment.

The shadows nip at Sophia's bare skin as she attempts to wrap the blanket fully around herself.

"My jacket!" Sophia's voice whips away from us as we travel, and she turns around as if she's going to go back.

My laugh is humorless. "I have your jacket. You don't want to go back there."

Sophia quiets and I shake my head. The fear morphing into something like frustration and anger. That was too close. I could have lost Sophia there; I might still lose her to the mark.

If I had known Sophia was marked, I would have taken precautions. If she had only confided in me—

We step into the bright lobby. The decorative tiles beneath us making beautiful patterns.

I turn and Sophia has the blanket wrapped around her tight, her eyes traveling over our location. Her brows knit together.

"I know this place—" she starts.

"Mace! It's been a while since you've dropped in. With a naked woman, no less." The man at the front desk smiles wide.

"Lowell." I nod in greeting. "Is Gideon around, by chance?" I ask.

"Gideon is with Rose in her office. The man doesn't seem to be able to leave her alone for any span of time anymore." Lowell squints at the harpy behind me. "Sophia, isn't it?"

I turn on my heel slowly.

"You've been here before?" I ask.

Sophia blushes. "I'm not supposed to be here."

My brows raise higher when some detail about Sophia's reputation clicks. "*This* is the bathhouse you were banned from?"

Sophia glares at me. "How many paranormal bathhouses like *this* are you aware of?"

Paranormal bathhouses that cater to individuals who enjoy public sex.

I bite my lip. "A few actually."

Sophia's mouth drops open.

Lowell reaches us. "None are quite like this one."

I nod in acknowledgment. The Love Bathhouse is an accepting community that has a resident matchmaker, it is by far the highest quality establishment of its kind.

"Mace! What a wonderful surprise."

We all turn to see Rose striding forward with a frowning Gideon.

"Sophia?" Gideon asks.

"He's your friend Gideon?" Sophia hisses.

I look back and forth and a laugh full of disbelief comes out of my mouth.

"Well, since it seems we all know each other, could we stay the night here? The bathhouse has a ward that blocks summoning marks, doesn't it?"

"Our wards should block something like that," Lowell answers. "The ward master is old school that way." The words sound bitter, but the man shakes his head as if dismissing his own thoughts on the matter.

"Of course you can stay here," Rose says, and takes in Sophia with a thoughtful look. "I can get you some clothes to wear but it will take a while."

"Clothes would be nice," Sophia says.

I raise a brow at Sophia. It doesn't seem as if she's banned.

"And I see congratulations are in order," Rose says, looking at the space between us, and I remember the woman has the ability to see soul bonds. "I'm glad you've found a mate. I didn't really want your ban to be a lifelong one."

Sophia's cool composure breaks. "Oh, we aren't—" She struggles for a breath before her shoulders fall. "Well, I g uess we kind of are, in a way. Partners?"

The anger that I had banked to deal with setting up our sanctuary flares. Partners don't hide key details from each other. A partnership has a level of trust in it.

"Summoning marks are dark magic." Gideon's words break through my thoughts before my emotions spiral.

My smile is more of a grimace. "We just need a little time to strategize and to rest. I appreciate the place to stay." I've teleported more today than I have in a long time and the drain isn't painful but each visit to the in-between is taking a little more out of me.

"Of course, you only have to ask." Worry creases Gideon's face and his eyes are on Rose.

I won't be calling on Gideon for assistance this time. My friend has more to worry about than helping me out of trouble. He has a mate and future young to protect.

While I have a harpy who refuses to trust me.

Chapter 21

SOPHIA

I step into the private room and fight to keep from gaping at the luxuriousness of it. The mosaic tiling covers the floor to the ceiling, black and dark green designs flow from organic swirls to geometric shapes and back again. A smaller bathing pool is in the center of the room, steam rising from water kept magically hot. An alcove of the room is fully padded with plush pillows for sleeping and *other* activities.

"Sophia."

My attention snaps to Mace, who glares at me with his hands on his hips. There's a coldness in his tone. He's *angry*.

"Who put that mark on you?" he asks.

Gone is the laid-back demon with teasing smiles. The male in front of me is strung tight with tension.

"It's not important—"

Mace curses. "Of course, it's important! Your life and mine are connected—"

"Whose fault is that?" My own anger comes sparking to life. "I didn't ask for this bond."

I was just dragged to another city in a blanket by this asshole.

"No, but you agreed to it. I didn't force this connection on you," he says.

He didn't, and all the things I could spit at him halt on my tongue. I struggle to say something. To stall. Saying anything else would be better than admitting to my biggest regret, my foolish mistake.

"You weren't ever going to tell me, were you?" Mace asks. "How are we supposed to work together if I don't know what dangerous people are after you!"

Mace runs both of his hands through his hair, not waiting for me to answer. Probably sensing that I won't.

"I can't talk about this right now." He shakes his head and heads for the alcove. Removing his suit coat in sharp motions before kicking off his shoes.

I'm left standing alone with a damned blanket wrapped around my naked body. The man who had whispered sweet nothings into my ear, now ignoring me.

"That's it? All that talk about worshipping me and now you're going to what? Go to sleep?" My voice cracks.

Mace freezes halfway through unbuttoning his shirt and casts me a look of disbelief.

"I just had to flee because I've spent the last two days with a woman keeping secrets. We aren't partners. Partners would have at least shared the bare minimum of information. I don't even think you like me as a friend. The goddess I was going to worship only wants me for a fuck anyway, so—"

Every item Mace lists sinks my heart deeper as he continues.

"I'm officially not in the mood. I'm going to get some rest before we have to run again." Mace's face twisting as he removes his shirt.

The broad expanse of his skin blurs and I close my eyes to keep any suspicious eye watering from becoming known.

"Fine," I say, my throat thick.

I toss the blanket to the side and head for the heated pool, hating the confusing emotions raging through me. Anger, disappointment, embarrassment, they all start to be drowned in shame.

Mace's rejection shouldn't matter.

It doesn't matter that he has a right to be angry with me. Lifespans are a precarious thing with soul bonds. If I died unexpectedly I could take him with me. The stubborn part of myself may claim that this soul bond hadn't been my choice, but Mace wouldn't have forced me to do it.

Unwilling soul bonds don't work out well.

He'd played on my pride, which is becoming my least favorite trait.

I step into the hot water and the vise that has been holding my chest tight loosens. Relief joins the quagmire of feelings and I run with it. I gather my hair in one hand and lower myself to my neck, enjoying the sensation of relaxing muscles that had been tight with frustration. My moan is soft, but a zing of arousal hits me through our bond.

The gaze of the only other person in the room is on me. The arousal has a bitter taste to it, reluctant.

I don't think about my actions, only the desire to sweeten the bitter need.

To hear praise from the demon who may now hate me.

I move to the shallow end of the pool, the water lapping at my ribs. My free hand massages the back of my neck and I drop it down my body. The hot water swirls around my fingers before I catch it and smooth it up my body, wetting my skin before reaching a breast. My nipples pull tight as I grasp myself in a tease.

The touch has my breath ghosting out on a sigh before my fingers trail down my skin once more.

The arousal becomes sharp.

"Sophia." Mace's voice is like gravel and goose bumps travel up my arms. It's a warning, but when have I ever heeded those?

I'm reckless. The most irresponsible harpy of my branch.

What's a little more castigation now?

"What? You said you weren't in the mood."

I cast a glance at him beneath my lashes. Mace stands right where I left him, his dress shirt still in his hands, his eyes fathomless. His eyes may be unreadable but the want pulling at me is clear. I'm walking up the steps of the pool before making the decision. Something in Mace's stance draws me in, or something working in the bond between us.

My wet skin chills in the air and before I question my intentions, Mace is in front of me.

I gasp, the smoky shadows of the in-between lingering longer in the air, as though he isn't focused on the task of teleporting.

"Sophia," Mace says again, softer this time. "I know the words I said hurt. I can feel it." He presses a hand to his chest, as if he could trace the line connecting us. "I'm sorry. I'm just still angry and I don't want to take that out on you."

Conflicting concern and arousal lines Mace's face.

"But you want to. And who better to take it out on?" My question has a sultry lilt to it.

Mace's laugh is humorless. I step closer to him, bowing my head as if I'm a coy virgin, unsure of myself or where this is going.

"Maybe," I start, cautious. "I want the bite of your anger."

"Maybe?" Mace asks. "Do you want the sting of my judgment too?"

My neck muscles seize before I can shake my head because… isn't that what I deserve?

Judgment, condemnation, the guilt gouging holes in my chest ever since my recklessness resulted in Zeph's abduction.

Mace continues, "Could you take away the choking fear that is behind my anger?"

Surprise has me taking in the angry slant of his brows, the helpless clenching of his fists. As if he wants to grab me.

"Fear? For me?" The question is out of my mouth before my thoughts catch up and I shake my head. Fear for what would happen to him if I'm killed is more likely.

Exasperation lines Mace's eyes. "Yes, for you. I care about you."

My nod is stunned. He had said before that he liked me, admired me. That he professes to care about me flakes away some of my need to keep him at a distance.

"We are friends." The words are soft on my tongue, denying the accusation he'd thrown out earlier to the contrary.

Mace's brows lift. "You tease all your friends like this?"

He traces a finger over my collarbone, and I shiver.

I try to implore him with my eyes. Let him see my own confusion. Reveal how it's never been like this for me. That

I've never been in this sort of situation. The kind where I like the man who tempts my body. "Maybe a little more than friends."

His hand comes to my cheek.

"Oh, fierce harpy." Mace runs a thumb over my lower lip, his nickname for me a growl. "The way you taunt me— it's as if you want to ask for something from me."

The words have me blinking, trying to figure out how this dynamic will work between us. The choices before me, to let him lead in this dance or to establish how a good harpy would go about sex and dominate our interaction.

That would mean keeping my emotions separate, instructing Mace in the exact way I want him to get me off. As I would have done for any other sexual partner.

"Maybe I want you to beg for something from me." My words are breathless as my mind dithers undecided. My instincts are unwilling to let this moment be dictated by the expectations of my kind.

His breath shudders over my face, tickling my hot cheeks.

"Do you want me to beg for you, fierce harpy? I would. I'd beg and beg until my voice grew hoarse." Mace leans in and his lips ghost over mine. "But that's not what you really want, is it?"

Tension strings me tight and my hands come to his chest. His skin hot and grounding under my palms.

Mace's words continue to seduce me. "No, you like pushing me." Sharp teeth nip my lip, and his next words flow over the sensitive spot. "You want me to break."

Yes.

Mace grips my hips and presses my wet body against his dress pants. The heat of his cock has a whimper escaping my mouth.

"What will it be, Sophia? Should I take out every fear stabbing me on your body? Should I use you to comfort me? Would you let me?"

Mace snarls each question and every one breaks down a little more of the guard I keep around my heart.

"Yes."

Mace's eyes darken with satisfaction. "Beg me for it."

I see red. The violent side of me wants blood but is also hungry for everything this demon is promising.

I do the one thing a harpy should never do.

I beg.

"*Please.*"

"Good girl," he says.

I rear back at the words, angry even as lust lashes me. Mace's mouth comes down on mine before I get the chance to snarl in defiance.

The kiss is feral. It's the breaking of control that Mace promised me. It's smoke and stars and when he opens his mouth and tastes mine, it pours every heated word into me and then some. The sting of his teeth on my lips, the slide of his tongue soothing the pain, brings me high until my blood is rushing under my skin, needing more of this pain-comfort combination.

Mace wraps an arm around me, and our bodies press together. His hand cups my breast, playing with the weight as his mouth explores mine. The sensations are heavy and my body responds, heat and hunger dragging me to meet him.

Mace's cock digs into my stomach, teasing me. My hips rock into him. I slide my arms around him, my fingers gripping his back. Needing the burn of him against me, inside of me.

When he breaks the kiss, I gasp at the absence, sinking my nails into his back to keep him from pulling away. Mace hisses in pain and I let go, horrified.

"Don't stop," Mace says. He sucks on my lip, his teeth raking it. "You're not the only one who likes a bite of pain."

Relief and lust ease my breath before I surge forward, showering bites on Mace's neck. My demon clutches me. We fall. I gasp at the rush as we move through the cold smoke and stars of the in-between before returning to this plane.

My back hits the plush bedding of the room. Mace on top of me, threading his fingers through my hair before pulling, pinning my head back and sucking on the pulse in my neck and I arch with a moan.

"Gods, that's such a beautiful sound." His hand runs up my inner thigh and he strokes a single finger up the lips of my pussy, the touch so soft I whimper.

"Mace, I need—"

"I know what you need, but this is about appeasing me. Isn't that what you want?"

I snarl. Mace laughs and plunges two fingers inside me roughly.

"*Fuck* you're wet." Mace curves his fingers, massaging a sensitive spot inside me without mercy.

"This is a familiar scene, isn't it? A harpy looking for a release, but you didn't moan so prettily for that shifter, did you?"

When I don't immediately answer, Mace stills his fingers.

"No!" I cry.

"I didn't think so. Tell me, have you ever begged for your orgasm?"

"Mace," I say his name in a whispered warning and he smiles, releasing his grip on my hair so I can watch him.

"Have no fear, harpy. I won't slot you into the position of a submissive. I know better." Mace presses his fingers into me harder with his words and my legs fall open wider. "But I think you like a taste of it."

I arch, rolling my hips with each wave of pleasure this demon sparks. He may be right.

"Just like I like the taste of pain." Mace drops his head and sucks a nipple into his mouth.

"Yes," I hiss when he draws hard on me. I grip Mace's dark hair with both hands, pulling on it in a way that has a moan escaping the man at my breast.

Mace slips his fingers from me, circling both around my clit. I gasp at the emptiness, squeezing my legs around his arm.

"Shhh," Mace says against my skin. "You'll get there."

"I want you inside me," I say, and feel him smile against my breast.

"I'm enjoying my position at the moment. Give me some more of those sweet words of yours and I'll think about it."

"Mace." The word is harsh and if anything, my demon smiles wider.

"As much as I like my name on your tongue, I was thinking of other sweet words."

"I don't—" I stop because I've already begged him once before so I can't claim that I don't beg. "Don't make me—"

Mace makes eye contact then. The bond between us vibrating with understanding. "You've given me such a gift, Sophia. Trust that I won't abuse it."

I swallow on nothing and some unidentifiable emotion surges in my chest. I nod and cry out when Mace slides three fingers inside me, his thumb pressing against my clit.

The tension in my belly dissolves as I climax. The sensations roll through me softly, and I want to sob.

Disappointment rises in my throat, choking me.

A gentle orgasm wasn't what I wanted. I must make a sound betraying my frustration.

Mace's laugh is throaty, and he starts to drop kisses down my body.

"Oh, don't be sad. We aren't done, Sophia. Trust me," he says, scraping his teeth against the skin of my hip bone.

Somehow, I do. This man who leveraged my debt to connect us soul deep, who seems to be able to read my every thought, who teases me and spoils me at every turn.

Mace presses his fingers up inside me again before sliding them free. The demon sucks them clean and the expression on his face has my legs squeezing in with a flush of heat. He smiles a wicked smile at me before dropping lower and dragging his tongue up the sensitive flesh of my pussy. I gasp, fighting the urge to draw away. He groans.

"I could write poetry about the way you taste, fierce harpy. Like fire and spite and every lush level in between."

His words dispel some of my nerves, I snort. "Like fire and spite?"

Mace's eyes glitter in mirth. "I'm not great with words, remember?"

"Then don't try and seduce me with them," I lobby at him, but my mouth is still curved in a smile. Clever demon, sweeping away my nerves with his ridiculousness.

"Ah, well, I guess I'll have to find a better use for my mouth." Mace slides his tongue gently through my folds.

Weaponizing the sensitivity of my climax until my lungs empty of all air and I whimper soundlessly.

Mace leaves no skin untouched. Working his hot tongue over my pussy, alternating hard and soft strokes to devour me. It takes until my legs start to kick out and he grabs the back of my knees to hold me open to realize that he's learning my body's responses.

I fight for breath. "I can't tell if your tongue is a blessing or a curse."

My lower body cants against Mace's mouth no matter that I try to hold still. One of his hands releases my knee and presses my lower stomach to keep me in place when he slides his tongue inside me.

"Fuck!" My body attempts to thrash but Mace's firm grip doesn't allow it and I curl upward instead when his tongue dives deeper. The sight of his dark head between my thighs only drives my arousal higher.

The demon slides his tongue from me and growls. The sound raising the hairs on my body and a pre-climax shudder travels through me.

"Mace—"

His dark eyes catch mine when I say his name and he licks up through me again, slowly.

"*Please,*" I beg.

A look of satisfaction curls Mace's mouth as if I've said the magic word. The hand pressing my lower body in place slides between my legs. Mace sucks hard on my clit in tandem with the thrust of two fingers inside me, pushing hard against a sensitive spot.

I shatter, the orgasm almost too much. My body moves mindlessly, my scream hoarse and sobbing.

The pulses go on and on until Mace softens his mouth on me and gently removes his wet fingers from me.

"So fucking tight."

I pant and Mace kneels between my legs, hands deftly starting to undo his pants. My trembling hands claw at the fabric, attempting to help, but clumsy with release. Mace catches one hand and brings it to his mouth, kissing it with affection before lasering me with his gaze.

"Still want more?" he asks. The hunger on his face rings a pang of need through me and I suddenly, desperately want him to fill my empty body. I nod and Mace's pants fall, releasing his cock. It's ruddy and thick, the end leaking precum that makes my mouth water.

I wrap a hand around his cock, admiring the shape and stiffness of him. Mace braces himself and slides a hand in my hair, gripping it. He pulls on my hair, letting me stroke him and I shiver at the tantalizing sting. I slow my strokes and Mace strokes a thumb over my lower lip in a way that isn't subtle.

I'm still in control of my body enough to stifle the urge to lean forward and taste him, lick up the bead of precum and swallow it. It's an urge I've never had before. Mace's eyes are hot and if I wasn't who I am, what I am, maybe he'd direct me to take him in my mouth.

But I am who I am, and Mace knows I'd have to bite on principle. I lean my head back and release the demon from my grip. The spell broken, but the concept leaving me even more wet than before.

Instead of annoyance at the nonverbal boundary, Mace smiles like a patient predator.

"Do you want me inside your greedy cunt?" he asks, teasing me with words. My breath halts before I nod.

Mace removes his pants and leans over me. His rolling movements are as smooth as any hunter. He slides a finger under my chin. "Words, Sophia, I need your words."

I spread my legs wider, brushing his thickness against my wetness in a way that has Mace sucking in a breath. He pinches my chin, and a dark look comes over his face. "Sophia."

He needs the begging. I groan in realization and my resistance dissolves.

"Yes, please, I need you inside me—" I gasp, breaking off when the head of his cock presses into me. My knees rise up around his body and Mace shudders before sinking deeper.

He's thick and the slide of us coming together is slow. The stretch of my body around his has whatever words I was going to say evaporating from my lips with the curl of my toes.

When our bodies meet, I tense around his girth with a moan.

"Oh gods, fierce harpy, so wet that you're practically sucking me into you. Perfection."

Mace rolls his hips. The measured motion is slow but the movement inside me sparks pleasure. I gasp when he hits even deeper.

"Oh gods. Please, Mace. I need it." My words escape me with no thought or decision, but each gets me a satisfying thrust just where I need it.

I don't quite know how or why, but I'm breaking again. Mace hisses and his next thrust smacks into me.

"Oh, just like that, *fuck* the way your cunt squeezes on me makes me think you want my spill inside of you. Is that what you want? For me to fill you up?"

Something instinctual rears its head at the thought of stealing this demon's essence, his strength. The thought of him filling me up. My talons elongate and I grab the sheets to keep from shredding Mace's skin on accident.

"Yes! Give me your seed." I'm desperate, my lower body tensing with the need.

Mace's thrusts falter before resuming on a slower roll of his hips.

His chuckle is dark. "Oh, my beautiful fierce harpy. How surprising. You want to be dripping with me, don't you?"

"Mace, please!"

His eyes dilate and he starts circling a thumb over my clit. "The way you beg makes me want to keep you here forever. Waiting for my cum."

The harpy in my blood sinks its teeth into me, and I snarl. Wrestling, I flip us, the world spinning until I straddle him, sinking his cock into me with a sharp smack of my body against his.

Mace laughs at the grappling and grunts when I drop myself down on to him again. I've lost all control, the burning need for this demon's seed riding me just how I'm riding him. My hands flatten against his bare chest. My talons curving wickedly against the designs of his tattoos.

Mace grips my hips, his face alight with delight and hunger.

"Take me, Sophia, claim me with all the ferocity you can. I can take it."

My movements falter. I'm not a stranger to this position, but it hasn't been like this before. My partners have never watched me like Mace does, with a face full of dark, hungry awe.

I circle my hips, searching for the best angle. He feels bigger like this, and a whimper builds in my throat, but I won't release it.

Then he opens his mouth. "So, *fucking* beautiful. My fierce goddess, conquering my soul. Take what you want from me, but you'll have to work for it."

I snap my hips down and Mace meets me. We both make a sound at the resounding impact, and I crave more.

I conquer. Our movements are fast, aggressive to the point of pain, but it feeds my harpy instincts. Instincts that desire blood, violence, and defeating the strongest opponent to capture strength for the next generation.

Every smack and groan drives me higher until I swear I can taste the very stars.

Sweat beads on Mace's upper lip and blood wells under my talons. I'm past the point of caring, only needing one thing that this demon is keeping from me.

I wrap my hand around Mace's throat. "Give it to me."

At my demand, the cords of Mace's throat tighten, and he throws back his head with a shout. His grip on my hips is brutal, as brutal as the depth of his cock, the heat that fills me and throws me into another climax.

Nothing exists anymore and I float, released from the driving need as Mace's release leaks from me.

Fuzzy happiness keeps me from thinking more complete thoughts than single inelegant words at a time.

Fuck. Gods. Mace. Wow.

I lay my body against Mace's heaving chest, gasping and covered in sweat. Spent.

"Oh, my gods, that was, I don't—" Words escape me and my face smears against more than sweat. The coppery scent of blood trying to yank my mind back into my body. "You're bleeding!"

I move to scramble upright, but Mace holds me still, blinking. "Hush, Sophia, relax, it's fine. Fantastic, actually.

Don't ruin my after-sex buzz by freaking out over a little blood."

"Don't you hush me! I just destroyed your chest." Panic and annoyance make my words shrill.

"It will heal." Mace sighs and the happy sound brings the level of worry down.

The shot of adrenaline has brought my mind back from the clouds though and I move, sliding Mace's cock from me. My cheeks heat at the dripping fluids even as a satisfied low moan escapes my mouth.

Embarrassment and confusion have my mouth opening. "I-I don't know what happened."

It's simple. You wrestled Mace for his seed, Sophia. My cheeks burn hotter at the thought.

Mace laughs in disbelief. It's not mean spirited, but I scowl on principle.

"Oh, you're being serious." Mace clears his throat, propping himself up on an elbow. "It seems as if we've discovered a little bit of a breeding kink in you."

My mouth drops open. "Definitely not! I don't want babies."

Mace smiles crookedly, he bends a leg. For a blissful moment my eyes forget the topic at hand and travel down his body. His form in repose is comparable to a renaissance painting, or a renaissance painting of a man still shiny from sweat and other fluids.

The blood smears on his chest glisten. I avert my eyes, though *his* blood doesn't have nausea twisting my stomach like the sight of blood usually does. Which makes just as much sense as me begging him to fill me with fluids.

"It has nothing to do with actually making babies." His dark hair falls into his eyes as he talks. "It's just your instincts pushing you a little. You can blame it on the soul bond if you want. Since I'm guessing it hasn't happened with previous partners."

The bond.

That must be it. Not that no other partner has ever spent the time to masterfully manipulate my body, or cause emotions to flow in time to the beat of our hearts.

The missing nausea from the sight of blood hits me. Fear twisting with indecision.

I have feelings for Mace.

"This is about having fun, right?" I ask.

My voice sounds weak to my own ears, but Mace tilts his head. His face soft, understanding.

"Of course, Sophia." He guides a piece of hair out of my face, smoothing it behind my ear with care. "I never dreamed of being able to keep one such as you forever."

The relief is instant even if something about that statement makes me want to scream. What are these emotions twisting me up inside?

Mace sighs. How much of my emotions can he pick up right now? Does he know how clueless I am?

Mace's arms come around me, and I yelp as he picks up and plunges both of us into icy shadows.

"Wha—" I start before we're both submerged in the hot water of the bathing pool. I sputter. "This can't be sanitary!"

Mace's laugh is deep with his chest against my ear. "There are spells for keeping everything clean. I'm glad they aren't interfering with your magic though. The ward master of this place must be excellent."

Now that Mace mentions it, the hum of the magics do brush against me, but don't grab at me like other magics do. I don't dwell any longer on it because Mace begins to massage me. Stress falls away under his hands on my back and I sink into the sensations, his heartbeat against my cheek.

Gods above maybe staying bonded wouldn't be a bad thing.

That snaps me out of it.

I push away and Mace releases me, starting to rinse away the blood from the wounds my talons caused. I sink into the water, trying to dispel whatever confusion is muddling my thoughts. My demon dunks himself in the water and heat pools in my belly as I watch the water droplets race down his body.

Exasperation flares at my reaction after everything. No more of that tonight. The hot water starts to dissipate my adrenaline and clusterfuck of emotions until my limbs are heavy with exhaustion.

"We should talk about that mark, Sophia."

That wakes me up, bringing another flush of emotions I'd rather cut out than deal with.

Mace wraps his arms around me, and I turn away. It's less of a hug now and more of him keeping me captive, but he doesn't release me yet.

"I feel your shame." Mace presses a hand against my chest, between my breasts. "I feel it and don't understand, but I want to. I don't want to lose you to forces I don't know about."

"You aren't looking for someone to protect," I repeat his words from earlier.

Mace's chest vibrates with his hum.

"No, but I'm invested in someone who could use a little help."

I want to scoff at that. Little is not an accurate description. I need a whole miracle.

"Can we talk about it tomorrow? I just—" Feel raw? Physically wrung out along with emotionally?

Mace kisses my hair. "Of course, we'll get some rest. It will all be easier in the morning."

I don't know if that's true, but I wish for it to be with all my feathers.

Chapter 22

MACE

The fact that I wake first is not surprising. I've never been a sound sleeper. In the environment that Elise and I grew up in it was better to be on guard at all hours, or at least up and out of the house as early as possible.

What is a surprise is that Sophia allowed me to hold her through the night. Her emotions after what we had done had been a roiling mess, most flitting past quicker than I could catch. I take comfort that none I identified were regret. Confusion, panic, and small bites of arousal in the bathing pool, but no regret.

Which is fantastic, I don't want anything to mar the memories of us together. Last night had been... I'm not in the practice of comparing sexual encounters over the years of my life, but nothing has ever been quite like it was with Sophia. The give of her body to mine, the growl of her aggression when she let loose.

I carefully slide from Sophia's grasp before I'm tempted to wake her with intimacy.

Intimacy.

This is dangerous ground. Ground I'm sure my fierce harpy doesn't want to trek at all, but that I can't help to stumble over. I'll enjoy having her while I can.

It will hurt when she leaves.

First, we have things to deal with. The hunting of the trafficking ring for one and Sophia's debt as another.

I dress quickly and am met with gifts outside of the room door. A bag full of savory croissants on a duffel bag with clothes for Sophia to choose from. I grab a couple of croissants before leaving the rest and the duffel where Sophia can find it when she wakes.

I moan at the smoky ham and tang of cheese of the croissant. Heaven. It doesn't compare to the taste of Sophia.

Like fire and spite. She thought I was joking.

I head to Rose's office. The bathhouse has an empty feel to it this early in the morning. The front desk is manned by a woman instead of Lowell. She gives me a polite wave and smile that I return.

I reach the matchmaker's office, knocking politely on the doorjamb to avoid interrupting anything.

"Come in." Gideon sounds grumpy.

Surprise.

I enter the office. Rose smiles at me from behind her desk, a monstrosity that dwarfs the space. It's truly a masterpiece that never fails to bring a smile to my mouth. Probably because it's carved with dozens of fiery figures copulating.

A masterpiece.

Gideon sits on a love seat in the corner, scowling at his laptop.

"Well, aren't you cheerful this morning," I drawl.

Gideon arches a brow, but Rose comes to her mate's defense.

"He's still upset that morning sickness isn't something he can stop." Rose's mouth curves. "This is reoccurring crankiness."

"Oh, did the candies I send not work?" I ask.

"They help, but sometimes it comes on quicker than eating candy in bed allows," she says with much more cheer than Gid. As if she's trying to make up for his glowering. "Small sacrifices—"

"It's not a small thing—" Gideon starts.

"Gideon." Some of Rose's cheer fades into exasperation. "How about you take Mace to the break room? You said you had something to discuss."

"But you're—"

"Fine—I'm fine and in need of a tiny bit of breathing space."

Gideon sits back, stunned, before his mouth curves into a small smile. "My apologies for being overbearing, my mate."

Rose waves her hand. "Go."

Gideon snaps his laptop closed.

"Thank you for breakfast and the clothes, Rose. You are incredible and if ever in need of someone who won't suffocate you with—" I don't try and dodge Gideon's smack to the back of my head. We leave the echoes of Rose's laugh behind in favor of the break room.

"You have enough on your hands." Gideon starts. "When you said you found someone to bond with, you did not say that it was with Sophia Shirazi."

I shrug, ignoring the comment. "You need to lighten up with the overprotective bit. You'll annoy Rose past the point that she'll continue dealing with you and I definitely don't want to deal with your grumpiness."

"I know I'm annoying her; I'm annoyed with myself. It's just…" Gideon trails off before sighing. "It's hard not to try to wrap her in cotton for the entire pregnancy. I didn't think she'd get so sick."

The look of helplessness that passes over Gideon's face is so out of place it almost doesn't register in my mind. Asa had been like this too with Zeph.

I always assumed that such powerful individuals were graced with never having to experience helplessness, but perhaps it doesn't matter how strong someone is. There are always moments where the tilt of the earth is uncontrollable.

We enter the break room, which, unsurprisingly, is just as beautiful as the rest of the bathhouse. A mahogany table with more carvings that I haven't identified yet has a lush houseplant as a centerpiece. The floor is tiled in the way of the rest of the building with this room having blue tiles with white lotus shapes.

Lowell is in the kitchen partition, measuring out loose-leaf tea. "I'm almost done," he says to us. "And then you'll have the space to whisper whatever secrets you want to each other."

"I'm telling Gid he's being overbearing," I say.

Lowell holds a finger up. "That is not a secret." He points the finger at Gideon. "But we love you anyway."

Gideon cracks a smile at that, and I take a moment to appreciate that my friend has found his place here.

"I'm happy for you," I say as Lowell is walking out the door. My words are soft, and Gideon's smile turns thoughtful.

"You'll have this for yourself one day," he says.

No, I won't, but I can enjoy my place in each of my friends' lives.

Gideon's face becomes serious, as if he knows my thoughts.

"I've been looking into other means of teleporting large groups of people," Gideon says, setting his laptop on the table.

I'm surprised at the turn of topic and take another bite of my breakfast. "And you've found something?"

Gideon hesitates. "There was a rumor going around a year ago about a demon with teleportation abilities offering services. Since then, there hasn't been a word about it other than the services are no longer available to hire."

I chew, mulling that over. We already know that this group has demonic assistance, but for the demon to be the one teleporting rather than them using a spell... Gods, that would make tracking and apprehending much more difficult and puts us back at square one with our portal spell lead.

Gideon watches me and a sense of foreboding has the hair on the back of my neck raising.

Gideon purses his lips before he continues, "I think it's Nero."

I choke on the croissant. It takes a moment of clearing my throat, but once I do, I cast a disbelieving look at Gideon.

"That's impossible," I say, my voice hoarse.

The wounds I carry on my heart that refuse to heal, bleed.

"Not impossible. From my understanding, you only banished him from this plane. You didn't kill him," Gideon says.

I should have killed him. People like Nero don't change, regret haunts me over my decision, but I was young and had just lost my only other family. It had been Nero's fault, but I still hesitated until Asa suggested a banishment.

Be reasonable, Mace! Logic is what will solve this. Not some latent fear of my own bogeyman.

"You never met him. Why are you so sure it's Nero?" I ask.

Asa had been my first real friend. We hadn't met Gideon until later.

"Mace, how many demons can teleport the number of people required to leave a signature as if a portal spell is being used?" Gideon asks.

My mind rebels. "It still might not be him."

"It might not be," Gideon says, but I can tell he doesn't mean it. What are the odds that there is another demon out there with that ability, working in an industry that my half brother dabbled in, and it not being Nero?

Not great. Our world is a small one and the others that I know of with the ability to teleport couldn't teleport as many people as we are tracking at once and teleporting a few people at a time wouldn't have left a signature of portal use at the location.

I finish the croissant. It doesn't matter how my stomach is turning at the news. Even after a couple centuries, wasting food is something I can't bring myself to do.

Gideon's brow creases in sympathy, but I'm not in the right state to accept it. I step back, considering the options ahead. A coldness rests over my shoulders.

"Thank you, Gideon. If you find anything else, let me know."

The opportunity to hold Nero accountable for Elise's death has been laid at my feet.

I will not fail this time.

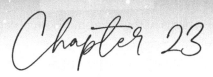

Chapter 23

SOPHIA

I wake to the sound of rapid tapping. The air is warm and humid, sticking to my skin in a comforting way. I stretch; the soreness of my body is quickly fading, but my cheeks heat with memories.

The tapping is constant. I rub my eyes and see Mace, reclining on a chair, fully dressed. How is this morning going to be? Will it be awkward now that we've given into our attraction, or will it be as comfortable as it has been? It's an interesting time to realize how well my demon and I work together.

Maybe I can convince him to join me for a repeat performance.

Mace looks up, the carefree attitude missing from his face. "Good, you're awake. I'm putting together details to send to Gage's team. Eat and dress so we can get going."

There's a pang of what must be hurt in my chest, but I keep from showing it. This option hadn't occurred to me. This disinterest.

Is this rejection?

The pang grows into an ache, and I focus on the pastry bag on top of a duffel Mace had pointed to. I place one foot in front of the other to get there without letting the emotions catch me. I turn from Mace so he doesn't see my face while I struggle to figure out the mood shift in him.

There's a sound of distress behind me and warm arms wrap around me.

"Apologies, fierce harpy, my mind is preoccupied. I didn't mean to distress you."

"You didn't." My words are constricted with my lie. I attempt to harden myself. Pull on the mask of being a good harpy that doesn't start having inappropriate feelings for a demon. Feelings that aren't returned.

Mace kisses the back of my neck and some of the physical response to my emotions starts to fade. "Your words can lie, but the bond between us can't."

I fall back against Mace. The bond between us is a violation of my mental privacy, but it's helpful when I don't know how to voice things. I don't know if I'd ever go so far as to call it a gift… but it keeps me from hiding and gets me talking.

"I thought maybe you had… decided against us now that you got what you wanted."

A pang of remorse reverberates through our bond and Mace takes a pained breath.

"Not at all, my fierce goddess. You'd have to run to the ends of the earth to get rid of me now, and I'd still follow like the saddest puppy."

I snort at the image.

Mace rubs his lips against the back of my neck. "Anyway, you got what you wanted too, didn't you?"

The sensual touch finally has the last of my tension leaving.

"Yes." It comes out on a shaky whisper.

Mace hums. "Get dressed before you tempt me away from our tasks for the day. I'll brief you."

* * *

"It's a demon? That's—" I break off and scrunch my nose. "That really sucks."

The suppliers of portal spells had at least been a solid lead. Now where do we go?

Mace makes a sound, his jaw clenches and the coldness I had caught earlier lines his face.

"There's reason to believe that the demon doing the teleporting is a demon born on this plane known as Nero."

"Wait, didn't Alton mention him?" Is it a common name? What are the chances it's the same person? That would mean that this Nero is Mace's—

Mace's face morphs into distaste.

"We have history." His words are slow. "We share a father. Asa and I banished him more than a century ago… He could have figured out a way to return to this plane."

Surprise has me straightening. "You think our target is your half brother. Why do we think he's responsible for the teleporting?"

Mace shrugs in a way that's anything but casual. "He's one of the few demons that can teleport on that scale."

I nod. "So capability is covered. What about motive?"

Mace's face goes so cold that I shiver. "This wouldn't be the first time he's dabbled in selling people. He has a history of doing easy jobs for money with little care for morality. Usually, it's to finance one habit or another, but with our last altercation, Asa and I cleaned out any resources he would have on this plane."

"So, if he's here to stay, he's going to need money." Something occurs to me. "Wouldn't he need an anchor to stay? Can we track him that way?"

Mace shrugs. "Anyone can be an anchor; with some demon born, they wouldn't even need consent to make or break a bond."

"Is Nero one of those demon born?" I ask out of curiosity.

Mace hesitates. "I've never witnessed it, but it's possible. Most people wouldn't even notice being bonded."

Scratch the option of trying to find this guy through his anchor then.

I frown.

"Other people don't notice being bonded?" I try to let the frustration go. "I guess I'm just the lucky one." I twirl a finger in the air, sarcasm coating my words.

Mace's stern face cracks into a smile. "Our bond is quite unique. Not many people can pick up so much through a bond."

Unique is a nice way of saying weird, but I let it slide.

Our bond isn't all bad, just the way it exists is destroying the life I have. I still need to find leverage on Mace, even if we're friends now… yeah, putting a pin in that.

"I'm assuming this is all going in that email for Gage's team. What are our next steps?" I ask.

Mace nods. "I've already sent Gage the info, along with some individuals Nero may contact and a list of his old haunts. We'll move down the list and see what we can dig up about this new operation."

Should I bring up my debt? The summoning mark on my wrist is always on my mind and now adds a layer of sticky guilt. Mace had said he wanted to talk about it, but there's nothing we can do about it right now. We don't have the exorbitant funds I owe, and I was unable to find any leverage to have it forgiven. The most we can do is to avoid being caught unawares where they can track the summoning mark.

What are the consequences to dodging my past employer's goons? Can I make sure Mace won't get hurt?

I stamp my guilt down before Mace can sense it. This new discovery is a much higher priority anyway.

"Where to first?" I ask.

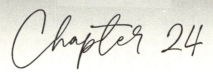

Chapter 24

MACE

"Alright, I've messaged all the contacts I can think of. Ready for a trip?" I ask, holding out my hand.

Sophia looks up from her phone where she had also been messaging her network, as fledgling as it is. "Don't you want to say goodbye to your friends? I was going to thank Rose for the clothing and ask… how much to send her for the sheets."

Sophia's blush is hot, and I grin as I cast a glance to the shredded bedding. My harpy really tore them up last night. The touches of memory threaten to have me carrying Sophia back to the bed to further destroy them.

"We'll be coming back tonight, I think. We still have your summoning mark to deal with."

A guilty look crosses Sophia's face. Good, she should feel guilty for assuming I forgot about it. It may have momentarily been misplaced in my mind, but avoidance won't help in solving that issue.

"As for the sheets, I'm sure it happens all the time. If anyone is going to pay for them, it's me," I say.

Sophia clears her throat. "What a gentleman you are."

I bite my lip to keep from laughing at her embarrassment. "I make a solemn vow to pay for every sheet you shred while we are lovers."

"You're not cute," Sophia says, but her eyes have a sparkle of humor.

I gasp. "You wound me. Shall we?"

Sophia's eyes light up the way they do every time we travel through the in-between. Will it ever get old to her? I hope not.

Sophia's hand firmly grips mine and we move into the shadows. The cold of the in-between is brisk in comparison to the warmth of the bathhouse. I focus on our destination, an old favorite dive bar of Nero's.

Sophia laughs and I look back, the shadows seem to be catching on her more now. The smoke moves almost with affection. The belief that the in-between is sentient becomes a little more real with the way the dark mist pulls playfully at Sophia's hair.

The idea that the plane I transverse noticing us may be frightening, but it likes my harpy, so we have something in common.

We step into rain. Of course it's raining. The stench of the empty alley is suppressed by the deluge and my hair quickly becomes soaked as I search for some sort of overhang to block the water from the sky. This may be the one location that Sophia doesn't look around in awe.

My heart stops when Sophia screams.

I whip back toward her as she drops to her knees, pulling her hand from mine.

"What—Sophia!" I cry.

My words drowned out by another soul-destroying scream as she cradles her wrist to her body.

No. I drop to my knees and pull Sophia into my arms.

"Sophia, my fierce harpy, you need to listen to me. *Breathe.*"

She tries. My brave harpy hiccups and sobs in a breath, curling in tighter.

"I-I can't—" Another hiss breaks off her own words and her body trembles with tension.

I attempt to order my thoughts even as helplessness jumbles them. To figure out a way to make the pain stop.

"It's the mark. You need to breathe through the pain as long as you can."

As long as it takes for them to find us. Running is no longer an option. There's only one person who can stop the pain she's in now.

"C-Cut it off," Sophia chokes out.

"Shhh." I cradle her, speaking into her hair. My heart in my throat. "That won't help. Just breathe for me, sweetheart. You can do it."

The air shifts around us blessedly quick and we are surrounded by dark shapes I barely make out in the rain. I stand, carrying Sophia, ready to go wherever they wish.

"What about the demon?" one asks another, their leader.

I snarl at the implication that they are taking my harpy from me.

"They're bonded. We bring him." The words are calm.

I let whoever is speaking grab me and rip us through the in-between again. This time the trip is rapid and nauseating, but we stop in a dry, well-furnished room.

"Harpy Shirazi, the pain will fade now. You'll be given a moment to compose yourself before your audience." The enforcer's voice is deep and neutral.

Sophia sobs into my neck and I rub her back.

"We'll need some towels if you have any. I'm sure whoever has summoned her doesn't want us dripping on their floor," I say.

The enforcer nods and disappears before returning with a stack of towels that he puts down on a sofa rather than approach me. So, this is the one with the teleporting ability. I can't sense what type of paranormal he is. The man disappears again, giving us what privacy we have.

I carry Sophia to the couch and start drying her, starting with her sopping wet hair, squeezing the dark mass. By the time I'm drying off her jacket, she's stopped trembling in pain and her breaths are merely stuttering now.

Sophia's amazing green eyes meet mine, full of sorrow and leftover pain.

"I'm so sorry, Mace." Her voice cracks.

"Hush. You have nothing to be sorry about." I sigh in relief that most of the pain had passed.

Sophia shakes her head. "I'm the reason you're involved in this."

"I wouldn't have let them take you. It's better this way. The two of us are more capable of paying off whatever you owe."

Shame drowns our bond. All of Sophia's emotions are fraught for the reading now.

"It was a stupid mistake."

"Undoubtedly," I croon. "We all make them."

My curiosity for the details of Sophia's debt is suppressed by the sound of her screams still echoing in my mind. Another thing to haunt my dreams.

Sophia sniffs, blinking rapidly.

"Stop it." I make my voice stern. "You need to use that scary harpy mask you wear for this, Sophia. I don't know who we're meeting with, but you need to get through this meeting without breaking. Later, you can break, and I'll hold you just like this, but you can't break now."

Sophia stops blinking and glares. "I will not break."

My mouth twitches. "Okay."

She takes a deep breath and then another.

"You should dry yourself off too," she says, distancing herself.

"What? No offer to towel dry my body?" I tease, trying my hardest to keep my tone light.

"Maybe later."

My smile comes out of nowhere and surprises me. "It's a date."

Chapter 25

SOPHIA

Dread pulls my stomach down. The deep breaths I take don't alleviate it, but at least I'm not on the edge of passing out. We're walked through the mansion by a blank faced man who looks a little familiar from the last time I was here until we get to a home office.

Everything is the height of luxury, as to be expected from an immortal of his standing. Kalos leans on his giant desk, nodding at us as we enter.

Even if I didn't have the knowledge of what he is haunting me, I would know not to mess with him. Some foresight I should have listened to when he'd offered me the job. Kalos wears a sharp three-piece suit, the height of formality even in his own den, only broken by his messy dark hair.

"Sophia, so good of you to finally come and speak to me." His gold eyes narrow in annoyance and if Mace hadn't given me a pep talk, I'd have shrunk under the scrutiny.

I lift a brow with all the bravery in my badass harpy heart. I may be facing an ancient, oversized lizard who

may or may not breathe fire in the form of a man, but if
he wanted me dead, I already would be.

"And how unexpected, Reynolds, it's been a while."

Of course they know each other. Everyone seems to
know each other in this world while I'm still the outsider
blundering my way through everything.

Mace lets out a whistle. "I doubt my presence was
unexpected. That would be unlike you. Almost like you
were losing your touch."

Kalos smiles, flashing sharp fangs. "I've always admired
your boldness."

Mace gives a nod. "As I've always admired your fairness.
Even if it is rather off brand at times."

Kalos shakes his head before heading to the liquor
cabinet. "Do either of you want a drink?"

I stiffly shake my head, but Mace blows out a breath.

"I'll take a whiskey. If I remember correctly, you have
excellent tastes."

Kalos nods as he pours. "In informants and in alcohol."
He gestures to the corner of the office outfitted in a more
casual seating arrangement than the one at his desk. "Take
a seat."

I follow Mace. Trying to make my movements as
relaxed as his. A pulse of comfort comes from the bond
and spreads warmth through my chest. I take the seat next
to Mace's and try not to tense when Kalos gives Mace the
drink and sits across from us.

The dragon crosses an ankle over his knee, tapping his
glass with a black reptilian claw. I have no doubt he could
make his hands match his human appearance, but then
how would he terrify his company with the mere tap of a
glass?

"I'm displeased that I had to resort to invoking the mark to get you to meet with me," Kalos starts. The coldness of his tone seeps into my already clammy skin.

"Me too," I say, sweetly. Mace's amusement reaches me through the bond and helps me push down the nausea.

Kalos's mouth twitches. "I'm sure. There is always a possibility that the pain will make the bearer of the mark lose their mind, so it's always a last resort for me."

A chill travels down my spine, but I don't comment. I didn't think he could cause me pain with the mark. It's not like the damn thing came with a manual and the magic is older than most use.

"I'm also sure you don't have the amount to repay me what you owe," Kalos says.

Mace straightens. "And how much might that be?"

A number rolls off Kalos's tongue.

My demon gags.

The impossibility of paying back the debt sinks my shoulders before I remember not to show my emotions.

"That's unseemly," Mace says. "How on earth did that happen?"

I bite my lip, my shame like water sinking a ship. Slow and insidious.

Kalos merely shrugs. "I entrusted Sophia with the task of retrieving information for the safe transportation of a shipment and the information turned out to be a trap. I lost a whole shipment."

I force myself not to rapidly blink. I will not cry.

I fucked up in such a large way. I'm lucky to be alive, for now.

"That's utter bullshit." Mace's hissed words break me from my spiral of self-castigation. "You would never trust one, untried informant for a shipment like that."

Kalos shrugs and Mace sips the whiskey though his rage fills our bond in pulses. As if he's trying to keep me from receiving the emotion.

"Still collecting people, are you?" Mace asks.

"You know how much I like a variety. Each particular task is best suited for a particular individual."

I'm not following their conversation, but I can clearly read Mace's clenched jaw.

Kalos continues. "And I have the best taste in informants. I can spot good talent a mile away."

His eyes fall on me even as Mace clenches his fist.

Things start to fall into place. *Collecting. Talent.*

"It was a setup." My voice transitions from disbelief to outrage. "You lost the shipment on purpose?!"

Mace catches my hand and I realize I've jumped to my feet. Kalos doesn't react to my outrage.

"I'm sure if you weren't the victim, you'd have figured it out much sooner, but being close to situations tends to put one in a blindfold."

I'm shaking my head. "I don't fucking owe you."

Mace squeezes my hand and pulls me back in my seat as Kalos's eyes chill.

"Careful harpy. There was no language in our contract that forbid my machinations, something you should revise."

I swallow and Kalos's eyes warm to his amused self again.

"I never intended to accept financial payment for the debt you owe."

"Then what do you want?" I ask.

Mace sits back. "Kalos likes having people who owe him at his beck and call." He starts massaging the bridge of his nose. "I'd say it's the last hoarding instinct he indulges in."

Kalos makes a hissing sound. "Watch yourself, Reynolds. You're lucky I'm in a good mood since I've just gotten a two-for-one deal."

"And you like my boldness," Mace says.

Kalos scowls. "That trait is starting to wear thin."

Mace salutes him with the whiskey. "Come now, boredom is worse than annoyance."

The dragon smiles, fangs gleaming at that. "That it is."

"Hey, we were talking about what I owe," I say.

Kalos sits back. "Mace is correct that I collect people in the case of having a particular task for them to do. One that no one refuses."

The suck in a breath. I can imagine that anyone would jump at the opportunity to have the debt forgiven, to have this mark removed. My body is still tender with the pain it had inflicted when the dragon invoked it.

But what would the cost be?

"The time for your particular task has come. I know of the traffickers you hunt."

Now Mace sits forward in interest and neither of us interrupts.

"Well, I know the group that is being funded by their activities anyway." Kalos flicks a hand.

"How?" Mace asks.

"They've been outbidding me in auctions." The dragon bares his teeth. "No one outbids me. I looked into them and how they've been able to get the artifacts I've been after even before some of the events go live."

I frown. "Why not just go after them yourself? Your organization is a force to be reckoned with."

The owner of my debt tilts his head at me in a reptilian way.

"The world is large, Sophia. I have no wish to rule over all of it. That way lies dissatisfaction. There are factions that exist, it's all sorts of political nonsense, but I can't take direct action without risking angering the other factions."

Mace's brow creases with suspicion. "Let me get this straight, to repay Sophia's debt you want us to take down a group we were already planning to? This isn't how one of your deals usually goes."

Kalos smiles. "I also want all of the artifacts they've outbid me on."

"Still hoarding—" Mace starts, and I cut him off with a shush.

"You want me to steal?" I ask.

"Would you rather I ask you to kill? Are you going to reject this opportunity to be free of that pesky mark?"

I put up my hands. "I'm not objecting."

Kalos nods. "Good. I'll send both of you a list of the objects. Congratulations on your bonding, Reynolds."

"Thank you," Mace says, rather than point out that our bond is a business arrangement, another debt I paid.

"I also have files of information for the two of you so that you can be successful in this endeavor," Kalos says.

My eyes widen and I nod, not wanting to jinx our sudden windfall of luck.

"Good. Ben will get you everything." Kalos stands, pulling down his vest. "You're free to go."

I'm not free yet, but I soon will be.

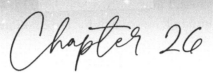

Chapter 26

SOPHIA

"I can't believe he played me like that," I say, scowling as I set the bag of clothing retrieved from my apartment on the couch. Not fleeing Kalos's wrath has its upsides. Not screaming in debilitating pain is one of the perks.

Since we don't have to worry about being tracked by the mark anymore, Mace opted to stay at one of his other properties. The cabin has a warmer feel to it than the penthouse. The furniture more focused on comfort than aesthetic, no one would notice the mismatched furniture when the windows are what really sell the space.

Floor-to-ceiling glass on one side of the cabin with a door to the deck. The view is a harpy's dream, rocky cliffs and pine forests. As high up as the cabin is on the mountain, I could jump and soar with no effort.

"It's a pretty minor play for that dragon. He's gotten quite the reputation for the practice. He must have salivated at the opportunity to trap you before you heard any of the rumors." Mace comes up behind me and takes the food we picked up to the kitchen.

I blow out a breath, rubbing my hands over my face. Every turn I take, I get smacked in the face with how unprepared for the world I am.

I sense him before his arms wrap around me, my back against his chest. I don't uncover my face. The world has stopped spinning long enough for my emotions to catch up.

I'm a walking disaster. Trouble wherever I go.

"Everyone has to stumble a little when they start out, fierce harpy," Mace says into my hair.

The words start to pour out of me. "Maybe Fairuza is right. Maybe I'm just as naive as she's accused me of and it's better for harpies to stay secluded—"

Mace shakes me a little. "None of that. Even if you were naive at the start, you've already learned so much. Think of all the people you've helped. People in groups that also keep to themselves, that trusted you because you are a harpy. An independent, impartial force that they could flock to."

I drag my hands down my face. "You heard about those?"

Mace's voice is warm. "Oh, fierce harpy, you are my favorite research subject. All full of contradictions of loyalty and violence. Bravery and heart."

I turn in Mace's arms and press against his front. The look on his face is one that destroys every poisonous thought in my head.

"You really believe that?"

Mace's smile is gentle. "Even you owing Kalos turned out to be a good thing. We have so much more information to go on."

I hiccup a laugh because it's true. All the stacks of files we received about the group we're targeting… because I was tricked by a dragon.

The smile fades from my face. Mace's arms around me and the softness of his face lull me into a daze.

Is this how Zeph feels about her mates? Do they also hold her head above water when the world feels like it's too much? Does she believe that they'll always be there for her?

I swallow, throat thick.

"If you keep doing these pep talks, I'll be tempted to keep you," I say.

Mace looks up at the wooden rafters, as if being offered something too precious and having to take a moment before accepting it, or like he's praying. Once whatever prayer is finished, Mace sweeps his mouth next to my ear as if imparting a secret.

"I'd give you so many pep talks that your ears would bleed if it meant being kept by you. I might not even be able to help myself."

The intense look on his face draws me in.

I kiss my demon before the screaming of my instincts register. A warning that this connection between us isn't momentary anymore. That this isn't about having fun, but consummating care.

My breath shudders in my chest as the kiss goes on and on. Mace groans and presses our bodies together. The sound flips a switch in my mind, and I want to force him to make it again. I rock my hips against his thickening cock.

Mace's hands drop to my ass, squeezing it as he lifts me to grind harder against him. I nip his lip and his hiss

of pleasure has the need to break him growing into an
inferno.

I claw Mace's shirt off of his shoulders and cold air hits
my own skin as he returns the favor, pulling off my bra to
tug at my nipples. He spins us and my ass hits the back
of the couch. Mace's head ducks, engulfing the flesh he's
teased into peaks.

I cry out at the first hard draw of his mouth. My legs
tighten around his hips, but Mace moves his body away,
releasing my breast to start unbuttoning my pants.

"Need to taste you again." His voice is a dark command
that has a whimper bubbling out of my chest, but his
words spur a different desire in me. A desire to cross a
previous boundary.

I dig my nails into his skin. "No."

Mace freezes. "No?"

My face heats and I force the words out into the now
awkward air. "I-I want to do something else."

Mace straightens and lets my legs fall from his hips.
"What does my harpy wish to do?"

"Give me a minute." I frown, trying to figure out how to
accomplish this while I kick off my pants.

Mace clears his throat and I'm momentarily distracted
by the movement. My hand runs over his bare chest,
running my fingers over the dark inked designs in his skin.

"Take your time," Mace breathes, and I do.

Fascination brings my mouth down on Mace's skin, I
lick and bite every tendon and dip that catches my eye.
Starting with my demon's neck, I explore him, moving us
in the space until Mace is pressed against the edge of the
kitchen counter.

I explore lower, letting my hands drag against the firm
skin of Mace's stomach, enjoying the friction of the hair

trailing to his pants. By the time my hand palms his stiff erection, my demon's breath is coming fast. He doesn't move to rush me, doesn't do a thing to dissuade the plans that are a mystery to him.

Until I sink to my knees.

My demon jolts in awareness, hands coming down to grab me, but I knock them away with a glare. Mace's brow creases in concern.

"Sophia—" Mace whispers, the awe enough for a syrupy heat to pour through my chest straight to my pussy. "Are you sure?" Mace asks, and I analyze his face. He knows. He knows the significance of this, a harpy doing this.

He knows how much I care for him.

"I trust you." The words crack with honesty.

The tops of Mace's cheeks redden further, and he closes his eyes, praying again. Who knew this demon was so devout? My mouth twitches to smile. Mace opens his eyes.

"I'm ready for you to destroy me," Mace says.

My laugh escapes me. "I might be terrible. I've never—"

"It won't be terrible." His tone is solemn. "I have no doubt, no matter your skill, that it will be the best thing that I've ever experienced." *Because it's you.*

The sentiment is unspoken and drives up the tension that I try to shake away. "Even if I bite you?"

Mace's smile is lopsided. "I like a small amount of pain, remember?"

My hands slide up Mace's cloth-covered thighs.

"I'll try not to maim you," I say.

Mace runs his fingers through my hair. "I'm yours to maim."

The sentiment resounds in the space between us, and I move to keep it from hitting my heart. The buckle of

Mace's belt is loud to my nerve-racked senses and has my core tightening unmercifully.

My fingers stroke against Mace's cock as I pull it out, the skin hot and soft. I grip him and the absolute hardness has me squeezing my thighs together. I'm not the only one affected, Mace's hips cant and he blows out a harsh breath.

"Fuck, goddess, you're going to be the death of me."

I hum but don't respond, the length in front of me has captured my attention. I've had many men before, sweaty, convenient hookups to blow off steam, but I've never been eye level with this part of their anatomy.

I admire Mace's sizable thickness in my hand. His member is almost pretty with ruddiness coloring the skin, I stroke a finger over veins I've never wanted to run my tongue along, until now. The small touch has Mace's body tightening. The head of his cock has the shine of precum, and I lean in and lick it experimentally.

It tastes the way that sex smells, salty with a bitter tang, but not terrible. Some instinct has me licking again and Mace groans. Some primal part of me wants this. Inside me or in my mouth, it doesn't seem to matter. Whatever secret desire in my mind that makes me want this man's seed, want to claim every part of him, has me moaning when I engulf the head of his cock.

Mace grips the counter behind him, and it creaks, his knuckles white.

"That's it. Fuck, Sophia, you like the taste of me? You can have it."

My body flushes with heat at Mace's words.

I take more of Mace into my mouth, running my tongue along him to suck away any new taste he gives me. I tighten my lips around him, dragging him out before sucking him back in again, trying to suck his cock in farther.

I repeat the motion, stretching my limits with every attempt to take more of him. Each one is met with a breathless sound from my demon. Sounds that have me trembling with a different want, the want to be taken. I'm so wet it smears against my bare thighs and adds more tantalizing sensations.

I whimper and Mace's hands tangle in my hair, clutching it before remembering not to and pulling away again. Something stutters in my chest at the move, I grab his hands and bring them back, moaning at the tug he gives to my roots.

The sensation makes me reckless, and I take too much of his cock, gagging and coughing. Mace doesn't release my hair but allows my breathing to return to my panting before tilting my mouth to take him again. When I let him press past my lips, he groans.

"You've got this. Take me to the back of your throat, relax."

Dark feelings of desire flow to me through our bond, but they're tempered with caution. I only need to let him know if I want to stop, and this all comes to an end.

Until then, I let Mace push me, allow him to take the gift I'm offering to the fullest extent.

The next rock of Mace's hips, I do as he says and relax, it makes it easier and the demon moans at the extra inch of depth. The sound has a needy moan escaping me.

I didn't think I'd like doing this action as much as I do. Every motion, every sound, spurs me on. The ache of my body to be filled grows in tandem with the strain of the demon plundering my mouth.

Mace clutches my hair as if to pull me away. "I'm going to come, goddess."

The primal part of me that wants all of this man's seed snarls and Mace's head falls back with a helpless sound.

"You want it? Want to swallow every drop? Want me to offer you—" Mace breaks off on a curse when my talons dig into the skin on his thighs and my demon comes for me. The long groan that reverberates through his body drives mine so high with arousal that it would only require a stroke of a finger for my climax, but I don't.

I absorb the sight of my demon breaking and swallow the rush of seed he gives me. Licking the excess away with soft strokes of my tongue until Mace pulls away on a sensitive hiss. He picks me up and sets me on the kitchen counter, kissing the taste of himself from me until stopping to gasp in air.

"Fuck, Sophia! You slay me."

I squeeze my legs around Mace's bare hips, rocking my bare flesh against his softened, slick cock. "I need—"

Mace laughs, breathless. "Oh, sweet harpy, I'm flattered but I can't fuck you at this moment."

I whimper, helplessly burning against his body.

Mace kisses the sound from my lips. "I'll take care of you."

"Please—" I gasp as he kisses down my bare chest, licking a nipple before continuing his path lower.

I cry out at the first slide of his tongue over my folds. Mace groans decadently.

"So wet, I could almost think you liked sucking out my soul through my cock."

"Less talking, more licking," I say, though I don't mean it. Mace's deliciously dirty words have a way of stoking the fire of my arousal higher.

Mace's laugh is dark and slow. He runs his tongue through my folds again before flattening it against me. My thighs come together, pressing uselessly against where his arms spread them.

"Need you." My voice is high and needy. "Need it inside me."

"Need what? My cock?" Mace asks playfully. "Or my cum? Is that what your body is demanding? To feel my seed fill you to the brim until it spills onto this counter."

I cry out, my body on the edge but not allowing me to take flight without stealing something first.

Mace notices it. His smile is greedily cruel. "I wonder how long your body would stay like this? Gasping and begging to be filled."

"Mace, fuck me."

My demon pushes his fingers into me with an easy slide, my wetness practically spilling over even without his. My whimper is almost pained. The pleasure sharp and unforgiving as he plays with me.

"You've absolutely destroyed me," Mace says. "The feel of you, the taste of you, nothing compares. No one else will compare, and I don't regret a single second."

Mace sucks on my clit and I scream, my body still refusing to climax. I grip his hair and pull.

"*Please, please, please.*" The words escape my lips, and I don't care. Pride won't save me from the fire burning me alive, only Mace can.

Finally, Mace snarls and yanks me against his body, lifting me. I cling to him, my legs clutching him, crossing at the ankles behind his back.

There is no slowly working his thick cock into me this time. The first thrust is complete, echoing through my body as loud as my shout, and it still isn't enough.

I claw Mace as my body fucks itself on his cock, needy. Mace lifts me and my back hits the fridge. When he starts thrusting inside me, it's everything.

He grips my hips and I take every sharp smack of his hips against mine.

I'm mindless, my only thought, the need to drip with this demon's essence. I beg over and over again, each one pushing Mace closer and closer to the edge until he's practically feral.

Mace roars and spills inside me.

As if accepting an offering, my body releases me from the captivity of endless pleasure. I *soar*. Heat and euphoria rob my mind of speech, of sight, and of time until the stroking of my cheeks and the soft murmur of words brings me back.

My vision is blurry. And Mace wipes more trickling tears from my cheeks.

"Oh, my beautiful harpy, clever, strong, and brave."

My eyes focus on my bond-mate. Mace must realize I'm comprehending his words now because he becomes serious.

"Don't let anyone tell you how to live your life. Not your aunt, not me. You are a phenomenon, a goddess beyond reproach."

Later I'll blame the fresh tears as an aftereffect of the mind-blowing orgasm, but I'll still know the truth.

Mace's words become soft. "You belong in this world."

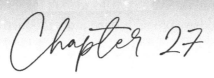

Chapter 27

MACE

Sophia says something, but it's unintelligible with the pen she has in her mouth. Her brow is knit as she flips through papers.

I pause in my own task of scanning documents to lean over the stacks of loose papers on the coffee table and remove the pen from her lush, bitable lips.

"What was that?" I ask.

Her scowl makes me want to laugh.

"There isn't any mention of a teleporting demon named Nero."

The urge to laugh flees.

"These are all the official records of the group. There hasn't been any mention of the trafficking side of the group's business. We only have Kalos's word that they are connected," I say.

Sophia frowns and I head off her question.

"Even Kalos wouldn't deter us from stopping a trafficking ring in favor of getting artifacts. They are connected," I say. "We just need to find out where they'd be holding captives."

Something that may take a while with this information in paper form. Paper is less traceable and Kalos doesn't want to be connected with this effort. I hope Gage can do something with the scanned versions to speed the process up. His team has more eyeballs to look for things at least.

It would have probably been more productive to search through the information at Gage's office, but I'm reluctant to share this time with Sophia. I left her long enough to run the documents through the copier there before returning to a napping Sophia on the couch. I'd have let her sleep off the stress of the morning, but my harpy woke ready to take on the world.

Now she has a pad of paper full of notes and a highlighter that spends more time being held in her mouth than applied to paper. When the pen isn't in her mouth, of course.

Sophia, in a state of focus, is one part adorable and the other arousing. I tamp down that feeling with force. We have business that needs doing and our activities earlier were wholly satisfying.

Amazing. Transcendent. Precious.

Harpies don't perform oral sex as a cultural norm. Their sexual encounters aren't to bring men pleasure. That may be untrue on an individual basis or maybe just something that is kept secret. That Sophia ventured into that taboo for *me* means more than she's vocalized.

I don't need the words.

Does Sophia need the words from me? I'd willingly tell her. I've already told her how much I like her, admire her. That I'm on my way to being truly besotted shouldn't be a surprise, but maybe it would be.

Maybe it would make her hesitate. Influence her to find a way out of this bond since our sexual relationship has never truly been just about having fun.

"You said that you and Asa banished him. Why? How does that even work?" Sophia asks.

I shake myself from my thoughts and focus on the conversation at hand.

"A banishment for demons simply involves unbinding them from their anchor and forcibly casting them from this plane."

Sophia's brows lift. "That seems like it would be intense."

I shrug. "The breaking of the bond is the hardest part. It can be done by demons with enough power and preparation. We ended up paying off the woman he was anchored to at the time and with her consent, the process was easier. The magic is similar to how people summon demons, with circles and spells."

There's a pause and Sophia tilts her head.

"You're not going to tell me why you banished your brother?"

"Half brother," I correct. I open my mouth to say more but hesitate.

"Huh," Sophia says. She puts down the paper and rubs her chest. "Do you know that I don't pick up your emotions very often at all? But, right now, I can feel... shame."

The weight in my stomach is sickening. It doesn't surprise me that Sophia can pick it up.

"You don't have to tell me," she whispers when I don't respond.

"Do you want to know, Sophia? It's not... a nice story."

The sensation of her curiosity tickles me through the bond and I almost smile. Of course the curious Sophia wants to know.

"I-I don't want to make you tell me anything you don't want to," Sophia says, exposing her soft parts.

Oh, fierce harpy, what wouldn't I give you?

"I told you I carry the guilt of not being able to protect my sister, Elise," I start. Her name still strikes a pang of grief through me. "Nero was responsible for her death."

Sophia gasps. "He killed her?"

"Not directly." It's harder to talk about this than I imagined. I cast my gaze down at my hands, remembering the sight of them smeared with blood, her blood.

There's a rustle and all I see is Sophia as she climbs into my lap. She runs a finger over my face, offering me physical comfort.

"Nero… raised us," I start.

"What happened to your parents?"

"They died. Nero didn't get specific; we were too young to remember anything about them. He said that our father went back to the demon plane and must have died. He and my mother were bonded. She was a witch with hardly any magic in her blood, so the bond killed her."

Sophia sucks in a breath but I smile sadly at her and shrug. It's hard to grieve people you don't remember, and I have few details about their bonding. Nero didn't share much about them other than he hated them for saddling him with us.

"Nero had sworn an oath to our father to keep us safe until our talents came in."

Sophia tilts her head, so I explain.

"Young demons don't need to have anchors until the magical talents develop. Usually when they become sixteen or seventeen years of age. The talents make it so they have to draw from the plane they reside in to continue existing."

"Nero made it very clear that as soon as that happened, we'd be on our own and that he was going back to the demon plane."

"Charming," Sophia drawls.

I snort and my tone took on a wistful note.

"I couldn't wait. Every day of my sixteenth year, I woke with the hope that Elise and I would get to leave him behind. It was the epitome of naivete. Just because a demon's talent develops doesn't mean they can control it, or do the magic required for forming a bond without instruction."

"And he was going to just leave the two of you?"

"I don't know. It didn't really come to that. Elise developed her talent first. Gifts follow bloodlines, and as expected Elise had the ability to teleport."

I swallow, remembering her dark eyes filled with worry.

"I was crushed." The words are barely a whisper, and I clear my throat. "It seems like such a small thing in retrospect, but Nero would constantly berate me for being a weak half-breed and when his friends came over, other demon borns, it would get worse."

"Friends like Alton?" Sophia asks, her eyes narrowing as if with one word my fierce goddess would smite the bullies of my past.

I love her.

The revelation has me looking away, struggling to stuff the words that I'll probably never say down. Being gentle with the soft feeling in my chest as to not break it.

It's a bad time for my feelings to crystallize, for me to know through my heart and soul that I love this harpy, right before I share with her my greatest shame.

I clear my throat, hard. "Uh, no, Alton wasn't that bad. He was actually the only friend of Nero's to try and get him to slow down on nefarious activities."

Sophia's brows crease and my heavy heart continues.

I sigh. "When Elise gained her talent before I did, I felt... betrayed and I... I left."

"Left?"

"I ran away. I was so upset. It felt like I had lost my only ally. I thought anywhere would be better than staying, so I left. I have never regretted anything more in my life."

Sophia's eyes are full of concern.

My throat swells but I push on to finish the story.

"I told you before that Nero had a history of running up debts and doing jobs for quick money. I think his vice must have to do with greed, or maybe gambling, because sometimes it didn't seem like he even had control of himself. It was a week before I went back. It finally got through my thick skull that it wasn't Elise's fault that she was a better demon than I was, and I didn't want to miss our birthday."

I thread my fingers through Sophia's hair, unable to look her in the eye.

"She was gone."

"Gone?"

"One of Nero's debts came collecting and he traded her."

Sophia gasps.

Anger at Nero overcomes my shame and grief and makes it easier to continue.

"He bonded her to a powerful man with a bad reputation to forgive his debt. I was furious. I wanted to go after her, but I couldn't do it alone, I couldn't unravel the bond. He said that we would get her, that it was all a part of the plan, but—" I shake my head.

"I could tell that this wasn't like any other con he'd done before. This was desperate. He'd traded our seventeen-year-old sister with no guarantees on how she'd be treated."

Sophia puts a hand over her mouth.

"The plan was to go in and steal her away, but it was already too late. She'd—" I break off, the grief of finding her coming back full force and I turn my head. Tears heat my eyes and I clench my jaw to keep them from falling.

Soft hands turn my face back and Sophia hugs me to her. The gesture is so heartfelt and comforting that soon the sobs I trap in my throat ease.

"Elise had taken her own life, killing her anchor in the process. The shock must have shaken something loose because that was the first time I entered the in-between." I'd accepted the darkness and stumbled somewhere completely foreign, covered in my sister's blood.

"I wandered for a while, teleporting to places I've never been, stealing what I needed to survive. Not knowing what I wanted to do, but I was unbonded. I started to fade. That's when Asa found me. He saved my life."

I'd crashed into the demon a few years older than myself, dressed for the theater, stinking of money and he'd haughtily asked who I was and what I thought I was doing appearing out of thin air.

"He hasn't been able to shake me since." I smile.

"What happened with Nero?" Sophia asks.

"When I entered the angry part of my grief, I confided everything to Asa. He'd been dealing with some issues with mutually acquainted demon borns himself. We devised a plan, a strategy to banish the worst characters at once, and enacted it."

I roll my eyes at my stupidity. "I told Asa that I wanted to be the one to get vengeance on Nero."

Sophia's eyes widen. "What happened?"

My chuckle is dark. "Nero nearly killed me. Asa swooped in with all his dark strength and saved me yet again. It's good to have strong friends. In the end, only a few demon born in that area were spared from the banishment."

I sigh out a breath. "Now you know my greatest shame. If I had been there, I'd never have let Nero trade Elise. If only I hadn't been—" *Weak.*

"A hormonal teenager bullied his whole life over something he couldn't control?" Sophia asks gently.

I swallow down the guilt.

"Yes that. If I hadn't let my hurt feeling fuel me, I'd have been there…"

"And that's why you don't connect with people you have to protect." Sophia's voice is solemn.

"Yes."

"It wasn't your fault, Mace—"

I shake my head, the motion sharp and Sophia stops. There are many things I'm willing to hear from her, but that isn't one of them.

Instead, Sophia shows her support in other ways, and it doesn't matter that I don't deserve it. When it comes time for us to rest for the night, my harpy allows me to steal her away to my bed, freely cuddling with me. Comforting me with physical affection and snarky words.

I pretend that someday I'll be able to tell her I love her without her running from me.

Chapter 28

SOPHIA

"Tea or coffee?" Mace asks.

I massage the bridge of my nose and shake my head.

We've combed through the files for days. Taking breaks to pop out for meals, connect with Gage's team, and sleep. And sometimes those breaks include playful teasing that always ends with me begging. Then we return to the files hoping to find the one detail that'll connect the puzzle.

I have pages upon pages of notes that almost seem cohesive if I squint my eyes. We're close to something. I feel it.

The sensation of being at the very edge of discovery motivates me forward and makes me all kinds of cranky.

"It's here," I say for what feels like the tenth time.

Mace only nods in understanding. He slides his hand under mine and threads our fingers together.

"Maybe another break? We've been at this for hours. You're no good to anyone if you burn out."

I bite my lip instead of lashing out in frustration. Mace smiles and kisses the back of my hand. The affectionate touches between us have sprinkled the days since coming to the cabin. Each time makes this relationship between us feel more real.

What we have is real. Inconvenient and messy and so real it makes my breath catch.

I don't know exactly when it happened but imagining a young Mace racked with the guilty sobs the man version had suppressed in my arms had cracked my defenses wide open.

Mace is in my skin, my blood beats in time to this demon's, my bones vibrate with him. I'm all in now.

The soft look on Mace's face twists into a wicked one. "A break it is."

I frown before shrieking as he throws me over his shoulder. A couple of papers scatter on the coffee table, but don't ruin the organization we have going.

"Mace!"

He smacks my ass as he carries me to the master bedroom we'd been sharing. "I know just the thing to refresh your mind."

I laugh and when he tosses me on the flannel-covered bed, I bounce. Mace shucks his clothes and I race him in getting naked. The tug of my pants rough against my skin in my haste. I'm bare when he climbs on the bed toward me.

I prop myself up on my elbows and look at the demon between my splayed legs. The way his dark hair falls over his forehead has something I don't recognize clutching in my chest. Tenderness?

Mace's eyes flash with a tease and he drops his face near my core.

"I have an idea." He breathes the words against the sensitive skin of my lower stomach. "Will you let me try something?"

His question is challenging and playful at the same time. I huff and he smiles.

I'll rise to any challenge this demon throws down.

"Do it," I say.

Mace's smile grows and the flash of his teeth has my stomach tightening in anticipation. He drags his thumb over the skin he'd dampened with his breath.

I gasp when I feel it. The pull on our bond. It's like the draw of a mouth on a nipple with the way it makes heat surge in me. All with one stroke of this demon.

It's a delicious amplification of sensation.

It stops as soon as it starts.

"What was that?" I gasp.

Mace is watching me carefully. The anticipation in his eyes showing just how much this play is affecting him.

"I can manipulate our threads, the ones that bind our souls together. Do you want me to do it again?" he asks.

It's probably reckless of me. I'm already too sensitive to the magic of our bond. But hunger blossoms in the absence of the draw.

"Yes—" My answer breaks on a sound from the back of my throat as Mace puts a hand on my skin and plays.

I quickly lose myself.

Each touch is a unique sensation. It's only Mace running his hand over my skin, but each strum of our souls reverberates in different ways, some tickle, others burn. Some threads have my back arching while my legs try to squeeze together from another.

Each caress brings me to the edge and has an ache of emptiness slicking my thighs.

I don't know how long I last before I start begging.

Mace squeezes a breast and I cry out. "Shh, I'm enjoying this," he says. His hard cock strokes through my wet pussy, the friction driving me wild.

My skin pebbles under Mace's chuckle. "Each time I pull on your end you tug back on mine and gods does it feel good."

He pinches a nipple at the same time as drawing on a thread and I groan, trying to twist away, but not wanting it to stop. Sweat has my hair sticking to my face even as my skin tingles with sensitivity.

"Please, Mace! I need you." I pull on his hair, whimpering.

Mace hums at the hair pulling, as if considering.

I snap.

I push Mace away and slide my fingers to where I'm empty. I'm so wet and needy, my first two fingers slide in easily and bring no satisfaction even as I grind the heel of my palm against my clit.

Mace leans back, watching me fuck myself with glittering hot eyes. "That's gorgeous, but my poor harpy needs more than that. Don't you?"

I'm an overwrought mess. "Yes."

"I've pushed you too far."

"Mace, please!"

Mace grabs my hand, pulling my fingers from my body. He sucks them and the stroke of his hot tongue almost has me wrestling him down again, but it's more fun when I don't overpower Mace.

He always manages to surprise me.

Mace finishes sucking my juices from my fingers and kisses my palm before a diabolical look crosses his face. He flips me over on the bed and pulls my hips up. His body leans over mine, the heat of his front against my back.

"My little cum slut wants me to fill her up, who am I to say no?" he says.

I groan into the sheets at the words, my talons digging into the fabric. Mace drags his cock against my ass and the wet smear of his precum has me greedily pushing back against him. Mace grabs my hair and pulls.

"I've got you, goddess," he says, and I believe him.

I bite my lip when the head of his cock nudges against my entrance and muffle my groan with the sheets as he sinks into me. I can't move much in this position, and it thrills some questionable part of me.

Mace grunts when his hips hit my ass and his next thrust smacks against me. I gasp each time our bodies come together. The primal nature of my demon rutting me has my climax coming for me with or without his release.

Mace curses before sinking as deep as he can go and clutching my hips. His cock throbs and when the heat of him floods me, I break on a scream.

My orgasm rips through me, a toe-curling rush and pulsing ecstasy. It's not just flying, it's the exact moment of swooping from a dive instead of crashing to earth. My pussy is still fluttering around Mace's thickness when I come back to myself.

Mace pulls himself from me and we both moan at the spill of us.

"Gods, Sophia, I think I could find the meaning of life in your cunt," Mace says, running his fingers through our combination and pushing it back inside me. I dig into the sheets at the action and gasp at the aftershocks.

"I didn't think I was into the breeding kink thing, but it's hard to deny the thrill of filling you."

I scrunch my nose, lifting my sweat-damp face from the bed. "Don't call it that."

Mace snorts. "Whatever you want to call it, seed stealer."

I flop on my side, grabbing a pillow and swinging it at the demon behind me. Mace cackles when it connects. I lose most of my aggression with it and tuck the pillow under my head.

"Don't make me hurt you. My body feels like cooked noodles."

He kisses my shoulder. "Do you want me to clean you up?"

I nod and the bed creaks as Mace leaves. Is it normal for the guy to clean his partner up? I've never been in a relationship. If I wasn't so relaxed right now, I might have frozen up at the concept that Mace and I are in a relationship.

But we are. There's no denying that we are connected. I huff, seed stealer.

I doze as Mace wipes away the evidence of our break. My thoughts scattering away to the case we're on.

The organization has so many small businesses scattered throughout the world on the edges of other entities. It's a wonder how they keep track of them all.

I shoot up in bed and Mace makes a sound of disappointment from the spot he took next to me.

"I got it!"

Chapter 29

SOPHIA

Excitement hums in my veins. I pat the emergency charms in my pocket in preparation of entering the building in front of us. The charms vibrate stingingly against my own magics but are muffled against the jacket, ready to be used just in case.

The jacket itself is hidden by the glamour I wear.

I'd been surprised that Gage's team had acquired such a finely woven spell that it's only giving me a headache to wear, rather than making me nauseous.

A drunken man comes swinging out of the door of the gambling den and Mace grips my waist. I get a vibration of worry from the bond. He doesn't like this plan, but everyone is already in place. Gage's team knows their roles and if all goes well, we'll get all of the locations the group is using to hold their captives.

"This is a bad plan," Mace says.

"It's a fantastic plan."

We enter the establishment, receiving a nod from the doorman. His eyes linger on the chest of my glamoured form. I appear as if I'm very endowed and dressed to show it.

It's an old trick, use boobs to distract, but old tricks are old because they work. The doorman doesn't even look at Mace's face, which displays an attractive man showcasing the slightly pointed ears of a fae.

I prefer Mace's imperfections to the pretty face he wears.

I think I may love this asshole.

The idea doesn't bother me as much as it probably should. As it would have a week ago.

Don't let anyone tell you how to live your life.

We walk into the main room that has tables spread throughout, the sound of cards shuffling and the odd cry of dismay permeates the space. Each table full of paranormals trying their luck even though this establishment has the reputation of the house always winning.

Yesterday I'd started sorting the businesses in this organization by digital security measures and found this establishment. During the day, this is a legitimate pub, but once the pub closes this operation starts.

There's nothing expressly forbidden about gambling, but the Council would want to be informed of any location where large amounts of magic beings gather. They'd want some sort of certifications of the spells put in place to protect patrons.

Expensive spells that this establishment doesn't have.

This is the largest business the group runs legitimately. I sent the information to Gage on the off chance that this building acts as more of a hub for the group. A truer den rather than just a gambling den.

"The digital security measures could be anything. There's no guarantee that they are storing information on the trafficking here." Mace frowns.

"No, but it's more of a lead to go on than checking your half brother's haunts. Stop being so negative. Ga—" I cut myself off before mentioning Gage. The disguises would be useless if I blurt out anyone's name. "Your employer thinks this is promising, and I agree."

Mace's pretty mouth twists as we start to head to the bar.

"It doesn't mean that you should be here," he says.

I would be hurt by the words if I didn't pick up on the thrums of his worry. I blow out a breath. "You have a task to do."

Mace is the distraction. It's best to have the person who openly causes problems to have the nifty skill of disappearing.

We'll try and get out of eyesight before teleporting since the skill is a rare one.

"And you and I are in this together. Like glue. I couldn't let you leave me behind and have all the fun," I say.

Mace scoffs but his lips twitch in a smile.

The smile fades when we reach the bar and Mace orders for us.

The bartender is an unrecognizable type of fae with green skin and red eyes that leer at my false cleavage as he gets us drinks. The ice clinks in the glass when the fae puts it down in a way that splashes on "my" exposed chest. I hiss as if hit with the liquid, the illusion so seamless that when I look down, I see the moisture beaded on my skin.

The fae smiles widely, exposing more teeth than I'd normally see in a mouth.

Charming.

Mace glares at the man, who visibly shrinks, before giving me a napkin from down the bar. We take our drinks and begin to stroll the floor, looking for an opening in the tables. There is a scattering of fae like the bartender throughout the space but the majority of people have or are wearing a human appearance.

"What game are you feeling tonight?" I ask.

"One near an escape," Mace mutters. As if the fates hear, a spot opens up closest to the back hallway.

The dealer of the table could double as a bouncer, with his size and human appearance I'd guess a shifter of some sort. He nods at Mace when he takes a seat at a stool and deals my demon in. There is no leer checking out my disguise and my heart rate picks up.

At least one employee in this whole establishment isn't taken with the false cleavage.

The card game begins. It's boring. Mace loses just as much as he wins.

I try to keep entertained by throwing myself into my act wholeheartedly, much to the disgust of the surrounding players.

I run my hands over Mace's shoulders in a sensual show of support. Fawning over any moves that are clever and even some that aren't until a male witch at the end of the table rolls his eyes. Mace eats the attention up, acting as if having a sycophant is his due.

It plays well into his disguise. It's rumored that the most human looking fae are of the noble class in that plane and are intolerably arrogant.

We're fully enmeshed in the dynamics of the table when Mace *finally* gives me a look. The look is accompanied with a pluck of our bond like the snap of a rubber band. It's go-time.

"Dearest," I purr, sliding my drink to him. "Hold my drink? I need to use the little girls' room."

Mace holds in a laugh. "Of course, snookums."

I keep my smile fake but glee sparks in my chest. I've missed taking jobs like this. The adrenaline sharpens my senses and I take in every detail as I move, taking note of every camera.

I walk down the winding back hall, passing the emergency exit, and enter the ladies' room. Going through the motions of looking at my glamoured face in the mirror. The sight of the buxom woman in the sparkly dress reflected is disorienting, but has anticipation thrumming in my veins. I've never been able to wear a glamour before.

My eyes are unaffected and they're bright with excitement.

Mace has already started cheating at cards, a skill he picked up in the centuries he's been alive.

This place may not have spells that ensure patron safety, but it definitely has spells that will alert the management of cheating if the dealer doesn't catch on first. It won't take long now.

I walk back through the hallway, sliding the charm Gage had given me into the crack of the emergency exit near the lock. A pop travels through the air, the wards of the building disturbed in that one location. I keep walking, not looking back.

The face Mace wears smiles at me when I return to his side at the table. The stack of chips already much larger than when I left. The dealer's face is sour, eyes narrowing.

"Look how lucky you've been!" I squeal.

A fur-covered creature on the stool next to us huffs in dissatisfaction.

"Now, snookums, don't be rude." Mace's dark eyes glitter. He's starting to enjoy himself.

My heart pounds as Mace plays another game. This time the creature snarls, but Mace smiles. "Better luck next time."

The dealer nods to the ceiling in an almost subtle way if one didn't know about the camera in the back corner of the room.

Perfect.

Mace flashes me a smile.

The air is flavored with thrill and danger. It's perfection and the worst possible time for confessions, but I can't help leaning forward.

"We make a good team," I whisper.

Mace smiles, his eyes on the cards. "That's what I've been trying to tell you."

For how large the feelings are in my chest, his reaction isn't enough.

"You keep saying that you expect me to be able to find a way out of our... connection."

Mace keeps his smile but looks a little sad. "Of course."

"Maybe we can agree to a permanent arrangement," I say, before leaning back. Now I have all of Mace's attention.

"What are you saying, So—" Mace cuts himself off before saying my name.

"I'm saying, maybe I like being with you."

There's a light of hope in my demon's eyes and I wish I could see his real face now.

There's a crash and we both snap to attention.

Reckless.

The hair-covered creature's stool is on the ground and he points a claw at Mace.

"Cheat!" The bellow silences the room.

Mace's hand grips mine at his elbow. My demon forces a laugh. "Now, that's something a poor loser would say."

The regular noise of the room slowly starts up again. The other gamers uninterested in the squabble. The creature growls, but after a moment sits back down, choosing not to challenge the fae Mace appears to be.

A couple of large men approach the table.

"Sir, if I could have you come with us." The management has arrived.

A spike of caution hits my chest, informing me that Mace has decided it's time to go. I hope Gage's person has had enough time.

Mace throws down his cards in feigned frustration. "I say! Is this how it is when someone here actually wins? Is that now against the rules?"

He's loud. Some people at the nearby tables still before whispering angrily to each other.

"Yeah!" some random person shouts from a couple tables away. The angry whispering grows to conversation level. Words about how rare winning is here start to be recognizable and the face of the large man in the nicer suit twists in anger.

Both men's attention swings to a screech of a woman throwing her cards down. "I'm done with this."

Mace and I take off in a run, heading for the emergency exit. Luckily, Gage's person won't be needing this door to exit.

"Stop!"

The clatter of pursuit behind us pushes my adrenaline even higher and a whoop of joy escapes my mouth. Mace flashes me a smile, hitting the emergency door to push us through.

"Don't start the building on fire!" The call behind us is confusing.

I'm halfway through the door when I'm hit with a whomp and a blast of heat. The force pushes me the rest of the way out the door. The searing pain takes a moment to reach me, but once it starts it rages like an uncontrollable fire. I stumble, my body rebelling against the sudden sensations, my scream is hoarse.

Mace shouts something I can't comprehend, and I'm pulled into the icy in-between. The touch of the shadows doesn't stop the cascade of pain.

Mace calls out my name. I try to lift a hand to comfort him, but a more complete darkness than the shadows takes me.

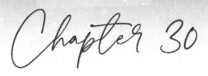

Chapter 30

SOPHIA

Fire. Pain. Icy shadows.

I waver like the reflection in water. Resurfacing for moments to bright pain and cursing before submerging again.

Peace is an illusion, nothing more than the bad reaction to other magics. An illusion I finally dispel with a gasp. The shadows in my vision recede and distant pain is my first companion. It radiates from my shoulder. My face is bruise tender when my hand brushes something stuck to the side of it. A bandage.

The confusion comes next but that quickly dissipates with the scent of my demon. I'm in Mace's bed. The one we'd shared in the days before I'd made the connection for the mission. *The mission.*

A ball of fire and the smack of magic before I lost consciousness. *Ouch.* I've never been hit by a fireball spell before.

The blurry world comes into focus. The light in the room indicates it's afternoon. *How long have I been out?*

I move slowly. Black marks catch my eye and I blink at the different runes painted on the skin of my arms.

It's surprising that the pain isn't as bad now that I'm moving. The kind of firepower I'd taken should have caused much more damage, perhaps it did.

There's a slight headache left over from the magic of whoever healed me and the world tilts when I sit up. The seat next to the bed is empty. Disappointment pricks over my skin that my demon isn't sitting in the chair next to the bed, worriedly waiting for me to wake up.

I dash the sensation away, who knows how long that spell took me out for. I can't expect that Mace would sit at my side the whole time. We still have an end goal to work toward. He's probably going through the rest of the files Kalos gave us.

It takes a few deep breaths before the world stops spinning but I get up anyway. My body demands to wash away the faint taste of ash on my tongue.

I stumble to the bathroom and blink at the bright lights. The skin under my eyes is dark but my face under the bandage is unblemished. I run my fingers through my hair, a little snarled but not burned as the scent of scorch lingering on me would indicate.

Magic. I'm grateful. We have too much to do for me to worry about having to explain singed hair to my family.

The magics on my skin itch, pushing me to the shower. The painted runes have probably done enough work by now. If I leave them on, the headache will just get worse.

I go through the process of showering, scrubbing off the marks until my skin is raw in spots. I wrap a towel around myself, concern starts to brew in my chest. Surely, Mace would have come to check on me.

Experimentally I reach through the bond but don't feel anything on the other side. The bond is still there but all the hints of emotions and presence I usually glean from it are gone.

Suppressed.

A heavy foreboding starts to weigh me down. He's probably just asleep...

I walk through the cabin, not bothering to get dressed yet. Some part of me needing to see Mace, make sure he's okay. Room after room I check, there really aren't many and I almost give up when I find him on the deck, staring at the view.

I succeed in not stumbling out the door.

"Hey, I was starting to think you left me here."

Alone.

Mace's eyes land on me like an impact and I stop. He gives me a closed-mouth smile. "How are you feeling?"

Something is wrong. I don't need to pick up Mace's emotions from the bond. It's in the stiffness of my demon's smile, the look in his eyes that resembles... grief.

I swallow and push onward. "Better now, I got hit by a fireball spell, right?"

Mace nods. "Your jacket saved you."

Note to self, get Alice a thank you present. It's a detail that I store in my mind before the weight of emotions in the air gets to me.

"I was surprised you weren't at my bedside, waiting for me to wake up." I blurt the words out.

Mace looks down at his hands and there's the deepest sort of ache from the bond before the sensation disappears.

The absence of it stabs me. *No.*

"I wanted to give you space," he says.

"Why?" It's not the question I really want to know, so I revise it. I will not cower from whatever this is. What my fears are whispering it is. "Why are you closing off your side of the bond from me?"

Mace's throat moves in a swallow.

"Let's not do this right now, Sophia—"

"Mace." My tone is sharp, and he winces.

He shakes his head before speaking again. "We need to focus on bringing down the traffickers. Later, we can talk about—"

I interrupt. "Mace, talk to me, please."

I see when my demon gives in. His shoulders drop.

"We shouldn't… be so personal in our arrangement anymore," Mace says.

"Personal?" I ask, the word is reedy when I wish it wasn't. I will force this demon to spell out exactly what he means.

"We should keep emotions out of this."

Keep emotions out of this. What does he mean? Is this about being lovers or friends? With the way he's acting, it's both. No more joking around, no adventures, no intimacy.

What is going on? What changed?

"Is this because I said"—I blink but need to know the answer—"that we made a good team?"

Is this because I said I wanted to stay together?

"You were injured. We can't be distracted while we do this," Mace says. The words make sense but don't account for the grief on his face.

He doesn't connect with people he has to protect.

"No." I hardly know what I'm saying.

"Sophia—"

"No." My throat swells with refusal. "You don't get to do this. You don't get to make me like you, trust you, only to decide to stop because I got hurt."

"I've seen you in unbelievable pain twice in the time we've been together—"

"It's been a bad week!" I shout.

Mace glares at me. "You stopped breathing!"

That throws me for a moment.

"I'm sorry," I say on reflex. I can't imagine how I'd feel if Mace stopped breathing in front of me.

"Don't apologize!" It's a pained hiss, vehement and direct when the rest of his words have been removed and bland.

"What do you want from me then? To say 'thank you' for getting me breathing again? Because thank you!" Tears sting my eyes, but I don't dare let them fall. "Just don't do this. Don't push me away. You saved me and healed—"

"Asa is the one who healed you—"

"Mace—" My eyes burn.

"I can't protect you."

"I'm not looking for protection!"

"I can't be *it* for you, Sophia."

I stumble back as if his words had been a blow. The railing at my back creaks and my thoughts over run my mouth.

"So what? Everything we did together was just about having fun?" I ask.

"Isn't that what you wanted?" Mace's words aren't unkind, just practical. It's as if he's folded all his volatile emotions up, hiding them from me.

"You know better," I snarl, wanting to pull his restraint away. "You know I—"

I stop. What am I doing? Mace knows I have feelings for him. I'm not going to prostrate myself.

He's decided I'm not enough. This is rejection.

The pain is deep. It cuts through every useless argument I want to make. Why would I think this would end any other way?

"So much for following me to the ends of the earth." My voice is hollow. *Like a sad puppy*, he'd said.

"I am sorry, Sophia, I truly am." And he sounds like it. "When we finish this mission, I'll restructure the bond—"

I make a cutting motion with my hand.

The bond? A future of us being connected, feeling the tug of Mace's presence in my soul and never being with him. Always remembering not measuring up, not being strong enough to be kept.

A living hell.

"I'm getting dressed," I say.

My vision blurs. I don't mean to slam the bedroom door behind me, but the echoing slam competes with the sensation of my heart cracking. The ache of loss spears through me. The ache of trusting Mace only to be found wanting tears at me. A sob escaping my mouth before I force it down.

I focus on stopping the hurt. *Stop it, Sophia. What did you expect, Sophia? Why did you give your heart away, Sophia?*

The roiling emotion chills, turning into bitter anger. I embrace the cold, embrace the numbness because everything else is too much.

I'm not running away. I'm not retreating, this demon has already given up the battle. I'm only preserving whatever is left of my guard until I can do what I intended from the beginning.

Get out of this bond.

Chapter 31

MACE

Sophia's pain destroys me. She's never been able to stop her emotions from flowing into me through our bond. As if what she feels is just so large that it overflows from her.

I could block it. I could stop the gouging sensation of the betrayal of her trust.

I won't

I deserve this pain.

If I'd only been faster, stronger, it wouldn't have happened. The memory of the bubbled-up flesh on her burned face, the moment when I held her in my arms and realized she wasn't breathing, haunts me. I caused that. Next time, she might not survive and the guilt and grief of that would be more than I can bear.

I hang my head and let the tears fall, wishing I could keep my goddess, knowing that stopping this now is better. Stopping this before Sophia tells me she loves me. It had been selfish to think I could keep her.

To let Sophia trust someone who couldn't keep her safe.

I may be weak, but I have the strength to keep my harpy from becoming invested in someone like me.

***

My tears are dry by the time Sophia exits the bedroom. My emotions have ravaged my senses, but I keep them from Sophia. I won't inflict my feelings on her now that I've drawn the line in the sand.

Sophia inhales and my eyes are drawn to her, no matter that I'm determined to distance myself. The ache of loss grows at the sight of her red-rimmed eyes.

"Sophia—" I start, my voice soft, but my harpy's eyes narrow.

"Stop it," she hisses, and I flinch at the venom of it. Sophia lifts her chin. "We still have work to do, and I have a debt to pay off so don't distract me with telling me how sorry you are. Save it for someone who cares."

We stare at each other, the sun beginning to set, all orange light and blue shadows. As if my mind wants to torture me further, it reminds me of that moment in the penthouse. The precipice of our relationship.

"I've been talking with Gage." Sophia's words startle me.

I'd heard her talking and just assumed it had been with one of her sisters.

"He didn't contact me," I say, though it's not as if I've checked. I've been too busy wallowing. To distract myself from that seemed like respite I didn't deserve.

Sophia rolls her eyes. "You didn't answer your phone. I'm sure you have an email in your inbox matching what was sent to me. We have a plan to implement. The ring is going down tonight."

The guilt that wells in my soul is poisonous. There are still captives missing and I've allowed myself to be distracted. Is there no end to my selfishness?

I clear my throat. "What's the plan?"

"Gage's team was able to set up a meeting posing as a vetted but mysterious seller. The individuals running the acquirement for the group have been trying to supply a particular type of creature for months."

My heart sinks. "A harpy."

Sophia nods.

"I don't like—"

"I don't care." Sophia cuts me off. "We'll go through the process of selling me and I'll lead Gage's team to the location, and we'll get everyone back. Game over for the group."

"The risk—"

"This is why you wanted my help. Don't stop this plan because you doubt my abilities. I can do this. I will do this." My fierce harpy glares at me.

I swallow. "Okay."

"And when I finish this job, the favor you're going to grant in payment is to sever our bond," Sophia says.

My throat constricts, expecting to lose Sophia's presence in my life doesn't make it any easier to accept it happening.

Veto it. Keep her.

Keep her when I offer nothing more than my company. Not protection, not safety. Keep her when I might lose her.

It's better to suffer this loss instead.

"Okay," I say.

Sophia rocks back on her heels. The placid features of her face breaking for a single second before she pulls her mask back down.

She turns from me, words traveling over her shoulder. "I wish you had been with me for me and not because you thought I was strong."

It's a stab in my heart, and I deserve it.

"I can't be the reason you get hurt," I say. The words are weak, like me.

"Too late."

Chapter 32

SOPHIA

Mace tries to avoid watching me, but he's terrible at it. My body reacts with each glance he gives me, and it causes a surge of anger every time.

"Everything settling okay? No pinching or weird magic interactions?" Leo asks, his questions soft.

"Yes." I rattle the restraints on my wrists, they hold. A clever bit of magic has the suppression collar on my neck humming as if activated, but it doesn't actually suppress my abilities. "Thank you."

Gage's team is incredibly proficient. It's only been ten minutes since they'd met up with us a short distance away from the meeting location and we're ready to go.

The spell caster of the group, Leo, had quickly become my favorite. His spells are seamless and custom designed to sit against my skin. They're almost as good as Alice's experiments, and he didn't have the benefit of trial and error to do them.

Leo is also incredibly cheerful and nice. Maybe he's dialing that up to combat with the awkward tension Mace and I bring to our huddle.

I had to leave my trusty leather jacket at Mace's. It had been partially damaged by the fireball spell and the charms set into it would have been obvious to anyone looking for them. I don't like the absence, it's like being naked.

Appearing as vulnerable as possible is my role. It's an essential part for this plan. We need our targets to bring me to the rest of their captives. I'll serve as a tracking beacon for our team. Leo meticulously painted a spell that he can track, a symbol the size of my hand in gold on my back. It's invisible to even those who can see magic.

The man who will be "selling" me to the group is a big shifter named Kane. He's been quiet since being introduced, but it doesn't seem to be unusual for him.

We'd all agreed, except for Mace, that with the possibility of Nero being involved, Mace couldn't be my partner for this mission. The demon is not happy with any of us.

I'm enjoying his discomfort more than I should. It's like having revenge and it's utterly ridiculous, but feelings are feelings.

"Is everyone ready?" Gage asks, his voice inspiring the hairs on the back of my neck to raise.

I don't know what Gage is, he hides it under a human-appearing glamour, but the reptilian quality of his movements and his yellow eyes make me think dragon. He won't be a part of the transaction. Rare species are better left unidentified by these groups.

My family is known in the paranormal community, especially after the business with Zeph. So the added danger of them recognizing me isn't an issue. I'm exactly what they're looking for after all.

We nod and Mace shoots a look to the rest of the men who wander a few steps away. He steps in front of me, and our bond vibrates to life with a throb of worry. I gasp and it quiets, ripping Mace's emotions from me yet again.

I glare but Mace leans his face next to mine, his posture communicating all the things the bond will no longer tell me. Worry, care, and maybe heartbreak.

"Be safe, my fierce harpy. May the winds favor you," Mace says, and I want to pull him to me, let the warmth of him soothe my racing heart. I want to find the solace he'd given me before. The type of solace brought by support.

I don't.

Because those soft feelings won't help me with this. Mace has already made his decision. I refuse to beg for affection.

"It'll be a walk in the park."

Mace arches a brow. "A dark park filled with vampires?"

I cough a laugh. "I'll be fine. Someone once told me they're snobs."

"You'd have to fight your way out. They always go for the highest quality."

How is it that this demon can always take my breath away?

Mace takes a step back, maybe realizing he's gone too far.

I start walking in the direction of the meeting, stopping to call out to Kane. "Are you ready to party?"

The giant's mouth twitches, and he nods, catching up to me quickly. I stop to let him slip a leash-like chain through the restraints. The tug drives home just how much I'm trusting Mace and Gage's team to rescue me. My breath is shaky, but I will not fail now.

"You've got to stop smiling like that. You have to be the scary one and I have to be the scared one." I tease to take my mind off everything.

That has a snort escaping Kane.

"Be good," he says, his smooth voice full of mirth.

"Never."

By the time we get to the meeting location, an abandoned warehouse, my adrenaline is pumping and the dangerous edge of excitement presses against my throat.

"You just walked here with a harpy on a leash?" The question comes from a man who steps into the light. More shadows move, more men milling around as if they've always been here and didn't just appear. My eyes count what I can. There are maybe five.

The speaker has thinning dark hair and a thick body. He'd look average if his sneer didn't make my skin crawl.

"You must be Frank," Kane says. "She's been obedient. Knows I have access to her phone and will go after her family if she makes even a peep." The big shifter on the other end of my leash is good at being the scary one. He makes his voice so monotone and chilling that Frank pauses.

Frank looks at a different man, this one rangy, his motions jittery. The jittery man sniffs the air and nods. I'd bet money that he's the spell caster. The nod must mean that we're clean of nefarious magic.

Thank you, Leo.

Kane shrugs. "But if you're not interested, I'll take her elsewhere."

He yanks on the chain leashing me as if we're turning to leave.

"Wait! Don't be so hasty, friend. We're interested."

Kane turns back. "Then transfer the money. I have other plans for tonight."

Frank's face scrunches in frustration, and he slides a thick envelope from his pocket, holding it out. Kane takes the envelope with a movement so quick it has me blinking.

"Cash?" Kane asks as he flips through the contents.

"We always deal in cash," Frank explains with a hint of condescension.

Kane sighs as if this is an inconvenience but tosses the end of my leash to the man who just bought me. I'm yanked forward when Frank hands the end to the spell caster.

"Should I contact you when I have more harpies? I've found quite the nest of them." Kane's tone is droll. Now it's my turn to perform. I try and manifest every helpless feeling I had when Zeph was taken.

"You said they'd be safe!" I yank on the chain, trying to simulate the strength I'd have if the suppression collar was really working. Even that much has the spell caster cursing, but he doesn't lose his grip.

"Not much you can do about it now, is there?" Kane smiles. It's so cold I shiver.

Frank makes a sound of annoyance. "So much for an obedient harpy."

Kane shrugs. "Your problem now."

Frank scowls and answers the question. "Yes, we have a buyer interested in harpies. It's got something to do with feathers."

Knowing my kind has been hunted for parts and hearing about it currently happening has a sick feeling rising in my stomach. *Feathers, really?*

Kane walks backward, exhibiting the correct amount of caution that this meeting entails. He waves on the way out. "Good doing business with you."

And I'm alone with the traffickers.

I suppress the panic. Mace will come after me as soon as I signal. This is a business group. They'll want to store me with the merchandise as soon as possible.

That's the clearest cut scenario we'd gone through as a team. There had been many other disgusting scenarios. Mace had almost lost it when we covered the options of sexual assault. This is a group dealing in people as if they are objects. The risk is present.

It's unlikely for a group this proficient to choose to do anything to me in an area that isn't secure. If these men had intentions of abusing me before transporting me… that's the reason my suppression collar doesn't work. It's the only thing that provides me any comfort.

"Be a good birdie. We'd hate to rough you up," Frank says, and a man in the shadows laughs. A different shadow smacks the laugher.

They seem to be all about business. Mace will find me; we'll save the captives. As if my thoughts summon him, he's suddenly there, strolling out of the shadows.

My heart jumps into my throat and I stare, looking away when the man narrows his eyes at me.

"Okay, demon, let's go," Frank says.

"She's bonded." Not-Mace's voice rolls lazily.

I freeze. I hadn't known that Nero would look so much like Mace. We hadn't even been sure he was involved, but the similarities are uncanny. Nero's face has a sharper quality to it, leaner and his eyes are darker.

Frank frowns. "A bonded harpy? Weird. Can she be tracked through it?"

The demon mulls the question over as if he doesn't care one way or the other about the answer. "Not by many."

"I don't care," he snaps. "Take care of it, but don't damage the merchandise."

Nero sighs. "If you insist."

I'm slow to react but Nero isn't. He makes a hand gesture in the air, and I come undone.

The threads of my soul snap. The impact of the slingshot of my own threads returning to me has a cry leaving my mouth with no volume. The pain is bad. I'm on the dusty warehouse floor, and I try to curl up to defend against it, but it's over quickly and all that's left is weakness.

Weakness and utter *emptiness*.

Chapter 33

MACE

Gage lifts me from where I'd fallen on the stained carpet of the motel room we've rented by the hour. The worst of the pain leaves but the shorn bond reaches out achingly for its pair. I wipe the tears from my eyes, clenching my jaw.

"They've broken our bond," I say.

Gage nods. It was a scenario we'd brushed on briefly. The bond between Sophia and I wouldn't be visible to any magic user, but there are a few types that would see it. The breaking of the bond doesn't change anything about our plan other than it's possible Sophia has lost consciousness.

Maybe not. She wanted the bond broken and if she didn't fight it, it wouldn't drain her. I'm a little dizzy, but the true effect of being without an anchor won't happen until I start traveling through the in-between.

Gage's brow creases. "Do you need a bond?"

My soul rejects the possibility of bonding to someone other than my harpy, but I press my hand to my heart, trying to quiet it.

"Your succubus would carve out my eyeballs," I say instead. Trying to figure out how many travels through the in-between I have left before I lose the luxury of being able to be picky about who I bond to.

Leo snorts and Gage looks uncomfortable. "It's not like that with Katherine."

The topic is successfully tabled and Kane bursts through the door.

"How is she?" he asks.

"They've broken the bond between her and Mace. We're just waiting for her to activate the beacon when they relocate her," Gage answers.

Kane curses. "They had at least five men. We'll need to take the Council Enforcers up on their offer, they outnumber us and undoubtedly have more at their main location."

Everyone makes sounds of aggravation, but Gage pulls out his phone and walks away to make the call. Enforcers are no one's favorite group of people to deal with.

After some quiet back and forth, Gage hangs up, his jaw tight. "They are on standby for when we have a location. Remember, our mission is freeing the captives and theirs is apprehending the culprits."

I nod. "Did you tell them it's possible that they have someone with teleporting capabilities?"

"Cooper didn't seem overly concerned." Gage's upper lip curls up in disgust.

My head falls back. Cooper had been the enforcer leading the team when Zeph was taken. I should have let Greg rip his head from his body.

The enforcer isn't a bad man. Just one with priorities about captives that I don't agree with. His the-end-justifies-the-means methods leave much to be desired.

As a reflex, I reach for the bond, only to wince at the gaping emptiness. I force myself to focus on the conversations of the room as we detail our plans now that the Council has been called in.

I will find you, my goddess.

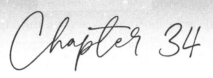

Chapter 34

SOPHIA

I tremble as I'm led down a cement corridor, still dealing with random waves of nausea and weakness from having the bond severed. I'd almost completely lost consciousness when Nero had teleported the group to this dank location.

The trip through the in-between had been more jarring than I'd ever experienced. As fast as the blink of an eye with no playful shadows pulling on me.

Seeing between the planes must have been an ability I'd been given from being bonded to Mace. The loss of our bond… *Stop it! This is what you wanted. Suck it up.*

My pep talk lacks conviction. I did want the bond broken. I just didn't realize how much I'd miss it. How lonely it would be.

We turn a corner, the spell caster leads me by the chain. Nero walks behind us; my skin crawls. Why is he watching me?

We finally get to a larger room with a few large jail cells made by bars going from floor to ceiling. People huddle in the cells, too many to count on one pass. The spell caster holds a hand in front of the door and the people cower, forcing them from the opening. Every person has a suppression collar.

"Hands," the spell caster says to me, and I offer up my wrists. He orients me behind the bars, and I make sure to stumble, showing the weakness strategically.

The spell caster snorts at my act and the anger that rises is hot. I fist my hands, trying to keep my talons from showing, the urge to disembowel him is strong.

"There was something familiar about that bond."

I freeze at Nero's words.

"What?" I force myself to sound confused. Could he sense it was his brother's bond that he severed?

Nero tilts his head. "I can't quite put my finger on it, but I'll figure it out."

"Don't touch the bars," the spell caster says, ignoring the interaction I'm having with the demon while he removes the wrist restraints and slides the cell door shut.

I'll figure it out.

What happens if he does? Could Nero outmaneuver our plans if he knows about Mace? Has he kept up to date on his brother? Would he know about Mace's past activities tracking down traffickers?

Fuck.

The possibilities race through my mind and I wait until my two escorts leave the room. I turn around and face my fellow prisoners.

There's a variety present. Men, women, children, and a few unidentifiable beings covered in feathers or fur, not able to glamour their appearance with the suppression collar. The time spent with Mace has been in an effort to find these people and I'm finally in front of them.

I take a breath and focus on activating Leo's spell.

Now would be a great time to get saved.

Chapter 35

SOPHIA

I slow my breathing and my heartbeat thunders in my ears as I count the minutes, waiting for the room to erupt in activity. Any moment now, Mace and the guys will come crashing into wherever this is and free us.

Any moment now.

The chill of the air sinks into my skin and poisons my thoughts. Have I placed too much trust in Gage's team? What if Leo's spell doesn't work however far underground we are?

I clench my hands into fists and stop my mental spiral.

Mace will not leave me here.

Why not? The bond was going to be broken at the end of this mission anyway. Why would he put himself in danger to save me? Everything we had is over. Our short time as lovers, the bond, our friendship—

I shake my head in anger and confusion. Where are these thoughts coming from?

I jump when someone touches my arm. A woman with silver hair and an ageless face pulls her hand away, her eyes full of understanding.

"It's a spell," she says, gesturing to the bars. "It amplifies doubts. To make us more compliant."

Just what I needed in my life.

I mentally grab on to the woman's presence. If I distract myself with conversation, my mind won't ponder on all the reasons why the calvary hasn't come yet.

"My name is Sophia. Who are you?"

The woman blinks slowly at me, assessing before a small smile stretches her mouth.

"Meri. People call me Meri on this plane."

At that comment, I notice the slight, pointed ears that peek through her hair. *Fae.*

I know almost nothing about fae except that many paranormal creatures originally came from the fae plane before settling in this one. Harpies could have very well originated there, but it would have been so long ago that the details have been lost to time.

"Well, Meri, I'm happy to meet you. Even if the situation sucks."

Meri laughs at that, and the sound is high and pure. People around us shift, but no one moves to join our conversation.

"I'm glad you are here, Sophia, if only to keep me company and distract me from the doubts," Meri says.

I let my eyes run over our fellow captives. Hollow eyes stare back at me. A few still seem to have some sort of cognizance but their features twist in grief. At our situation or the spiral of doubts plaguing them?

A thought rings in my head, one tainted with frustration more than doubt.

Where the fuck is my rescue team?

Chapter 36

MACE

Sophia smiles at me, the sun bright on her face and the sky a vibrant blue behind her. The wind picks up her hair and I watch her take in the sight of Paris from the Eiffel Tower in my mind's eye. The memory a beautiful moment that I'll treasure even after we get her from the bowels of hell. She was so slow to trust me when our relationship started. I failed to keep her heart safe, but I will not fail in getting to her.

No matter how this plane grabs my energy away.

"Gage." My voice borders on threatening. "You have a single minute more to figure out this arrangement with the Council Enforcers or I'm leaving without you."

Gage's yellow eyes glow and a curled lip communicates that he's holding back an inner beast. I doubt he gets many people challenging his dominance but I'm past the point of caring. It's been ten minutes since Sophia revealed her location.

A scrying crystal glows on top of a tablet, a seamless mesh of magic and technology.

Online maps of the location are up on every screen.

Ten minutes of recon of the underground base, of posturing and planning with the Enforcers, time that Sophia could have needed help without me knowing. I can't feel her anymore, and it's torture.

I have no right, either by strength or dominance, to challenge Gage, but I am getting my harpy, with or without his team's help.

Gage surprises me by nodding and ending the phone call, he quickly types a message on it before sliding it away.

"You're right. We go now. I let the Enforcers know that we won't wait any longer. Are you sure you can do this?"

Teleporting without an anchor isn't ideal but a portal spell can't be used to go to a place it hasn't been set up to yet.

I make a sound in the back of my throat. "I will do what it takes."

Even if it requires eventually making myself bond to someone other than Sophia.

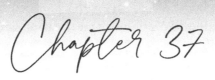

Chapter 37

SOPHIA

Meri and I talk about inane things.

Anything to keep the doubts from getting to us.

"The *internet* is your favorite thing?" I ask.

"I'm sure you can't imagine how things are on the fae plane. It's not that we are behind on technology." Meri frowns. "Okay, so we actually are. We have the modern comforts, heating, lighting, and such. It's just done with magic instead of electricity. What we don't have is some universal collection of information available at the fingertips of anyone who wants it. It's truly amazing that I am a click away from learning anything from how to cook a pie to a dissertation on nuclear science."

Meri's brows raise, morose. "I'll truly miss it… if I ever get to go back."

The subject is one that we've stayed clear of, but the downswing of the conversation and my curiosity is too much to ignore.

"Why are you on this plane?" I ask. "Did you get brought here as a prisoner?"

Meri shakes her head with a wince. "I fear that I'm in this mess very much by my own doing. I thought I could find someone here. Convince him to return and be back home before my mates were any the wiser."

My brows shoot up. "Your mates?"

"I'm sure that I have two very worried, rightfully angry mates back home," Meri says with a lopsided smile. "I don't think they'll ever forgive me. Leaving with just a note and all."

Dear gods, I don't envy Meri. Putting the closest people to you through hell like that.

What about me? If Mace fails to save me, my family will be left to wonder—I stop the thought there. It's just another doubt. I trust that if anything happened to me, Mace would tell everyone what happened. No matter the risk of angering an entire branch of harpies.

"You came here alone?" I ask. I know that the travel for fae back and forth to this plane has been normalized, but the details of how and where are kept quiet. Fae aren't keen on sharing those details.

"I'm not proud of that. I really did think it was going to be a quick thing, but this world turned out to be vast and the person I'm looking for would be operating under a disguise anyway." Meri runs a finger over the suppression collar she wears. "A stupid decision for the sake of a little hope that turned out to be for nothing."

That statement rings a chord in my heart. As someone prone to making stupid decisions, I sympathize with Meri's predicament.

"Hey, stop it," I say, trying to inject surety into my tone. "We're getting out of here before either of us gets sold. I'd rather keep all of my feathers."

A spark of delight lightens Meri's eyes and I see the mischievous fae that landed on this plane with big plans. "What do you have planned, Sophia?"

I hesitate, not wanting to jeopardize the mission or give false hope if Gage's team isn't able to track our location.

Boom!

The explosion sounds above us, and the ground vibrates with the intensity of it.

"Thank *fuck*!" I say as we both jump to our feet.

A cluster of familiar men appear in front of us, the shadows of the in-between are quick to dissipate. Mace stumbles hand in hand with Gage and Kane, Leo hops off his back.

"If you're here, who is blowing shit up?" I ask.

"Enforcers," Kane says.

I roll my eyes. *No wonder they are so late.*

"I totally didn't think you guys left me out to dry," I tease.

Gage grins at me. "Your confidence leaves much to be desired."

"So does your timing."

Gage makes hand gestures to his team, and they move quickly.

"Please remain calm. This is a rescue." Gage raises his voice. "We need to be quick."

Leo does something to the cells that open all the doors and Kane starts ushering the people in the other cells to ours. The captives move with no hesitance, some of the hollow-eyed people looking painfully hopeful.

I pull my attention away from the action. Mace's eyes are unfocused, as if he's dizzy, and he sways on his feet.

I grab his arm on instinct. Needing to hold on to my demon. "Are you okay?"

Mace finally looks at me, and relief breaks over his face.

"Sophia." Mace pulls me in and presses his face into my hair, inhaling.

I choke and wrap my arms around him. My worries drain even as the adrenaline of the moment has my heart racing. The bond between us is gone but being in his arms is perfection. It soothes every doubt that preyed on my mind, every hurt he inflicted.

If I had ever wondered that our soul bond compelled my feelings for him, the worry is gone now. My demon won my heart fair and square.

"Keep him on his feet." Gage interrupts my thoughts. He gestures to the people around us to huddle closer. He raises his voice. "Are there any others?"

"No! They've kept us all together since the beginning," Meri calls back.

"Good, everyone, get close and take note of who is around you. We only have one portal spell and don't want anyone getting left behind."

His words are incentive enough and all the people crush together as much as they can.

At the crush, Mace raises his head and frowns, as if finally becoming aware of everything. He looks down at me and starts to loosen his arms and I scowl.

"Alright, let's blow this popsicle stand," Leo says, and I catch Gage rolling his eyes as the witch activates the portal spell. The sensation isn't like walking through the in-between at all. It's as if the world spins and my ears pop.

We all stumble but stay upright. We're in what appears to be a respectable-looking office. Heavy desks have been moved to the edges of the space to make room and an unfamiliar dark-haired woman stands next to a stack of blankets and boxes of water bottles.

"Welcome! Is anyone injured?" the woman calls out. No one answers, probably too stunned at the abrupt travel from the dank jail cells to this calm space with generic decor. "You're all safe now." Her voice exudes comfort. "I'm Katherine, and I'm going to be the one contacting your families while Leo begins deactivating the collars."

Someone in the crowd begins to weep.

We did it. We really did it.

Chapter 38

MACE

Sophia's eyes gleam with happiness as she whips her gaze around, taking in the details of all the rescued people realizing that their ordeal is almost over. I don't do the same. I only see her.

Teleporting to the underground base had felt like being sucker punched, leaving me in a daze. It had taken some time to be cognizant of our surroundings and then Sophia had been in front of me, and my soul and heart had rejoiced.

I'm still holding her. I don't want to let go, but I must.

Sophia makes eye contact, her entire being lit up with almost a tangible joy. The severed bond keens in loss. Our bodies press together and my chest aches from with the want to prolong this moment forever.

Sophia's face softens, her mouth parting in the tempting way it does. She leans in to kiss me and I've never wanted anything more, but my conscience cracks like a whip through me.

I can't. I pull back and Sophia stiffens.

I gesture to the rest of the room and finally release my hold on her. "Not right now."

Sophia frowns but nods

"Later," she says, as if our company is what keeps me from embracing her.

I don't have the heart to correct her.

***

Later ends up being hours later.

All the freed individuals have been funneled to places to stay, have had family come collect them, or are set up to make their own travels. The work is monotonous, but necessary. Twenty-six people had been retrieved from that pit and I'm grateful that Sophia is one of them.

The last person to leave is a fae woman being driven to the nearest fae door by Kane. The woman embraces my harpy—Sophia, not *my* anything, and they share words I don't catch.

The team are all in states of tired relaxation. Katherine has her feet kicked up and Leo munches on a granola bar from the supply boxes. Gage is the only one still vibrating with energy. Angry energy.

The door to the main office space closes and the team leader closes his laptop.

"The Enforcers didn't get them all," Gage says.

It takes a moment for the detail to settle, and I curse. Of course they didn't.

"Do they know who they missed?" I ask.

Gage sighs. "They have a man who confessed that the boss of the ring didn't get taken, they also don't have a demon who can teleport in custody."

I curse again but start to feel hopeful that Nero really isn't involved in this.

"Nero was there," Sophia says, dashing my hopes.

She continues, "He was the one to sever our bond."

I nod. He's still out there.

"We have to go after them," Sophia says.

Gage is the first to shake his head. "We were hired to get these people back to their families. I wanted to take down the operation, but these people are our priority and there is still a lot of work left."

Sophia's brows knit. "Then just Mace and I will go."

"Sophia—" I say.

"We can bond, again." Sophia puts a hand over her heart. Does she feel the same loss as I do? "We can bond and start going after them. With your ability to teleport and knowing Nero's usual places, we could—"

"No."

"But—"

"We aren't bonding again, Sophia."

Katherine stands. "Leo, Gage, I need both of your help to… get a box down from storage."

Leo blinks once before he's on his feet. Gage frowns. "But it's my office."

"Now." The demoness glares.

Gratitude swells that we have a little bit of privacy for this. When Gage closes the door, grumbling, I turn back to Sophia.

"Your part in this is done," I say.

"What do you mean? We're so close. All we need to do—"

"No, Sophia, there is no *we* anymore. Our bond is broken, just like you requested. Our agreement is over." I force my words to be firm even as the ache of loss grows.

Sophia blinks at me.

"You're going to bond with someone else?"

The question hits me as if I've been slapped but I refuse to draw Sophia in more. This is over.

"It's a fact of my existence," I say.

I'm a parasite, weak and needy. This is for the best.

Sophia shakes her head. "We could be so good together. You just need to—"

"Fierce harpy, I can't be the reason you get hurt." The words flay me, leaving my heart open and vulnerable.

Sophia snarls in denial. "What's so different now than when we started this whole mess?"

"I didn't have the same feelings about you then that I do now." This is as close as I'll ever get to being able to express my love for this fierce harpy and it's not enough. I'm not enough. "It would kill me to lose you."

"So you won't allow yourself to keep me?" She sounds broken. I deserve to burn alive for being the cause of this pain.

"I'm sorry," I say, so soft that I can't be sure she even hears it.

"But—" Sophia stops, and I watch the grief turn to anger. I watch the strength of my harpy and wish she'd gut me with her beautiful talons. It would hurt less than this.

"You're a coward!" Sophia spits out.

I don't deny it.

Chapter 39

SOPHIA

"Sophia, I'm glad you set up this meeting." Fairuza gestures to the chair opposite her large glossy desk and sits. Each item on the desk is ordered and angled, from the crystal paperweight to the fancy pens. The office Fairuza keeps in the city is generic perfection with just the right amount of accent pieces and precise modern furniture.

I take a seat. I don't take off my jacket because this won't be a long meeting.

"I thought you were going to keep ignoring my messages until the next family gathering." My aunt arches a sharp eyebrow.

I lift my chin. "I was trying to figure out what to say to you."

It's been a day since everything had gone down with Gage's team. A day since I turned my back on the demon who is letting fear rule his actions. Anger and hurt have churned the soil of my heart into an unrecognizable mush but there's something else there too. Confidence.

I triumphed. I saved twenty-five people and dealt a blow to the insidious practice that preys on my kind. And I didn't do it alone.

I've repeatedly met and worked with paranormal beings who are determined to look out for each other.

"Oh?" Fairuza asks, her brows crease.

I straighten in the chair. "I'm coming to you as my branch matriarch to formally express opposition to the beliefs that are perpetuated by the elders and matriarchs in our community."

Fairuza's eyes widen slightly but she sits back in her chair and steeples her fingers.

"Go on," she says.

"I think the way harpies are raised, our lack of knowledge and interactions with the communities around us, is dangerous." *Remember to breathe.*

"Harpies are small in number. The plan to combat that by procreation is not a solution I believe in. My work has brought me face to face with many other beings who suffer the same issues that harpies do and ally with other communities to remedy it."

Fairuza's face shows me none of what she thinks.

I continue. "Isolation puts us at a disadvantage when trouble does come, and cuts us off from beneficial connections." And now to the personal issues.

"When the time comes for my sister and I to train our nieces, I'll instruct them on how to navigate the paranormal world in ways that won't align with our community's views. As for the position of matriarch, if it comes to me, I'll do what I think is right for our community. I refuse to be trained in maintaining beliefs I don't agree with."

I take a breath. The office is silent.

"Are you done?" Fairuza asks.

I blink. "Yeah, I'm done."

My heart is pumping as if I'm facing an enemy. I considered the possible ramifications in being open with my thoughts and intentions. Our immediate family won't ostracize me, but the community at large…

"I know about you and your witch friend's business. The making of charms that are compatible with harpy sensitivity," Fairuza says.

My heart drops. Now my eyes are the ones widening. "Oh?"

My aunt is matriarch. If she prohibits me from spreading the charms throughout our community, it would mean trouble for Alice and me to break the rules.

"And I heard about the trafficking ring you disrupted… I'm proud of you," Fairuza says before scowling. "Stop gaping."

I close my mouth, but my face must still show my shock. Fairuza picks up a pen from her desk and fiddles with it.

"I know I don't always express it and I know I am—" She clears her throat and looks down at the pen she's squeezing. "—manipulative."

Fairuza blushes. "I don't think it ever occurred to me that the next generation would be just as stubborn and headstrong as my own and I'm coming to realize the consequences of trying to get my own way at all costs."

The confession is a vulnerability that fills the space between us. I've never heard my aunt get this close to saying that she was wrong.

Fairuza narrows her eyes at me, the vulnerable look on her face disappearing. "I will try to be more flexible in my thinking and explore our options. Thank you for your insight."

It sounds like a dismissal, but I don't move.

"Thank you," I say. "For not—" I wave my hand. For not getting angry? For not banishing me?

Fairuza nods, her lips twisting in a small smile. "I'll see you at the next family dinner."

Chapter 40

SOPHIA

I scroll through my messages. Emails from incoming jobs, a text from Amara about her employee, but nothing from a certain demon. I don't know why there would be, there's been nothing for the past week.

"How did that new job go?" Alice asks.

"What?" I blink in confusion and set my phone in my lap.

Exasperation tinges Alice's voice and she puts down the charm she was painstakingly inscribing. "The Nelson job? How did it go?"

I watch the swirling dust in the air catch the sunlight illuminating Alice's workshop.

"It was quick." And bloody. The amount of blood had almost been therapeutic. Maybe not therapeutic, it didn't make me feel happier in the long run. Cathartic.

"Did you really castrate someone?" Alice asks.

"Well, yeah, it was the job."

Alice's face scrunches.

"It grew back," I say. "The man is an absolute menace. The only way to stop him from trespassing until the

Council could take action was to make charms from a piece of him."

"Couldn't you have taken a finger?" Alice asks.

I roll my eyes. "I gave him options."

That shuts my friend up for a single second before she opens her mouth again, eyes wide in horror. "He chose for you to slice—ew."

"I know. Honestly, I think he enjoyed it." Which is a detail I have to live with, and now Alice gets to as well.

Alice gags. "Oh gods!"

I snort. "Careful. Don't be yucking anyone's yum or anything."

Alice scowls. "Don't lecture me about kink. There are other people he would have been able to go to for that that would have been a mutually beneficial arrangement. I thought that blood made you…"

"Throw up? Yeah, it still does." The vomiting after had been less cathartic. "And it was a mutually beneficial arrangement… just not in that way."

Alice looks down at the charm she'd been working on. "I think it's going to be a while before I feel like leaving for dinner."

"You asked!"

"I was trying to break the ice! I didn't think I was going to get that kind of visual with it!"

"What ice?" I ask, but dread draws on my stomach.

Alice chews her lip. "It's been a week, Sophia."

A week since Mace had rejected bonding with me. A week since I'd seen that annoying demon that could make my heart race with just a crooked grin. I've heard from Gage and the rest of his team, but not a word from the person I'd been bonded to.

I'd retrieved the artifacts for Kalos without issue so there was almost no pressure on that debt. The mummified parts of *something* were not what I'd expect him to want. There was just one piece unaccounted for, but the dragon didn't seem to be in a rush for me to find it. He said it would turn up someplace and I'm sure he's right. There's a light at the end of the tunnel for that whole situation.

"Do you think that you should call *him*?" Alice winces while she asks.

And just like that, my mind is back on Mace.

"Why would I call him?" I'm honestly confused. "He's the one that broke things off with me."

Alice and I stare at each other in silence. The expression on her face looks like she's struggling to explain something glaring.

"Sophia, you're fucking miserable."

"I'm *aware*." I just hadn't been aware that it was so obvious.

After living with the constant presence of the bond for months being without it… hurts. It's not always an active hurt. The first day or two the absence of the bond had been like a stab wound. Sharp and painful, each memory ripping me open. The pain dulled over the following days until it's more of an ever-present throb.

I fiddle with the seam on the pillow next to me on the couch. Looking for any way to avoid the fact screaming in my mind and dreams.

I miss him.

"Whose side are you on anyway?" I ask.

"Yours. Always yours."

That's nice to hear and soothes my feathers.

"I just think that maybe you guys could work it out," she says.

I throw the pillow at Alice.

I thought so too. And if I, a harpy who shouldn't be getting attached to any man, thinks that, why can't he?

"I won't beg him to be in a relationship with me," I say. *You were fine with begging for other things—shut up.*

Alice looks sad. "Then you don't get to keep him."

The possibility of it truly being over stings like needles in my heart.

"He has issues," I say.

After the pain of rejection faded, time and distance had given me perspective. The whys of Mace's rejection. He wanted to be with me. Every hopeful look and moment of happiness between us spoke volumes to that.

His feelings for me aren't the problem.

Fear. Low self-worth. The all-consuming guilt of how he lost his sister. Mace doesn't want to be open to loss. He doesn't want to carry the burden of guilt for another death. Am I being too hard on him? Asking for too much?

No. I deserve someone who is willing to fight the world with me. *He was willing to fight the world with you, just not risk losing you.*

What's the answer then?

"If he was brave enough to be with me, this wouldn't be a problem," I say.

Alice makes a sound in her throat. "Are you going to wait for him to realize he's being an idiot? That doesn't sound much like you."

Alice is right. It sounds so *passive.*

"I'm not waiting for anything." *Right? I'm not going to bed at night wishing that he'd call me.*

Alice's brows raise and irritation spikes.

"Is your suggestion to go into it thinking I can change him?" I throw my hands wide. "I may not know much about relationships, but that sounds like a bad idea."

"Well yeah, I guess that's the conventional wisdom of it. I don't know. Are they issues that you think could be resolved? You guys aren't some theoretical situation. You're Sophia and Mace."

A vice squeezes around my heart. *Sophia and Mace.* That sounds too good to be true. It probably wouldn't work out. I could call him, go through all the effort and have it lead to nothing.

That's not right, it could lead to even more hurt.

"Sophia." Alice's whole demeanor softens. "I want you to be happy and sometimes it seems like you're just waiting for people to reject you. I'm sure growing up with your aunt did a number on you even if she's trying now."

My first reaction is denial, but I keep my mouth shut. Alice deserves to be heard. I let the idea roll around in my head and… it's not wrong. Had I been waiting for Mace to reject me?

Has Fairuza's conditional acceptance marked me in that way?

Maybe.

Love is conditional. Or it's what I'd thought.

When Mace had pushed me away, I thought it was because I'm not as strong as he wants, but that's bullshit. It doesn't matter how strong someone is, there's always the risk of losing them.

I can't still say that love is conditional. If it was conditional, my heart would just stop feeling the stupid emotion now that Mace has broken it.

"If I wait long enough, will this go away?" I ask.

"What?" Alice asks.

"The hurt... the heartbreak."

Alice's face falls. "Yeah. It will go away, but do you want it to?"

"He doesn't want me." I shake my head. "He says he can't be responsible for my safety."

"He doesn't want to be responsible—what old-world garbage is that?"

I snort. "I told him I wasn't looking for someone to keep me safe."

"*Responsible.* Gods help the idiot." Alice's brow creases. "I mean, I guess that's the language I've heard some people use. As if in order to claim what they want they need to be able to provide safety and care."

To avoid guilt as much as loss.

Claim.

A proverbial light bulb goes off. It can't be that simple... but maybe...

"Oh, you've got a look on your face," Alice says.

I definitely have a look, because I have a plan. Kind of a plan anyway. I have a deal to offer my demon. One that he might take me up on.

"I'm calling him," I say and press my speed dial before I let any doubts weigh me down.

"Oh wow, you're taking my advice?" Alice smiles. "This almost never happens."

I point at her while the phone rings. "Don't make a big deal about it or it won't happen again."

Alice laughs. "Well, here's to hoping the man has enough sense to pick up your calls."

The phone rings and an eerie feeling creeps up my spine. "He hasn't picked up calls from you?"

"Nope." She pops the 'p.' "To be fair, I berated him in text message first, so it could be that he didn't want to get lectured by me."

"Maybe," I say, the voice mail ends and the call disconnects. No personalized message with Mace's voice. I hang up. My stomach starts to fall.

"Alice, when's the last time you heard from Mace?"

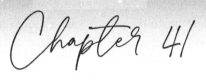

Chapter 41

MACE
Five Days Ago

I curl my hand into a fist to knock on the door and freeze. It's an inconspicuous apartment door. The better to hide in plain sight. This man is the perfect candidate to soul bond with. A person hiding a juicy secret who will agree to a temporary bond. I have no wish to have a long-term bond with someone I've blackmailed.

Temporary. I repeat it over and over again, hoping to ease the tightness in my chest. Make this whole situation feel less like a betrayal of my harpy.

I drop my hand and leave the plain apartment door undisturbed. I can't do it.

The sky is gray and miserable. It matches my mood. The rain soaks my hair and coat while I walk. I need the time moving to think. I'd say I need the time alone, but all I've been lately is alone and it's my own fault.

You're a coward!

Sophia's words haunt me. She's right.

I'm stuck in a between place. The thought of sharing a bond with anyone other than Sophia makes my heart sick but I'm still too frozen in fear, in past guilt, to reach out to the woman I love.

So I walk.

The streets pass in a blur, and I let my thoughts spiral. It had almost been two days of being unbonded and as long as I don't try to do any tricks, I should have at least a day or two more before the fatigue starts.

Can I let myself be with Sophia?

Bonding without a relationship isn't a possibility, I hadn't thought the option through when I mentioned it to her before. I hadn't realized how torturous it would be to feel her through the bond and not have the ability to hold or tease her.

No, if Sophia is kind enough to forgive me for my missteps and bond with me, it won't be a temporary arrangement. I'd want a mate bond.

Can I be bonded with Sophia if I'm unable to protect her? Can I open myself up to that kind of possible loss?

Can I face the guilt haunting me from the last time I failed someone?

I blow out a breath and stop, tilting my head up to the sky I let the raindrops hit my face. My emotions are a mess. I need to contact Sophia. Maybe if I listen to her this time, she can talk me into letting us both be happy without my doubts souring the whole thing.

I miss her.

The scrape of a boot on concrete, a footstep where there hadn't been one before, has me whipping around.

"Hello, brother," Nero sneers.

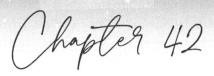

Chapter 42

SOPHIA

"You think Mace is missing?" Asa asks.

I saved asking my brother-in-law until last. With the triplets, I'm sure his life is hectic enough as it is.

"That can't be right," Asa says. "I just received a text from him the other day..."

I suck in a hopeful breath.

"Dammit. The text was six days ago. Gods dammit." Asa's voice drops. "Tell me someone else has heard from him more recently than that."

My hope deflates and I try not to let anger rise. Asa is one of Mace's closest friends, Gideon is the other, and neither of them had recognized the gap in time from the last time they heard from him.

"The leader of the group we were working with had an email update from him five days ago, but that's it. No one has been able to contact him since," I say.

"*Fuck.*" There's an edge of guilt in Asa's curse. "I should have realized something was wrong. It's just that no one has been sleeping and—there's no excuse."

Yes, someone should have known.

I push down the urge to heap even more guilt than Asa is already experiencing. People get busy. Five days isn't that long between hearing from someone. Top it off with the fact that Mace is usually the one reaching out to people instead of the other way around and it's easy to see how the man could be missing so long without anyone noticing.

Still, my hand flexes with the need to dig my talons into something.

Mace has been taken.

"Asa, did Mace tell you if he bonded to anyone?" I ask.

I push down the illogical jealousy. It's better if he has an anchor, even if we don't know who it is. If he has an anchor, then he's not as vulnerable.

"No," Asa says. "Last I knew, he was bonded to you. He's without a bond?"

I swallow at the horror in the demon's voice. It expresses just how vulnerable Asa considers Mace.

"Yeah. He—we're currently not bonded." I clear my throat, trying not to let my emotions rage out of control. "I've got to go. Alice and I are taking a portal key to meet up with that team that we were working with so we can start trying to find him."

"I'm coming," Asa says. There's a darkness to his voice that has a shiver running down my spine.

"Fine." I spout off the address. "Don't make us wait too long."

I hang up the phone.

Alice nods at me. "Asa's coming?"

"We're going to need all the help we can get," I say.

How does one go about finding a demon that can be anywhere in the world in the blink of an eye?

Chapter 43

MACE

Drip, drip, drip.

All I want is to sleep. To find solace in my dreams while I still can. Dreams full of a certain harpy with flowing dark hair and blazing green eyes. Even if the dreams are me falling away from her, her hand outstretched, begging for me to take it.

The sounds of the godsforsaken dungeon always bring me back to reality. Or the jangle of my chains.

I readjust my seat, leaning against the cold stone wall behind me. I'm sure it's cold anyway. It isn't always. Sometimes my being is too incorporeal to feel much of anything. Anything physical, that is.

I can still feel plenty of emotions. Regret, rage, frustration, helplessness. It all whirls around in my soul with the boredom of being chained to a wall in an empty room for days.

I've had a lot of time to think since Nero brought me here. He hadn't needed any help to overpower me. I try not to dwell on the humiliation of just how weak I am. At least only a select few have played witness to my current state. Nero, a couple of henchmen, and the boss of the operation who had sneered at me before they chained me to the wall.

The anger the boss expressed toward me has me betting that my capture was in a small part revenge. I'm aware of how they found me.

Asa says I'm a master at finding people, tracing them to their exact location. But my skills only work with a few types of beings with varying levels of success depending on how connected I am to them. I'm an amateur compared to Nero. Because he knows the way my soul threads "taste" he can find me wherever I go.

I forgot about that ability. It didn't seem like something to worry over while I wandered empty streets, bondless.

The chains are overkill. I'm too helpless to fashion with a suppression collar and the room they've placed me in stops my ability to teleport away. As if I could enter the in-between without losing myself completely. I've already started to fade.

The question is if my captors will find a buyer for me before I cease to exist.

Sound carries off the stone walls. This cell is right next to the meeting room for whatever is left of the operation Sophia and I had tried to bust. I've heard all about how they are going to sell me to try and recoup the costs of losing their inventory. My skills are valuable after all.

Nero appears. The wards on the rooms are personalized to allow his ability. It wouldn't do for their own to get stuck. The shadows of the in-between oddly cling around him, as if clawing him with aggression. He bats the darkness away with a huff.

I'd rather have an empty room.

This isn't the first time my brother has come to blather at me.

The first time, I'd been so full of rage I'd barely listened to a word he'd said. I'd been too absorbed in trying to find a way out of my chains so that I could stab the bastard.

The times since then, I sit, conserving my energy in the small hope that I'll find a way out of this place.

And since I have nothing to do but sit, I end up listening to Nero. Sometimes I even talk back. It gets repetitive though because I've come to a realization over the days I've been stuck here.

Nero isn't quite right in the head anymore.

I don't know what has caused the cracking in his psyche. He's anchored from what I can tell. His soul threads weaving back in on himself in a way that confused me until I realized he must be bonded to a physical object. It's rare for something to be so immersed in the energies of this plane to be able to act as an anchor, but they exist.

The lack of an anchor can't be blamed for his instability, maybe something happened in the demon plane?

"You just had to go and ruin it. I had a good thing going, a great one actually," Nero says, glaring at me.

This is a road we've gone down before. Instead of retorting anything about the trafficking which leads to infuriating loops of logic, I take a different approach.

"I'm surprised you came back to this plane. I thought you hated it here."

Nero sneers. "I was told in no uncertain terms that my presence in my home realm is unwelcome."

"I can't imagine why. Rack up debts with the wrong person?"

Nero twitches, which I take as a yes. All these years and he's still at it. And for what? The rush of the gamble? A terrible vice, but vices are merely strong inclinations.

The quick funds Nero always schemed for define him completely.

"Did being responsible for your own sister's death not slow you at all?" Some of my rage seeps through my words. "Does the guilt not bother you?"

"The death of a half-breed." Nero's words are ugly but halfhearted at best. Not even he could hate Elise. There's some sort of emotion muddling his eyes, but I can't define it. Nero appears lost in thought.

"It wasn't supposed to happen," he whispers to himself.

"It wouldn't *have* happened if you hadn't *sold* her," I hiss.

"It wasn't supposed to happen," Nero repeats louder. His frown carving deep grooves in the face that looks so much like my own. "Elise knew I was going to get her out of the bond."

"Then why?" It's as much of a shout as I can manage, and it echoes with bloody memories. "Why did she kill herself?"

I don't expect an answer. I have no idea what she experienced while that man had held her captive. Nero spins in place, tearing at his hair.

"Because she was too good!" His words are manic. "She wasn't the princess waiting to be saved. She was the white knight and she slayed the monster."

Nero shouts her name, and it bounces off the stone of the walls. The mumbles of the rest of his group in the next room barely pause as if accustomed to the mental swings of their employed demon. Each pacing step has my brother looking more and more deranged, but confusion clouds my mind.

"What?" I ask.

"I didn't know! I didn't know why they wanted her ability so bad. I offered them anything else, but they refused."

Nero had resisted selling our sister. It's a small detail that doesn't change the result, but it does settle a small vicious detail in my mind.

Nero continues his ranting. "I didn't know that they chose her because she could lure children in. I hadn't heard the whispers about the lender."

A cold weight takes the place of my heart. "No."

Nero isn't listening to me, his face twists in a grief I didn't know he could express. "By the time I found out, it was too late. All that blood—but it worked. The bond killed the monster."

"That's not what happened," I say quietly, but I'm suddenly not sure. I shake my head. "She-she couldn't take the abuse—"

Nero laughs. It sounds crazed. "Is that what you thought? That our bright, beautiful sister turned the dagger on herself because she just couldn't go on?"

The concept shatters. The reasoning of a grieving child doesn't stand up to the truth of the experience. The pieces stab my heart with regret. All this time. I'd been wrong all this time. Elise had chosen her fate. My twin had to make a terrible decision, but she wouldn't have hesitated.

Her kind heart went along with her ferocity.

Slowly the picture of her in my memories repaints itself. The times she smiled weakly at me when I'd paint my fantasies of us being free of Nero and I promised I'd take care of her, move over to make room for the times she stood between Nero and me, brandishing a knife. Protecting me.

How could I distort my memories of her to that extent? How could I forget how strong she was? A different type of guilt wells.

Elise was a victim, but that wasn't all she was.

It takes a while for my emotions to settle. When I look up, Nero is pacing.

"It's still your fault," I say.

"I'm aware!" Nero's voice is angry, and he points into the air around him. "They are all aware. They tell me constantly!"

My eyes widen and I look around the empty room before slowly asking. "Who?"

"They whisper about it. That I should stop. That I've hurt enough people. Sometimes even Elise tells me," Nero says, almost as if he's talking to himself.

The hairs on the back of my neck raise. A ripple in the air has the shadows of the in-between appearing as if in acknowledgment before disappearing.

The in-between is haunting Nero?

"Every time I travel through the dark, they grab on to me. The ghosts tell me I need to stop."

Ghosts.

Do souls reside in the in-between? I don't want to know, but it shifts my understanding of the moments the shadows played with Sophia's hair. The way they reached out to her, as if they liked her.

Will my soul go into the in-between if I fade completely? I've never thought about what the end would mean. I figured I'd be gone.

Nero takes deep breaths, and it seems as if the madness in him recedes for the moment.

"Nero, are you going to let me fade away?" The other option would be for Nero to forcibly bond me to whoever buys me. It would take a lot of time to gain the power needed to break such a bond in my current state.

My brother's eyes focus on me and there's something wild in them that belies his measured words.

"It's fitting, isn't it? The fact that you were left in the world without Elise almost seemed like the most egregious thing. Now the world will be in balance." Nero casts his gaze to the shackles on my wrists, musing. "As if the two of you never existed."

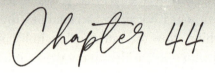

Chapter 44

SOPHIA

It's chaos.

But chaos is my element.

Gage is helping coordinate with Asa's and Gideon's networks while I work with mine. It's a little tedious but we've narrowed the possibilities to four locations that could serve as safe houses. One from the legitimate business files Kalos gave Mace and me, one from the files taken from our infiltration of the gambling den, and two from sources getting back to me from my original information seeking about the group.

It's progress. I can't allow myself to think about what Mace has been suffering. I only hope that they haven't sold him to someone else.

I grip the pen in my hand tighter.

If they've sold him, it won't matter. I'll find him. I won't stop until I find him.

"We need to narrow down the locations." Gage twirls a marker in his hand as he faces the list on the whiteboard. "I, for one, think that they won't go to the legitimate business location. If they taint that business, they'll have nothing left."

I nod in agreement. We didn't have enough evidence to give the Council to link the legitimate business to the trafficking. The files we'd gotten from the gambling den were stolen and wouldn't be accepted.

Gage looks around to take in other nods before crossing that location off.

"That leaves us with three," Asa says, his brow creased in thought. "Sophia, can you eliminate either of the locations that came from your sources?"

I glare at the board, hesitating. If I pick incorrectly, we may lose our chance to take them by surprise. If I don't choose… it's the same end. I think of the details.

"The one in Chicago is a bit of a reach. The informant was trying to be helpful, but I don't think the location would be a good one to broker a deal. Too many opposing bigger factions they'd have to appeal to or work under their noses."

Various people nod in agreement and Gage crosses the location off. "And then there were two," he says.

My phone buzzes in my hand with an incoming call. It reads "Fire Breath" and I answer.

"Kalos, I'm a little busy right now."

The dragon's chuckle isn't nice sounding. "I've heard that you're looking for something."

I freeze. If Kalos has information… I'm already indebted to this creature, but what would I trade to get Mace back safe and sound?

Anything.

I close my eyes. "You heard correctly."

"Don't sound so much like a martyr, harpy. I've come across some information about the missing artifact that I think you'll find very useful."

I grit my teeth in frustration, trying not to snap at the dragon.

"I can't retrieve the artifact right now. I need to find Mace," I say as calmly as I can manage.

Kalos huffs. "The location is one and the same."

Chapter 45

MACE

Ghosts.

Souls in the in-between haunting Nero. Talking to him. The possibility is frightening but it's something else too. The idea that Elise isn't really gone after all. The concept that she is listening.

Nero left me to my thoughts a while ago. There's no one to hear me, the other room has gone quiet. Even still, I keep my voice low, feeling stupid and hopeful all at the same time.

"I think we're finally going to meet again," I say. I breathe out a sigh. I can't sense the cold of the room at all anymore. If that isn't troubling enough, the tips of my fingers are see-through. "Don't take it the wrong way, but I'd rather this not be the end for me."

The brush is so faint that if it were any other moment, I wouldn't notice. If I could sense anything else, the soft stroke to my cheek wouldn't register at all. As it is, my throat swells and a sob chokes me.

"Oh, Elise, I've missed you." Tears well in my eyes and I lay my head back, letting all the words trapped in my throat free. "I'm so sorry I left, that I blamed you. It was stupid. I should've been there—"

A warmth stirs around me that isn't from a physical temperature change, and I can't go on. The words float away from me, as if accepted and there is nothing else to say on the matter. I close my eyes and focus on the sensation of not being alone.

There's a peace that takes the place of the heavy words I've carried.

"Maybe it wouldn't be the worst thing—ow!"

Something pinches my side as if to argue with me, and I breathe out a short laugh. Pestering me even from the grave.

"Fine. I won't give up yet, but it isn't looking good," I say, no longer feeling stupid for talking to the empty air. The shadows hold more mysteries than I've ever known. "I don't know how I'm going to get out of this. I don't know if anyone has even noticed that I've gone missing yet, but I'll keep my eyes open."

I sigh, trying to do just what I said, not give up. I'll let myself be distracted with the overwhelming emotions of this whole strange interaction after I get out of this.

There's a bang of a door opening in the next room and then a voice I recognize as the boss. It's not until he continues into my cell that I can make out his words.

"This room will work for the time being. If all goes well, we can replace the cost of the lost inventory within the week." The boss looks around with a sneer, counting the shackle placements on the walls of the room and Nero enters after him.

"I finally have a buyer for this one." The boss gestures to me. "So we'll have some more space. No one wants to buy someone with the reputation he has."

I roll my eyes at the refusal to acknowledge my presence. Nero shrugs. "The skill to teleport has value. I figured at least one person would overlook his reputation."

"We still need a gods damned harpy. I promised the buyer we had her." The boss glares. "We don't want to get on his bad side."

Nero hums. "I could find the one we had before."

My brother makes a snipping motion with his fingers and fear floods me. Nero was the one to sever my bond to Sophia, he'd be able to find her based on that contact.

The boss nods.

"Yeah, let's plan on that. Take Troy and Chad with you, be sure to fit her with one of our collars this time. I don't want a repeat of that raid." The man spits. "Fucking Council."

My ears ring as the men talk logistics. Sophia is in danger. If they take her, there won't be a rescue team coming for her this time.

I can't let that happen. I won't.

It doesn't matter that the only thing I can think to do will take more energy than I have. I don't even have the ability to sever the bonds let alone go toe-to-toe with Nero.

But I have to try.

I clench my fists. Something brushes my cheek again and I understand. I won't be doing this alone.

"I'll see you soon, Elise," I whisper.

I focus on the threat to my harpy. Nero's eyes are glazed over as if trying to listen for something as his boss walks toward the door. I don't have time to plan anything complicated. If Nero teleports now, I'll lose my chance.

I love you, Sophia. I wish I had told you.

I breathe in and the shackles pass through my wrists as I enter the in-between. I'm on Nero in the next moment. Launched forward by the shadows I traversed with so much ease over the years with no thought as to what they were before now.

Nero's eyes widen as we collide, and he laughs. The force of my body against his probably a fraction of what it should be with how much I've faded. I barely feel the impact but it's not important.

As if possessed, I reach for Nero's link to his power. His anchor. I throw everything I have into the action, my hands claw at the fabric covering the object that sings with power. We fall to the ground. Tears run down my face, but I don't feel them.

This is it. I'm going to fade from existence and Sophia will still be in danger.

Some force cradles around me. I gasp in a breath at the *push* of power, and *something* snaps.

Without hesitating, I bond to the object in my hand. The object that Nero is no longer bonded to. The sensation of being solid is welcome. Pins and needles prick over my skin as the power of this plane flows into me.

Nero lays flat on his back under me, cackling. I lift my fist and open it.

I broke his bond to his anchor. Or something had anyway.

The anchor in my hand looks like the raptor claw from Jurassic Park strung on a cord to be worn around a neck. A cold sensation runs through my veins at the thick pulse of earth magic. Where did Nero get a dragon claw?

Nero is still cackling like a madman. "Seems like you've gained some skills over the years."

I squeeze my hand into a fist again and punch him. Rage moves my body and each time I connect my fists to his face is satisfying. I don't know how long I hit him. Every ugly memory with Nero rises out of me, like lancing an infection.

It's when he stops laughing and loses consciousness that the rage finally leaves me. I sway as if drunk. The outpouring of violence so unusual for me.

Where is the rest of Nero's group? Someone had to have heard the ruckus we're making.

A slow clapping sounds through the room and catches my attention.

A woman stands in the doorway. A woman with dark hair and fiery green eyes. Am I hallucinating?

"Sophia?"

Sophia smiles at me. "And here I thought I'd be swooping in and saving the day."

I swallow the impossible emotions clogging my throat. "Y-you could take credit."

I stand, still wobbly from the ordeal.

Sophia wrinkles her nose. "Nah, you would have gotten free and—you look like shit."

I look around in disbelief but we're alone other than Nero's still form. "What happened?"

"We found you," Sophia says. "The others restrained the rest of the ring. We made sure to get the boss this time. You were… preoccupied. They wanted to give you privacy."

All that had gone on while I was lost in beating the shit out of Nero? A detail strikes me.

"You found me," I say.

"I found you." Sophia's eyes shine with pride. "Kalos confirmed, but I found this location."

"I just didn't think you'd come after me."

Now those green eyes are angry. "We all came after you, Mace. Asa, Gideon, Gage's whole crew—"

My heart swells with emotion, but I interrupt. "I'm talking about you… we didn't part in the best of ways. *You* came for me."

Sophia glares at me. "*I* came for you. We need to talk."

I blink at her. Stereotypically that phrase is supposed to strike fear in a person's heart, but I can only be hopeful. She wants to talk. Do I have another chance at being with my fierce harpy?

"Reynolds, you've looked better," a voice says.

We both jump and Kalos strides into the cell. Grace and power in every move.

I dramatically react. "Kalos, you shouldn't have."

Why is this dragon here? I grip the talon in my hand harder. *Oh.*

Kalos snorts. "I couldn't have let the Council bungle getting rid of this ring you mean."

"I didn't think you cared about the ring itself," I say. "Just the artifacts."

Artifacts… or pieces of dragon? A puzzle I hadn't identified starts to make sense. Dragon body parts are strong in magic even centuries after the creature's death. Dragons are of the few paranormal beings that are solely from this plane going back further than anyone can remember. They are so entrenched in this world's magics that their inanimate bodies are objects that can be used as anchors.

Kalos raises a brow at my fist, and I immediately offer the talon to him.

The practice of selling parts of creatures have declined over the years, but it hadn't occurred to me how awful it is. I've always been concerned over the trafficking of the living, but how would I feel if the pieces of someone I cared for were sold to the highest bidder?

Murderous.

Kalos gingerly takes the piece, turning it over in his hands in thought. His yellow eyes flash.

"I see you've already bonded with it," the dragon says.

"I am so sorry, Kalos." Regret makes my heart heavy. "I didn't mean any offense. It was Nero's anchor—"

Kalos makes a motion with his hand, and I stop talking. "I understand. I don't like it but it's the reality of being what we are in this kind of world. Our bodies are commodities in the end. I would like to lay the owner to this piece to rest. Finally."

Kalos clears his throat. "But I suppose the situation is a little complicated by it being your anchor. I'm not a tyrant enough to demand you weaken yourself at this very moment. I'd like to keep doing business together."

The dragon holds the talon back out to me.

"You can borrow it. Sophia will return it to me when you've figured out who or what you're going to bond to." Kalos's eyes soften with old grief. "I may be a bastard, but she wouldn't mind helping the two of you before her final rest."

A groan from the floor breaks the moment and our gazes drop to my bloodied brother.

The grief leaves Kalos's eyes and his smile is chilling, as if finding joy in the distraction. "Oh, allow me, it's been an age since the last time I've gotten my hands dirty even if it's just to deliver him to those idiot Enforcers."

The dragon grips his talons around the back of Nero's neck. The air charges with some ancient magic. The kind used before suppression collars came on the market. There is no escape for my brother now.

Nero hisses as Kalos drags him up by the arm. "So, this is how it ends, brother mine?"

His face is slowly starting to heal, and even as blood drips from his mouth we look uncannily alike. The blood we share strong even in the face of our differences.

"I'll attend your trial," I say.

Nero laughs in a way that brings the memory of his manic state to mind. "Don't be naive. I won't last long enough for a trial."

It sounds dramatic, but always a possibility.

"Then this is farewell. I hope you find peace, Nero." I realize I mean it. The poison of fury I'd felt toward this demon has run dry. There's nothing left but to expect Nero to stand accountable for his crimes.

There's a glimmer in Nero's eyes, a surfacing of the brother I'd known and hated, but ultimately who raised me. He nods and Kalos drags him away.

Chapter 46

SOPHIA

"Are you good to—" I wiggle my fingers as Kalos leaves with Nero.

Mace's brow creases in confusion. There's dirt smeared on his face and tear tracks mark his cheeks. I get lost in the details, the tear in his jacket, the smear of dried blood on the back of his neck. I push my emotions down. The urge to throw myself in his arms purely in relief.

"Forgive me for being slow on the uptake. I'm still a little floaty," Mace says, interrupting my perusal. "But what are you asking?"

Floaty. Mace is bonded to the dragon talon now, but how close had he been to fading away?

"Teleport. Are you good to teleport?"

Mace gives me a blank look and mimics the finger wiggling action. "How does that mean teleport?"

I scowl at him until he clears his throat.

"Yes, I'm good to teleport." He points to the door. "We just need to leave the warded zone."

We walk out of the room; through the garbage-cluttered room the group had been using as a hideout and into a cramped hallway. Mace stops us with a nod.

"Where to?" Mace asks.

"The cabin." I don't question the instinct, but Mace's brows raise.

"As you wish." Mace offers me his hand and I grasp it. It's solid and I breathe out a sigh in relief. Nothing happens for a moment, and I tilt my head at him.

Mace looks hesitant. Does he not want me in his space? Touching him?

Mace takes in my frown and winces. He shoots me a sheepish smile.

"Sorry, um, a lot of things have happened. I'll tell you about it when we get there," he says, and with that, we leave.

Traveling through the in-between happens in a jarring instant. I'm bereft. Will I ever get to see that place with its shadows and distant stars again?

Not much has changed in the cabin since I was last here. The notes I made from the files are in a neat stack on the coffee table, as if Mace couldn't bring himself to throw them away. The sunset filters through the giant windows and paints the walls and furniture in oranges and reds.

"Sophia..." Mace's eyes have some open emotion that I can't interpret.

I guess that's my cue to talk. I asked for him to bring me here. Maybe because of all the memories.

But now that I have my opportunity, the words tangle in my throat. Where do I even start? Mace rejected me a week ago, what can I say to make him believe that we're possible.

Mace steps forward, his hand coming up to stroke my cheek in awe. "I missed you."

The statement is simple and yanks my words free. "You rejected me."

Mace winces and takes a step closer. "All I wanted while I was shackled to that wall was to dream because in my dreams, I saw you."

I take a step back.

"What does that mean?" I stop and shake my head. I'm messing this up. I need some time to put the words I want to say in order. "You probably want to clean up. Let's—can we pause this conversation?"

Mace's face cracks into a smile and he rubs the scruff on his face. "You should have just told me I stink."

I snort and blush, tempted to tell him to leave the scruff, but not wanting to get ahead of myself. "Just give me a minute."

Mace takes my hand and raises it to his lips, echoing the gesture from not even a month ago.

"For you, fierce harpy, I'll give you all the time in the world."

My heart softens a little.

"Don't make promises you can't keep," I say.

"Never."

***

It feels like the shower runs forever. I can only imagine what it's like trying to wash away five odd days of captivity. The first few minutes I fidget and worry over what I want to say until I pace the floor one too many times and decide to keep busy other ways.

The motions of food preparation slow my heart even when the shower finally shuts off. I take breaths, waiting. Why am I so nervous?

Because I don't want to leave this place empty-handed.

I also don't want to make all my demands while Mace is still reeling from being held prisoner… but I'm impatient.

"I didn't know you cooked." Mace exits the bedroom and dramatically groans as if he's scenting ambrosia. I blink at the shirtless man with damp skin, distracted by the sight of black ink on pale skin until I shake my head.

"It's pasta sauce, from a bottle. Of course, I cook. I'm a Shirazi." I might not cook well, but it's to be seen if Mace will find that out.

"It could be a Twinkie after the week I've had, and I'd still drool."

"Now you're being insulting." I point at him with the spatula before retrieving bowls.

Mace smiles while he dishes up the food. His body steps into my space, bringing the scent of clean man and smoky shadows. My mouth waters as my skin heats. My fingers itch to slide over his exposed chest.

"Shall we?" Mace asks with a grin.

"What?" I ask, feeling stupid when I realize he's holding both bowls and gesturing to the deck. "Oh, yes, that would be great."

Focus, Sophia!

I follow him into the cooling air of dusk. The scent of pine and the view of rock face mountains taking my breath away. I turn toward the clink of the bowls on the low table and Mace holds out his hand.

"Let me enjoy your company before we speak of unpleasant things. I know I have things to make up for— it's just so nice to see you. To be next to you."

I missed you. There were words I didn't say when he stated that.

"I missed you too," I say.

Mace's breath shudders out in relief, and I join him on the double chair instead of the opposite seat. I grab my bowl and turn facing him, leaning my elbow on the back cushion and tuck my feet under me.

"So, how was your imprisonment?" I take a bite of pasta. The man doesn't want to talk about *us* yet.

Mace laughs. "I could tell you, but I don't know if you'll believe me."

He starts to eat, and the conversation fills with the sounds of forks against bowls. After a while, Mace twists the stem of the fork between his thumb and index finger in thought before breaking the stalemate.

"It was mostly boring," he says.

"I believe that." I raise a brow.

"I've been mistaken about things." Mace looks down into the red sauce, his mouth curving sadly. "And I spoke to my sister."

Both of my brows lift. "Oh, so just small stuff."

Mace's laugh is soft, and he tells me. Tells me the real story of Elise Reynolds. The sister who protected him from the worst of Nero's cruelty growing up. The woman who sacrificed herself to stop a child predator.

At the last, pinpricks of stars start to shine in the purple sky.

"How are you doing with…" I trail off. I've never been good at comforting people. I'm all action and fire, not the steady foundation that offers support.

"With finding out that the guilt that has haunted me for two hundred some odd years isn't… real?" Mace finishes.

I huff out a breath. "It's real enough to hurt you."

"The guilt of leaving her alone with Nero still weighs on me. But meeting Nero again forced me to reevaluate old wounds. The events that happened… I couldn't have stopped them. Nero said Elise agreed to the trade because she knew he was coming for her. She made the decisions she did and to let myself dwell as if I was a big player in the situation takes away from Elise's sacrifice. My guilt doesn't honor her memory."

"You do a lot of good in the name of Elise. All the trafficking you've stopped with your sister in mind. I think she'd be proud of you."

"Oh, well, that brings me to how I got free," Mace says, looking up at the sky with a laugh. "She helped me."

"Um, what?" I ask.

"Nero said that the ghosts in the in-between were haunting him. That Elise haunts him."

So, Nero lost it.

"And… on the off chance she'd hear me, I spoke to her. I'm pretty sure she answered."

Goose bumps break out all over my skin and Mace glances at me.

"I couldn't have severed Nero's bond on my own. Severing a bond of an individual who doesn't consent takes a lot of power and isn't a skill I have."

My mouth drops open.

"You think Elise helped you win against Nero?"

Mace looks out into the night. "I don't know for sure. Maybe Elise's and my bloodline is so connected to the in-between that we become a part of it when we die. Or it could have been a delusion from my own fading mind… but I don't think it was."

Mace takes my empty bowl and sets it down with his.

"It felt like she was there." He swallows, the grief of his words striking me deep.

I grab Mace's hand and kiss his palm. Mace smiles sadly at me. "Do you think it was a delusion?"

I hum in thought. "I think it doesn't matter. If she did help you get free, good. If it was a delusion and you came out on the other side alive and well, good. Your experience and whatever closure you gain from it is real to you, and that's what matters."

I lean forward and put my head on his shoulder. "No matter what it was, I'm grateful." We sit in silence before I break it. "For what it's worth, I think she saved you."

The sky darkens and the stars shine brighter.

I hug my arms around my demon as he weeps.

Chapter 47

MACE

I blink at the morning light and push the blanket down. Sophia stirs next to me with a cranky grumble. She has a right to be cranky, I kept us out here late into the night.

Birdsong joins the quickly rising sun.

I feel... lighter. As if the act of talking about Elise's and my early years until evening had turned into early morning had been a type of vigil. The stories had ranged from heartbreaking to humorous and Sophia had urged me for each one until we both must have fallen asleep.

This woman... I rejected her and instead of forgetting me like I deserved, she found me. Some feeling fills my chest. I have a name for it and at the same time, it's too large to comprehend. I stroke my finger over her face, catching the dark strands of her hair and tucking them behind her ear.

Sophia squints against the light. The green of her eyes strikes me.

Words that have existed in my mind for weeks are on the tip of my tongue, wanting to be released. Wanting to proclaim the love I have for this harpy from the rooftops.

I clear my throat.

"It's too early for it to be this bright," Sophia says and snuggles her face against my bare shoulder. "If you're going to say anything important, save it until after caffeine."

The warning comes across loud and clear. I laugh, a little breathless. "That can be arranged. Tea?"

Sophia grumbles in answer, her breath tickles my skin. How on earth had I ever thought I could let her go?

But what could I possibly offer to keep her?

***

Sophia is halfway done with the tea I brewed before she sets it on the counter and *glares* at me. Her spot on the stool at the counter is across from me, but that look cuts through the space and the sensation of having trespassed tightens around me.

"Yes?" I ask.

"You rejected my offer to bond."

Oh. I suck in a breath.

"Yes."

"Why?"

I fumble for words. "I wouldn't be able to protect you, keep you safe."

"And you think I need protection?"

"You almost died, Sophia." Stale pain stabs my chest. Memories of Asa working healing magics on her injury. "I can't—I can't lose you because I'm weak."

Sophia nods at my words.

"So, it isn't that I'm not strong enough?"

"No!" I shake my head, wanting to grab Sophia in my arms but I don't have a right to. "I-I can see why you'd think that."

We both go silent and Sophia watches me with narrowed eyes.

"Does finding out about Elise change anything?"

I stop. *Does it?* I let my mind go over every jagged piece of this puzzle. The guilt of not being able to protect Elise is still there. There are extra details now, nuances to my original memories.

Can I let it go to keep Sophia?

I want to say yes but the harpy deserves the truth.

"I've carried around guilt for that instance for so long it's worn a groove in my soul. I want to move on from it, but it's going to take time."

The brutal honesty of it weighs on me. I can't be the partner Sophia deserves right now, and my heart rejects that vehemently.

Sophia tilts her head and nods. "I'm going to claim you then."

"Claim me?"

Sophia shrugs. "You don't want to be responsible for protecting me, so I'll protect you instead. You've said I'm the stronger one anyway. I'll bear the responsibility of keeping you until you figure out how we can bear the weight together. I want us to be a team."

A team.

"Even if I'm weak?"

Sophia scrunches her nose. "A weak demon wouldn't have been able to do what you did with Nero, no matter if you had help. I think it's time you flip the script on what you believe about yourself; power isn't the only way to measure someone."

The smile that threatens to break free is one of hope. Something occurs to me, and I frown, needing to be specific.

"A team sounds… nice, but I don't want only that. I want a mate bond."

Sophia's mouth twitches. "You want to be stuck with me?"

"I want to earn your heart every day."

"What makes you think you don't have it?" Sophia asks, her eyes soft.

Her words are a punch to my chest and I slowly round the counter.

"Don't tease me, goddess," I say.

Sophia stands gracefully before I get to her. She tilts her head back and I lean into her space. Her hands smooth up the T-shirt I'd thrown on to brew us tea before gripping it.

"I'm claiming you. How is that teasing?" Sophia asks but there is a cheerful glint in her eyes.

My hand presses into her lower back and our bodies press together, fitting against each other perfectly. I brush my lips against her cheek and her eyelashes flutter.

"Have I earned your heart, fierce harpy?"

"Do I have yours?" she asks.

My grin probably looks vicious. "Yes, it's yours just as much as it would be if you tore it from my chest."

A flash of disgust on her face has me laughing but she pulls my shirt and her lips on mine breaks the laugh off. The taste of black tea and Sophia has me moaning. She breaks the kiss with the nip of my lip.

"How bloodthirsty of you and gross. Keep your heart in place please." Sophia pats my chest.

I thread my fingers through the hair at the base of her skull and steal another kiss. Tasting and enjoying every brush of her lips, slide of her tongue, pulling a moan from her.

I break the kiss; her eyes are glazed over in a daze.

I don't want there to be any misunderstanding. "I love you, Sophia. I loved you when I thought I had to send you away and I love that you're battling all my faulty preconceptions. I want to spend every day earning the privilege of standing beside you."

A blush spreads across Sophia's face and her eyes shine, and then she tackles me. She grabs my shoulders, nails digging in, and wraps her legs around my hips. The sting of pain is glorious, and I want her to dig in harder. I grab her ass and hoist her against my body. Our kisses are feverish and the thin fabric of my shirt rips under the hunger of my harpy. My mate.

I press her into the edge of the counter to grind my hardening cock into the cradle of her thighs with a groan. Sophia breaks our kiss.

"You're mine," she says. "I claim you and will destroy anyone or anything that gets in my way."

It's a vicious snarl that has my soul singing.

Sophia pulls my ruined shirt off and I slide my hands under her top, groaning at the heat of her skin and exposing her.

"Break your bond to your anchor," Sophia says. It's nothing less than a demand delivered breathlessly.

"Are you going to claim me?" I taunt, the wicked thing that likes to hear her beg riding me. "Are you going to connect our souls? Will I get to feel your emotions flow through me while I'm inside you?"

Sophia chokes. "Yes."

The kitchen counter under Sophia is a far cry from a holy altar. I pick Sophia up and walk toward the deck.

"Wha—"

"If we're going to enact a mate bond. I want the memory to be special." I'm blushing, but don't care. My harpy is ethereal under sunshine. Her grace and power are too big to be stuck inside a room during a moment like this. I set her on her feet and fall to my knees before her. Pulling down her pants.

Sophia snorts. "You romantic sap."

I growl. "A hungry romantic sap."

Sophia finally stands before me naked and I'm ravenous. I move to taste her, devour her. My hands slide up her bare legs, but Sophia stops me with a hand to my shoulder.

"Lie back," she says.

Something soft hits my head and I realize she's snared the blanket we used to ward off the chill of the night. My lips twitch. "How sweet of you."

"Can't have splinters in that ass," Sophia says, unbuttoning my pants with a yank.

I spread the blanket under me with little patience and lie down. Sophia finishes removing my clothes and we are bare before the world with my harpy astride me. My hands smooth over her skin, wanting to grip.

Sophia bites her lip.

"No one can see us, right?" Hesitant even though her arousal is painting my stomach.

"No," I say, circling my thumb around her clit, groaning at how wet she already is. "There are no trails nearby. Is the harpy I saw having relations in a nightclub really worried about some extra eyes?"

Sophia's face is fierce. "I don't want to share this with anyone else."

Happiness surges in my heart. "Just you and me. No one else and no other bonds."

I take a deep breath and release the bond to the talon anchor. It's a clinical sensation in the unweaving, none of the messy emotions of being bonded to another. All that's left is empty loneliness.

"Mace?" Sophia asks.

I open my eyes and take in every part of her, committing this moment with her to memory. The tangle of dark hair lifting in the mountain breeze, the swell of her breasts tipped with tight brown nipples to her weeping sex, both parts have my mouth watering.

"It's done." I grip her ass and lift her up to straddle my face. "And now, I'm ravenous."

I lick her and she gasps. I moan at the taste of my harpy, tart and full of need.

"Oh, Sophia, you slay me."

"Whispering sweet nothings to my pussy isn't going to get you anywhere," Sophia says wryly.

My grin is quick. "I forget you don't like my words. I'll have to settle with action."

Sophia cries out as I stroke my tongue through her folds. The sound pushes me onward and I grip her hips to keep her in place, swirling my tongue and sucking. My harpy groans above me, wrapping her hands around her breasts and squeezing. The sight intoxicates, my cock leaks with need.

I eat my harpy like I'm begging forgiveness because I am. Begging for forgiveness, expressing happiness, and hungry to have her pleading with me for more. And she does plead.

"Oh fuck, Mace, your tongue please—" She breaks off on a cursing moan when I slide my tongue inside her and out again to suck on her clit. Each beg pushes my arousal higher.

My harpy grows impatient.

Sophia pulls away from my mouth, sliding down my body with purpose. Each touch of her skin is at once too much, and not enough. I ache for my harpy.

Sophia presses her palms on my shoulders, pinning me. She leans down and kisses her own taste from my lips with a groan. My cock jerks at the erotic action.

She breaks the kiss. "I love you, Mace."

My breath shudders out of my lungs. Relief and happiness make my eyes sting. I assumed that she must love me to want a mate bond, but there is nothing like hearing the actual words.

"And I love you. Do you know how to do the bond?" I ask, desperation edging my words. "I need to feel you again."

Sophia hesitates, a blush darkening the skin of her cheeks as she sits up. The heat of her wetness less than an inch from my throbbing cock.

"It should be like fertility. Willing what I desire into being," she says.

I smile, massaging the muscles of her legs. "I'll help if you need it."

I won't need to. I have a feeling that Sophia's methods will forge our bond the way it was supposed to be forged. The last time I wove our soul strands together, Sophia had been hesitant, pulling on the bond, yanking it too tight.

This time, the bond is mutually, enthusiastically welcome.

Sophia makes a *pfft* sound and I tighten my grip on her hips.

"Conquer me, fierce harpy," I rasp.

Sophia arches her back at my hungry words and rocks her hips. She grabs my cock and slides her wet folds against me. The muscles of my body draw tight. I start praying to make this last but there are stars in my vision when she forces my cock inside her.

I throw my head back at the tight heat surrounding me. A sensation at the base of my spine has me gritting my teeth, holding back my climax before I embarrass myself.

She moves, sinking down on my cock and dragging it out with every fall and rise of her hips. I can't help watching the erotic slide of it even though it's almost too much. The stretch of her wet cunt to take my hardness leaves me transfixed.

A puff of breath away from emptying myself inside her.

"Where's my demon?" Sophia teases, not stopping her slow ride.

"Wanting to fuck you until you feel me in your throat." It's a growl. I focus on not squeezing her hips too hard, of thinking any thought more than being a rutting animal.

She laughs, the sound victorious. Holding back the wave of need in my body almost hurts.

"Then why don't you?" she asks.

It takes a moment to understand what she's asking for. I'm distracted by being balls deep in her. She's all around me, her scent, her cunt. The clarity comes from familiarity, like before, Sophia is pushing me, pushing me until I snap.

I sit up, almost dislodging Sophia from straddling me. I wrap my arms around her, capturing her to me and gripping her hair in a fist and taking her mouth with mine. I kiss her with every hungry echo of my soul. She moans at the scrape of my teeth against her lip.

I tug her away with my hold in her hair.

"Stop taunting me, Sophia. Let me feel you," I say.

She moans, helpless and yet the driver in all of this.

Her eyes flutter shut, and I move her body in a rocking grind that has my eyes crossing as she starts the process. Our threads start to weave together and the drawing sensation on my soul lights a fire. I groan and fall back to the blanket, needing the leverage to roughly fuck up into my harpy. The need grows with each tangle of our souls until Sophia is gasping.

With the last draw, the ending knot of our commitment, a new urgency takes over my body.

Sophia gasps as my fingers dig into the flesh of her hips. I thrust up, but she brings herself down on me just as desperately. Her talons digging into my chest, the pain driving me to the edge of my self-control. As does the flow of emotions against my soul.

Love, nerves, and *hunger*.

I gasp at the connection. No longer alone in this world. It's perfection. But the hunger is clawing, and I groan. "You want something, goddess?"

Sophia shudders at my question. "Yes, please, Mace."

My lips twitch at the beg and her seed-stealing kink making an appearance. Or maybe it's more of a take-no-prisoners urge, sucking everything I am from me. The thought of her dripping with seed has my body moving with contained tight violence.

"*Fuck!*" I hiss. My cock kicks inside Sophia, filling her, and my harpy screams. The squeeze of her around me has spots blooming in my vision.

Large shapes unfurl, casting a shadow and my breath catches. Sophia's wings are gorgeous things. Gold and black markings, similar to a bird of prey. Striking and dangerous.

Sophia sways, her cunt fluttering around my softening cock and I shiver. She hums and lies down on my chest.

Her happiness reaches me through our bond, and I know mine reaches her. Mentally I inspect the bond. It's a lovely thing with an equal draw on the both of us.

Good, I don't think I'd survive a second attempt.

Sophia tucks her wings to her and snuggles into my chest. I have an extreme *urge* to pet them. It won't be suppressed.

"You can touch them." Sophia's mouth twitches in a smile. "I can't seem to keep them contained if I wanted to right now."

"You could pick that up from the bond?" I ask, gently placing a hand on a wing, the smooth slide of soft feathers is delightful.

Sophia opens a bleary eye at me. "It feels… more equal now. I can pick up your feelings more."

"I thought so too. We can work on shielding if it bothers you."

Sophia yawns. "Maybe later. Now, I'm enjoying feeling your presence."

"As I am yours."

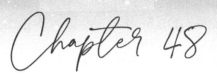

Chapter 48

SOPHIA

I walk back into the main area after a much-needed shower, towel drying my hair. A delicious aroma from a brown bag on the counter has my mouth watering. Mace didn't seem to want to press my cooking skills another night, smart man.

I stop in my tracks when a weird sensation squeezes at my heart. It's a distant thing in the way that I recognize it being Mace's emotions. I change course and find my demon on the deck, pressing his phone into his chin, lost in thought.

"Is the food bad or something?" I ask, knowing that's not the case but needing to break the silence. The last time there was a morose Mace alone on this deck my heart was shattered to pieces.

He starts at my question. "No, sorry. That was Gage. Nero was right. He and his boss were found dead in their cells this morning."

My brows shoot up. "Right under the Council's nose?"

"Almost right in the Council's face."

I mull over the options. If there was someone offing people apprehended so they couldn't talk, then it's likely there is another rung of the ladder we've missed. "Well, fuck."

I make the decision then and there that we'll eradicate this operation. I know Mace will feel the same. The sensation of before comes to mind and I want to jump off the deck railing. His brother is dead. "Oh gods, Mace, I'm sorry."

Mace shakes his head. "It's strange."

"It's okay to grieve him."

"It's not—not that. Nero and I were never going to get along." He frowns. "It's as if I'm grieving what could have been. If Nero hadn't hated me from the start, hell, maybe if we'd talked out the Elise situation years ago—"

He breaks off. Confusion coming off him in waves. "We were technically family and now he's gone."

"You have more family. It may not be by blood, but blood isn't required. Asa and Gideon came to your rescue, you've practically been adopted into the Shirazi family, a feat not many manage let me tell you, and I'd like to think what we have now is starting our own family."

Mace's mouth twitches. "A family? Have something to tell me, harpy?"

It takes me a moment to understand what he's implying. When I do, I smack his arm and he laughs.

"A family of two, thank you very much! See if I try and cheer you up again."

But Mace is laughing, so I'll let him keep his joke.

"So." Mace clears his throat after his chuckling subsides. "Do I get to be there when you announce to your family that we're mated?"

Fuck.

Epilogue

MACE

I finish the last of the gelato with a hum. Sophia drops her hand from shading her eyes and flashes me a smile. Smiling back is a compulsion even amid the sounds of honking cars and the odd Italian exclamation that peppers the sunny day.

"Delicious," I say.

My sun goddess steps closer, ignoring the tourists around us and steals a taste with a kiss. She hums in agreement.

"You know, we don't have to do the guided tour," I say.

The tour guide drones on, gesturing to the colosseum behind him.

"I could give you an excellent tour—"

"If I let you give me a tour, we'd end up at home touring the bedsheets." Sophia rolls her eyes.

The cabin was one of my favorite properties before, but now, with Sophia's presence, it's home. When we're in one place for any stretch of time, that is. My harpy does love to travel.

"Our bedsheets are very interesting." I lower my voice and speak into her ear. Sophia snickers and bats at me, a blush staining her cheeks.

"I want to enjoy our vacation to the fullest. Out of bed this time."

I bump my body to Sophia's in suggestion. "That can be arranged. I'm not much of an exhibitionist, but I know a place."

Sophia's composure dissolves on a loud laugh, and the guide stumbles over his words. Sophia waves the man on, embarrassed.

"Behave!" she whispers. "We have the weekend until we're back at the grind and I want to see something new."

We'd finished a job gathering information for a shifter pack looking to move and I convinced her to take a break. Otherwise, she would have tried to pick at tracking the organization that Nero had worked with. The case had gone cold, and I refused to let my harpy burn out when these people would come back on the scene again, it's just a matter of time.

The ruins look especially dusty today and my mate is focusing very hard on paying attention. I clasp her hand; the bare skin of her wrist never stops inspiring relief in me. Kalos had released her from her debt, and we still do business with the dragon, under much better contracts.

"My fierce harpy," I murmur. "You only had to say the word. How about meeting someone new?"

Sophia's eyes brighten and I bite back my smile. With her, I'm at peace. I have a home, a family, and a partner. We are a team.

It's only fair that I know exactly how to bring my mate happiness.

***

SOPHIA

After a quick trip through the in-between from an alley, always alleys with this demon, Mace leads me to a bronze-decorated door and uses the knocker. I squint at the weathered metal, making out the shape of what appears to be a spider.

"Where are we?" I ask.

Sometimes on our adventures, he'll tell me what I can expect, others he keeps a surprise. It doesn't matter which it is. When Mace takes my hand to show me something new, he never disappoints.

Mace rocks on his heels. "I thought you might want to meet a lace maker from a very long line of weavers."

The door opens and reveals a tall, very thin older woman. Her face creases in a warm smile and her hair is long and bright white.

"Mace! What a wonderful surprise. And who is this you've brought into my parlor?"

Mace laughs. "Very funny. This is my mate, Sophia."

Every time he says those words with happiness and reverence it makes my heart skip a beat. As a harpy, this isn't something I'm supposed to have.

The woman puts a hand to her mouth, and I can't help smiling at the honest joy.

"You are so beautiful, my dear. And your threads are so strong. Come in! Come in! You'll stay for lunch. I'll teach you to make lace."

The woman is a force of nature. We're whisked inside the building and into a cozy courtyard shaded by some type of tree at the center.

"I am Maria Arachne. Welcome to my home," she says.

Something tickles the back of my mind until the spider on the door makes sense.

"As in *the* Arachne?" I ask.

Maria laughs. "Not exactly, no. My family is spread from here to Greece and we have our own story, passed down over the years that doesn't match the human mythology. I'd love to tell you it over lunch."

My face must show my excitement because the woman pulls me forward with enthusiasm and Mace gives me a knowing look. Leave it to my demon to gift me something so unique.

Maria's multigenerational family accepts us with warmth. The story of their ancestor's sacrifice and boldness pairs beautifully with the lunch and knowing smiles of Maria's daughters. After much laughter and good conversation, we set up in the courtyard.

My third attempt at lace goes better than the last couple, but I end up losing my place and mixing up the ordering of the tiny bobbins.

"I don't think this is a hidden skill of mine," I say with a wry smile.

Maria snickers. "As with any skill, it takes time and patience." She eyes my progress. "Though this one might not be one you have an aptitude for."

I don't take offense.

Maria started me on a bobbin lace process that she used to teach beginners but explained that her own method, and that of her family, is more a hybrid version of that and needle lace. Though, I'm sure there isn't any technique quite like the fine strands of silk Maria produces from her wrists and weaves into designs with the tips of her nails.

She controls the thickness of the strands by will and skill. The result is an ultra-fine weaving that catches the light in a way I've never seen in a fabric. I could spend days watching the older woman work.

Mace dozes on nearby cushions after eating every one of the pastries Maria's granddaughters had offered him and giving loud compliments.

I snort at the sight and Maria's dimples deepen. "I'm glad your threads found each other. Mace did a service for my family years ago, it's good to see him so happy. It's good to see the tangles in his heart resolve."

I tilt my head. "Do you see soul threads?"

"Oh, not really. Not in the way demons do. What my kind sees are more the way people interconnect with the world they are in. I can see a little of how those connections were in the past and a little of what they may become in the future too, when it's clear."

I stop myself from asking her to tell me my fortune, just barely. It's at the very tip of my tongue, but I'm experienced enough now to know that it's only polite when those things are offered freely

"The future is bright, young harpy." Maria's eyes crease with a knowing smile. "You were tangled, and now your strings are free to become what you wish to be."

She doesn't elaborate and I don't ask for more. I thank her and join Mace, leaning over him and running a finger over his face. The demon wakes and looks like he's going to wrestle me down to the cushions before remembering where we are.

It's better not to scandalize our host even if she's seen worse in her time.

Mace wraps his fingers around my hand and kisses my palm. The casual affection is commonplace with us now.

"You seem like you've enjoyed your new experience." Mace's tone is smug even as his voice is raspy with sleep.

"I'm very glad I owed you a debt," I say.

If I hadn't stumbled into owing this demon, none of this would have happened.

Mace blinks at me and his grin takes on a wicked edge.

"Oh, my fierce harpy, there will never be a moment in our lives where I'll pass up granting you a favor. You and I are truly stuck together."

My lips twitch. "Like glue."

Mace squeezes my hand. "Like the finest weaving, unbreakable until the end. And maybe not even then."

Forever with my demon sounds like the perfect amount of time.

Extended Epilogue

AMARA

This is a bad plan.

Dale's basement apartment is lit up. The fae had told me that he'd be home. Had offered the invitation with the curve of his lips. It had been a dare. A safe dare to make because he knew I wouldn't come.

Then why am I here?

The door is one that has wavy glass in higher cutouts and the yellow glow radiating from them is cheerful. It doesn't help the clawing anxiety that constricts my chest or how unsure I am about this.

Is this the mistake or would not doing this be worse?

I bite my lip.

At the very least, this would be a step in the right direction. I think.

Fairuza's words haunt me. *Amara isn't a good choice for matriarch. Timid. Hasn't shown the mettle required.*

I've spiraled since the moment I'd overheard exactly what my aunt thought of me. She's messaged me since then, tried to make whatever amends she can without admitting fault or apologizing, but there is no taking back something like that once it's been released in the world.

The effect has been visceral, like I'd had a protective blanket ripped from me, leaving me exposed to the elements and raw.

It hurt. And after weeks of focusing on anything but her words, the reason why it hurt is clear.

She's right.

For years I've tried to hide, show the world the harpy I thought my aunt wanted. But appearing as something doesn't make it a reality.

I've stagnated, too fearful of everything to make a decision, to commit to a plan. Even the catering business I'd started had been noncommittal, lacking any major gains and floundering until offering my services under Greg's bakery just made more sense. Running Greg's bakery made more sense. It's safe, stable.

In the face of risk, I freeze.

And somehow, the fae who works for me knows it. Dale teases me with it. There's a darkness that peeks through when he smiles at me, something hungry.

A predator hunting its prey. Cat and mouse.

It sparks something I don't recognize in myself. Even as uneasy as the man makes me, there's something there that makes me want to lean in.

I'm here to do something I've never done before to prove to myself I'm not a mouse. I'm a harpy. I descend from warriors known for their viciousness. It's time I acted like it.

And if I succeed in getting pregnant, all the better.

Right?

***

THE END

To keep in touch and find out when Amara's book releases, join Lillian Lark's newsletter!
LillianLark.com/newsletter

Harpies of a Feather:
Three of Hearts
Pair of Fools
Amara's Book Title TBD

Curious about Gideon's and Rose's story?
Monstrous Matches:
Stalked by the Kraken
Deceived by the Gargoyles (Releases January 2022)

NOTE FROM THE AUTHOR

Hello Dear Reader!

Thank you for taking a chance and reading Pair of Fools!

Author note means truth time: this book was the most challenging book I've written to date. I had to take a creative detour and write Stalked by the Kraken to even get my thoughts straight. And when I returned to this project and finished the first draft, it was a month later than it was supposed to be.

Straight up, Sophia and Mace were a handful. Every step of the drafting process they defied what I thought their stories should be until finally I stopped fighting with them, and let their characters take the wheel. I have to say, I'm glad I did. Sophia and Mace deserved their happily ever after on their terms.

A thank you to Cattaleya Giraldo for not only beta reading this book but doing it in haste so that I could make my editing deadline!

As always, thank you, Dear Reader, for reading my book. It's always a marvelous thing that people read the books that I create and I'm grateful to you.

L. LARK

ABOUT THE AUTHOR

Lillian Lark was born and raised in the saltiest of cities in Utah. Lillian is an avid reader, cat mom to three demons, and loves writing sexy stories that twist you up inside.

More information about Lillian can be found on her website at LillianLark.com

Made in United States
North Haven, CT
28 April 2024

51872291R00193